INFORMED CONSENT

BY

R.M. FIX

To Sarah, Lindsey and Whitney

Acknowledgments

This book would not have been possible without the encouragement and support of my wife, Sarah. I am forever grateful.

Steve Nicholson and the dedicated team at Frontline Publishing deserve special thanks. They believed in my story and worked exceptionally hard to get this book published.

I have had two of the best assistants in the business, Sarah Wilmoth and Karen Hinson. They were very helpful with this project and they deserve special thanks. Tom Helm provided invaluable assistance with marketing and I appreciate his hard work.

Finally, I would like to thank my parents, Jim and Ilse, for giving me the support to succeed in life.

1

Robert Lunden didn't make mistakes. He couldn't afford them. He had a plan, devised through extensive study and preparation. Like always. Now, the time for planning was over. He would start tonight.

He rotated the tight steering wheel of the classic '65 Mustang Fastback and veered south onto the coastal highway. The noisy engine and crisp night air blocked the sound of the ocean's assault on the shoreline, a few hundred yards to his east.

The full moon's glow swallowed up the postcard town of Ponte Vedra Beach. His charted route carried him past one oceanfront estate after another.

But he wasn't out for a scenic drive. No, this was business.

He slowed to a crawl in front of a two-story shingled house set back off the road. A metal gate guarded the drive entrance. He eased the car forward until he could spy the house through an opening in the palmettos and scrub pine. Only a dim porch light shined.

No activity. Perfect.

He drove a quarter mile south and wheeled off the road into a public access lot. He scanned his surroundings before stepping outside.

All clear.

The salt mist bonded to his skin. He yanked a mask over his face, trotted across the road and out onto the beach. His legs churned through the loose, cold sand.

He ran north, closer to the water's edge. A wind gust nudged him from behind. Each exhale clouded the air in the early morning chill.

Almost there.

He stopped and observed his target home. Waves stretched to reach his feet from behind, but fell just short.

The beach was empty. House quiet. No barricades blocked the rear. Why would they? No self-respecting owner would think of it.

A wooden deck jetted out fifty yards and led to the beach. A smaller deck hung from the second floor. The master bedroom.

He watched and waited. No movement. No lights. Nothing. He had stood in this same spot every night for the past two weeks. Tonight was different.

He'd not come just to watch.

Entry was easy. No alarm to disable. They had it, but didn't use it.

The razor's circular motion sliced through the glass and he reached through the freshly carved hole. A quick turn of the latch and he was in.

Hardwood floors. No place for shoes. No mistakes. He didn't make mistakes.

He glided through the stainless steel kitchen and its scent of leftover roast. He slid down a narrow hall to the stairwell. Only a short climb remained.

Not a sound. No creeks. No loose boards.

The bedroom door was open. Why wouldn't it be? The elderly couple lived alone.

His sturdy frame covered the doorway. He focused on the rhythmic rise and fall of the white sheets covering the size and shape of a man. Deep breaths echoed through the room. The man posed no threat. A freight train wouldn't wake him.

The other body, much smaller, lay perfectly still. Perhaps too still.

His eyes penetrated the dark static and focused on the woman. A faint beam of light snuck through a window blind and splashed her face.

Her lids opened, then quickly closed.

She was awake. Probably in shock. Maybe pretending to sleep, praying he'd grab some jewelry and disappear. If she was going to move, she would have done so. Awake or asleep, she was no threat. Not to him.

A rush of adrenaline poured through his body. He loved the feeling. Power, God-like. Time to move. He slid into the room.

The pinpoint blow to the old man's stomach ripped him from his sleep. He cocked for another strike when the woman lunged at him. A quick stiff arm launched her to the unforgiving walnut floor.

He positioned the palm of his right hand on the old man's chin and grabbed a clump of hair on the back of his head. One rugged twist sent a dull snap through the air. The man's limp body fell to the bed.

The woman collapsed. Silent tears washed down her face. She gasped for breath. He removed a pistol from his pant leg and took aim. She focused on his clear, blue eyes and whispered, "please."

There would be no mercy.

One shot. She was gone.

He slung the old man over his left shoulder and carried him to the stairwell. He tossed the carcass and watched it plunge head over feet down to the bottom.

He poured through his victims' personal possessions. Drawers rattled open and shut. He collected some rare coins and a jewelry box from the bathroom counter.

He scoured the remaining rooms on the second floor and discovered a collection of crystal figurines that he stuffed in a bag. He returned to the bedroom and lifted the phone off the nightstand. He dialed 911 and stuffed the phone in the woman's hand.

Time to go.

He sprinted to the car and kept watch for any trace of his earlier footprints in the sand, but saw none. Nature had already covered his tracks.

A banging noise greeted him. He popped the trunk. Shoehorned inside lay a small, haggard man with thinning gray hair in a ponytail. The man was gagged-his arms and legs tied.

He ripped off the duck tape covering the man's mouth. "Goddamned son of a bitch. What're you doing?" the man shouted with a raspy Southern drawl. "Get me out of this trunk. And get this rope off me. Who are you?" His bourbon-breath penetrated the air.

Lunden leaned forward, "Not to worry. This will all be over soon."

He slammed his fist across the man's chin. Discussion over.

He lifted his victim by the collar and pitched him to the ground like a piece of airport luggage.

He leaned back into the trunk and found a bag with a duplicate black sweater and ski mask. He stripped the man and re-dressed him.

He drew the .25 caliber pistol again. He wrapped the man's fingers around the handle and trigger and squeezed off a round into a dune. Then he forced the dead-weight body into the driver's seat.

He tossed the booty bag on the front seat and dropped the pistol on the back floorboard. He cranked the car, threw it into drive, and idled toward the road. When it was perpendicular to highway, he jammed the gear from drive to park. The car jerked to a stop.

He moved to the edge of the road, knelt and waited. Three minutes passed. Two headlights materialized from the north. The height and spacing of the lights signaled it was a truck. Probably a pick-up. He timed the headlight flashes against the mile markers, then hurried back to the car. He forced the unconscious man's foot on the gas and wound the engine.

The truck approached and he jammed the gear into drive, slammed the door, and watched the car emerge onto the roadway.

His timing was perfect.

The pick-up driver had no time to react. Impact. Sounded like a violent thunder clap.

The truck's bulky front-end barreled into the Mustang's

driver-side door. Glass, metal and other debris showered the highway and the locked metal masses skidded off the road.

Then silence.

He approached the edge of the highway. The pick-up driver's bloody head rested on the steering wheel. Didn't matter whether he was dead or not. The other driver didn't make it. That was all that mattered.

Flashing lights appeared in the distance. He turned from the scene and disappeared.

2

8:34 A.M. The office was already in full sprint. Secretaries pounded computer keys. Starched, white dress shirts and conservative red ties bobbed and weaved through the maze of hallways that connected the 150 attorneys who comprised Parker, Jones, Brandt & McDowell, the largest law firm in Jacksonville, Florida.

Alex Weaver, an associate with Parker Jones, was alone on the elevator. The ride down from the 24th floor of the Riverside Towers highrise wouldn't take long.

The gold, reflective elevator door allowed for a few last minute adjustments to his appearance. He had to look good for this meeting. An important meeting—perhaps the most important of his young career. One that had bred jealousy among his peers. Everyone wanted this case. He got it.

The man looking back carried a wiry build just over six feet in height, brown hair that was a bit long for a conservative lawyer, and dark green eyes. Eyes that drew smiles from the opposite sex. Inspection passed.

The elevator doors opened. He checked his watch and paced quickly to the parking garage. Michael Murphy, head of the firm's litigation department, was waiting. He dared not be late. Murphy would introduce him to a new client—one who would change his life forever.

3

Lunden slid his key into the door and entered the sterile apartment. Fresh sweat from a long run soaked his body. Nothing about his place felt like a home. The apartment was sparse: no pictures on the wall, no magazines on the coffee table, no loose clothing lying around, no dishes in the sink.

He tossed his keys on the coffee table, walked to the kitchen, and opened the refrigerator. A bottle of cold water greeted him. He guzzled it down.

He moved out of the kitchen, down a hallway, and into the bedroom. The closet door opened to a thick, metal bar attached to the doorframe. He took off his shirt, grabbed the bar, and pulled his 6'2" body up and down. He stopped at fifty.

He rotated from pull-ups to push-ups, to sit-ups, to lunges. A relentless workout.

The moisture on his muscle structure highlighted a build resembling a middle-weight prize fighter. Like clockwork, he finished exactly one hour after he started and grabbed a towel from the laundry. He ran the towel across his face and the stubble on his closely shaved head.

"Time for the last milking," he said, moving back to the kitchen. The refrigerator contained a small clear beaker of yellowish fluid. He drew back the plastic wrap across the top and replaced it with a wax-like paper. He wrapped rubber bands around the paper draped over the beaker's neck.

He returned to his bedroom and grabbed a potato sack off the closet floor. The bag was tied at the top. "I need you one last time little girl."

Back in the kitchen, he untied the sack, aimed the open end into the sink, and lifted the opposite end in the air.

"Come on out, baby."

A black head emerged from the bag, followed by a yellow stripe, then black, then red, then yellow again—a coral snake dropped into the sink. She curled into a tight ball.

The coral snake's bite is distinct from other poisonous snakes. A rattlesnake bite produces immediate pain. Skin swells to large proportions. The venom causes internal hemorrhaging, readily detectable during autopsy.

The coral snake's venom is a neurotoxin. It stays undetected in the system for several hours before symptoms develop. After doing its damage, the venom simply dissolves out of the system. Like it was never there.

"Hold still now," he demanded, pinning the snake's head with a wooden kitchen spoon. He grabbed behind her head and lifted the reptile from the sink. He carried her to the beaker on the table.

"Okay, sweetheart. Let's take a good bite."

He pinched the snake's head to force open her jaws. She plunged her top jaw into the beaker cover and bit down hard.

"That's it."

He squeezed the snake's head. Small drops of fluid slowly trailed the side of the glass. The snake wiggled her jaws back and forth. He held her head to the beaker until he no more drops remained.

"Good girl."

Over the past week, his small companion spit out enough poison to kill five men. He sucked the fluid out of the beaker with a syringe. Time for the next job.

4

M urphy rolled down the window of his shiny charcoal Mercedes. "Get in," he said to Alex. "Charles asked us to be there at nine sharp and he has some other people joining us. Don't want to be late."

Murphy was a compelling man. Immaculate appearance. He sported perfectly coiffed silver hair. Small rounded glasses complemented a slender face. A neatly knotted blue silk tie accented his pressed, white dress shirt.

Alex carefully placed his briefcase in the back seat and hopped in the car. The scent of new leather dominated the interior.

Like his office, Murphy's car was pristine. Alex was grateful he didn't have to chauffeur. His boss would have been appalled at the empty water bottles, stray coffee cups, and wadded-up fast food bags that cluttered his old Beemer's floorboards.

They left the concrete parking garage, the same square and dull garage found at five locations in every city, and looped onto the highway. The morning sun burned the side of Alex's face. He thought twice before pulling down the visor. Wasn't sure whether Murphy wanted anyone messing with his $80,000 toy.

Eventually Alex's discomfort surpassed his fear. He folded down the visor and fanned it across the side window.

Relief.

Murphy didn't react. He kept plodding along, eyes on the road.

Murphy seized the opportunity for a brief training seminar. "Rule one in getting new business in this and any other industry is knowing your customer. When you go to a meeting, you go prepared. Know everything you can about that customer's business. Make smart points and ask smart questions. It impresses the hell out of them. Put your answers in terms they can best understand—money. Whatever you do, don't ask them 'What is it you do here?'"

"I know a little about the company," Alex said. "Van Doren Pharmaceuticals sold 40 billion dollars worth of drugs last year. Net income on paper was 3.5 billion. Research and development budget was 2.5 billion. It has manufacturing plants in the U.S., Australia, Belgium, Canada, England, Germany, Japan, Singapore, Puerto Rico, and Ireland. Of its 12 production facilities in the United States, the largest is here in town. In the last five years, VDP lost substantial market share to the other drug companies because it hasn't developed any hot new drugs. Despite the company's big R&D investment, a couple class action lawsuits and FDA non-approvals contributed to Wall Street's loss of confidence. Sales are slumping and rumors are rampant. The company looks good on paper, but in reality, it's in a down cycle and needs some good news. Perhaps some good legal advice could have prevented many of the company's problems."

His words served their purpose. Murphy stopped his patronizing lecture.

With a few minutes to spare, they arrived at Van Doren Pharmaceuticals' office complex.

Impressive. Two twenty-story towers connected by a limestone cladding. Two-hundred acres of yellow pine forest encircled the sprawling corporate campus.

Conference Room 5 resembled a modern classroom with enough seating for 50 people. Theater seats looked down at the lecturer's podium. Two men were seated in the first row when Murphy and Alex entered.

"Michael, it's good to see you," Charles Van Doren said standing. His tone was low and deliberate. "Who do we have here?" he asked, turning to Alex. Van Doren was a tall, slender man around sixty with intense, blue eyes. They seemed to bore into Alex's thoughts.

"Alex Weaver," Murphy answered. "He's the attorney I told you about. He's helping out."

"Good to meet you, Alex." Van Doren's grip was firm. "I've heard good things about you." His eyes stayed on Alex just long enough to create a little tension. "I'd like to introduce you to our General Counsel, Wilson Gates," Van Doren said, turning to his left. Gates was well-groomed, early fifties, he wore a dark suit, white shirt, and blood-red tie. Definitely a lawyer.

"We're still waiting on Jim Schofield." Van Doren said. "He's our Director of Research and Development,"

As if on cue, the door opened and a short, ruffled man entered hauling a battle-scarred attaché. He plodded down the steps.

"Speak of the devil," Van Doren called out, "here's Jim now."

Schofield looked every bit the absent-minded professor. Disheveled white hair and a ruffled suit, probably ten years old. This man obviously didn't concern himself with fashion. He was all about the business of science. If he was in charge of research and development at VDP, he had to be brilliant.

Van Doren didn't waste time starting the meeting. "I've asked Michael and Alex to help with our problem. Before Wilson explains the legal issues, I've asked Jim to give a brief background of the wonderful discovery that's led to our current problem. Jim? Please . . ." Van Doren motioned Schofield to the podium.

Schofield shuffled through paperwork and wandered to the podium. "As Charles alluded, we've made a wonderful discovery, which I'll share with you now." He spoke with a tilted head as if he pulled each thought from the air.

The old scientist cleared his throat and removed a remote from the table in front of him. He pressed a button and the lights dimmed. He pressed another button and a large viewing screen lowered from the ceiling. Four bold letters appeared on the screen. A-I-D-S.

"I think we've all seen these letters before and they've obviously had a profound impact on our world. What exactly is AIDS? Most people haven't a clue. The answer is—it's the very nasty disease known as Acquired Immune Deficiency Syndrome. HIV stands for Human Immunodeficiency Virus, which is slightly different. Some quick facts: More than 47 million people have been infected with HIV since 1970. Last year, ten people acquired HIV every minute. One million people in the United States are HIV positive. Over 300,000 are currently living with AIDS."

Schofield brought several cell diagrams to the screen. "The human body can acquire HIV in several different ways. The most common virus carriers are blood, vaginal fluid, semen, and breast milk. So how do we become infected? The virus is simply fascinating. Once the HIV bug enters the body, it goes to work immediately, assaulting the immune system."

"The immune system is a miracle invention, comprised of millions and millions of small white blood cells that fend off intruders-germs, bacteria, and viruses. If we didn't have an immune system, the common cold would be fatal. HIV knows this fact all too well."

"The virus enters the system and seeks out lymphocytes, which are groups of small white blood cells. T-cells. HIV does its harm through replication and destruction. First, it binds to the outer core of the host T-cell."

"The virus contains a molecule called gp-120, which attaches to particles that surround T-cells called CD4 and CCR5 receptors. These receptors must be present in order for the virus to enter. Otherwise, it's the equivalent of having the wrong key to your car. It won't start."

"Once the virus enters the white cell, a series of complex genetic transactions transpire, ending with the virus replicating itself and moving on to attack other cells. Over 10 billion new copies of HIV can be made every day in a host body. If the virus isn't stopped or slowed, body's immune system will be dispatched quickly because our supply of white blood cells is limited." Schofield employed his pointer masterfully, moving from diagram to diagram.

"So how do we treat people to slow the virus from spreading? Well, VDP, along with others, have developed a variety of drugs to delay the inevitable—death." he paused for effect.

"Imagine HIV as a very determined burglar with a sophisticated set of tools. The burglar's goal is to rob every house in a city. When all the houses have been robbed, the game is over. We cannot prevent him from entering the house: he's too powerful and smart. He'll eventually find his way in. The only thing we can do is make his entries more difficult. We must make him expend more time and energy to prolong the game—board the windows, install multiple locks, use deadbolts, get a dog. Keep in mind; once he breaks into a house, he converts all inhabitants into his assistants. Though he starts as one, before long he has an army that multiplies exponentially. Into millions."

"And it gets worse. This burglar's army is intelligent. It adapts to every roadblock and barricade we build. This is why we developed 'AIDS cocktails.' Patients take different drugs in different combinations. If only one drug is used to treat the virus, it will adapt and modify its DNA to render the treatment worthless. Inevitably, the virus becomes resistant to all treatments and the host's T-cells are decimated. Once the T-cell count drops to 200, he has full-blown AIDS and his prospects are grim."

Schofield cleared his throat and continued, "HIV has baffled scientists for 30 years. We learned to slow it down, but we could never stop it—until, perhaps, now." His eyes widened. "Most people don't know that for every virus out there, someone probably carries a natural immunity. This applies equally to HIV. For that person, you could inject him with HIV and he'd never get sick. With today's medical technology, if we find the person who is immune, we have a chance of developing a cure through genetic engineering. We simply generate synthetic cells through gene splicing and related techniques that use the same DNA and RNA mapping as the immune host's cells."

"But finding that person is like finding a needle in a haystack. The HIV-infected population is not overwhelming when compared to the population as a whole. Let's say, for sake of argument, 50 people in the world are immune to HIV. What are the chances of us finding them? Think about it. They won't test positive. We wouldn't know they were infected. We could never explore their bodies for a natural cure."

Schofield played his audience like a Barrymore. "Five years ago, Dr. David Rabinowitz, a physician and researcher who ran an AIDS clinic in Chicago, applied for a patent and for FDA pre-market approval for a drug called Transviazine. Rabinowitz's patent application claimed the drug could not only slow down the HIV process, but could stop the virus all together—a complete cure."

"The scientific community was skeptical about Rabinowitz's discovery. We had the brightest research minds in the world looking into this and a treating physician from a small clinic supposedly found the answer. How was that possible?"

"The answer," Schofield paused, "is he found the needle. Based on his patent applications and his FDA submissions, we can tell Transviazine was developed with human DNA from a person whose white blood cells were HIV-resistant. The genetic codes identified in the filings are a scientific certainty. I refer to this person as Mr. X since we don't know his identity."

"How can we not know who Mr. X is?" Murphy asked. "Didn't Dr. Rabinowitz disclose this person's identity?"

"Rabinowitz wouldn't tell," Schofield said. "The DNA donor preferred to remain anonymous. It's not surprising given the stigma attached to the disease."

Murphy followed up. "Doctor, I noticed you referred to Mr. X in the masculine. Do you at least know the DNA donor is male?"

Schofield looked to Van Doren.

"Very astute observation," Van Doren said. "You listen well. You have to understand, however, Jim comes to us from the Stone Age. He doesn't find women qualified for anything except sewing, nagging, and screwing."

Schofield's face reddened.

"Dr. Schofield, can you explain how we get from Mr. X's blood to a cure?" Murphy asked.

"Let me see if I can put this simply—Mr. X has a unique DNA structure. His T-cells have a mutated group of receptors distinct from typical CD4 and CCR5 receptors. If you remember my earlier discussion, HIV has an outer core component known as gp-120 that acts as a key for the virus. To open the host T-cell, gp-120 needs CD4 and CCR5 receptors. If these receptors are missing or altered, the virus can't gain entry into the lymphocytes or T-cells. In essence, Mr. X's DNA changed the locks."

"Now comes the tricky part," Schofield's zeal resurfaced in his feet as he paced from his notes to his visuals, "getting infected victims' white cells to act like Mr. X's cells. Again, I'll try to keep the explanation simple. I presume you each went to law school because you couldn't tell a periodic table from a picnic table." Schofield's condescension thickened, but his audience was too caught up in the discussion to be insulted.

"You've heard the expression 'fight fire with fire?' Well, that's what Rabinowitz did," he continued. "He applied various gene splicing and cloning techniques to replicate Mr. X's genetic makeup. Simply replicating the DNA and RNA patterns was not enough, though. He had to change the genetic makeup of the person infected so his or her host T-cells would have the same outer core as Mr. X."

"How do you change somebody's DNA?" Murphy asked.

Schofield smiled. "With a virus, of course. Rabinowitz used HIV against itself. He recreated DNA components of the virus responsible for targeting the white blood cells. He then added genetic components of a few other viruses known to be fast acting and powerful. The result—Transviazine. I like to call his creation a virus on steroids."

"When injected into the body, Transviazine rapidly bonds to the host's lymphocytes. Just like HIV, Transviazine passes through T-cell receptors with its own gp-120-type key and reproduces itself, creating a new white blood cell with mutated CD4 and CCR5 receptors. These receptors block HIV's entry. Like the HIV cell, Transviazine replicates itself and travels from cell to cell. Eventually the body's chemistry changes so all new white blood cells are formed with the mutated receptors that block HIV transmission. The Transviazine cells eventually outnumber the HIV-infected cells and allow the immune system to drive them out of the body."

Schofield stopped talking, surrendered his pointer, and turned up the lights. He plopped down next to Van Doren.

"Does it work?" Alex asked. "Has it been tested on humans?"

Van Doren nodded to Schofield to direct him to answer.

"The FDA has not issued its final approval. We anticipate that coming within the next year, so the drug isn't available for commercial marketing and sale. It has, however, been used in clinical trials on animals and had success. Three months ago, the FDA granted limited approval for experimental use on humans. We are setting up research centers and recruiting appropriate candidates for testing. We anticipate testing within the next few months. As you know, though, nothing moves quickly with the government."

Van Doren motioned to his General Counsel, "Wilson, why don't you tell these gentlemen why they're here."

"Sure, Charles," Gates responded smoothly. "Michael and Alex, as

Dr. Schofield told you earlier, we began following Dr. Rabinowitz's discovery shortly after his patent was filed. When we realized the drug was viable, we started negotiations to buy it. Rabinowitz was a tough shell to crack. He was independent-minded and ran his own testing labs, even though his budget was limited. When we offered to purchase the drug, he hedged at first, but eventually agreed to sell. Of course, he held us hostage in the process. Generous terms—for him. We paid a twenty million dollar lump sum."

"Charles," Murphy said, "perhaps you should tell Alex what happened to Dr. Rabinowitz."

Van Doren peered at Gates and Schofield, who both glanced down. "Dr. Rabinowitz was murdered." Van Doren gave him a moment to process the information before continuing. "Here's what we learned from police reports and news clippings. Rabinowitz was a strong liberal who spoke out on a variety of social issues, including homosexuality and AIDS. I suppose you could call him an activist. His clinic drew protestors and hate mongers with whom he regularly butted heads. A few weeks before his death, he received some disturbing threats from a hate group known as Aryan Nation."

"In January, only days after signing our agreement, Dr. Rabinowitz was shot and killed in the parking lot of his medical clinic. The killer, or killers as the case may be, dragged his body inside the clinic, mixed some chemicals, and set the office on fire, which destroyed the lab and most of the clinic. They had to identify Rabinowitz with his dental records. All of the patient files in the clinic were destroyed. It appears Mr. X's identity may have died with Dr. Rabinowitz."

"Did they catch the killers?" Alex asked.

"No, not yet. Still being investigated. Only thing we can do is get Dr. Rabinowitz's drug to the market. I'm sure that's exactly what he would want."

Van Doren refocused his attention to business. "Wilson? Tell

Michael and Alex where we stand right now."

"Rabinowitz signed a contract that transfers all rights in Transviazine to VDP. If things go as we expect, this is going to be the biggest drug to hit the market since Penicillin. We anticipate Transviazine will not only cure HIV and/or AIDS, but will also become a standard vaccine. It will likely evolve into a treatment for numerous diseases outside the HIV context. A drug certain to catapult VDP back to the top. Bottom line? It's worth billions."

Gates reached down to the briefcase at his feet and pulled out a packet. While he arranged the papers, Van Doren excused Schofield from the meeting.

Gates handed documents to his guests. "I made several copies for each of you. I'll give you a moment to review them before I continue."

The form of the pages was a dead giveaway as to the contents. A demand letter with a lawsuit attached.

"I know you need to look through these materials more thoroughly," Gates said, "but let me summarize. The letter is drafted by an attorney in Chicago named Gary Hudson. He represents a class of people treated for AIDS at the Great Lakes Clinic where Rabinowitz practiced. Hudson claims Rabinowitz used his patients' blood and other bodily fluids in research projects that led to the development of Transviazine. According to the complaint, Rabinowitz didn't obtain informed consent from his clients to use their blood or bodily cells for testing purposes."

"Hudson alleges his clients have property rights to the cells taken from their bodies and used in the Transviazine research. As a result, he claims his clients are entitled to any and all royalties derived from the commercial use of their cells, including royalties received from the sale of Transviazine and all drugs that become the natural offspring of Transviazine."

"He also claims Dr. Rabinowitz's sale of the patent to VDP is invalid because Rabinowitz didn't own the rights to Transviazine."

"Now the punch line . . . he is willing to settle this dispute for $100 million, plus a 15% royalty on all future sales of Transviazine for the next ten years."

Alex and Murphy moaned and rolled their eyes.

Gates continued. "Hudson's complaint is captioned in the U.S. District Court for the Northern District of Illinois. Neither the Illinois court system nor the state legislature has issued a legal ruling on the topic, which makes us nervous. This'll be a case of first impression, where law of other jurisdictions will be used as persuasive authority. As I'm sure you know, getting the right judge is a crapshoot and without law on point, we just don't know what's going to happen. To compound matters, the records from the clinic were destroyed in the fire. We're going to have one hell of a time confirming these plaintiffs were even patients of Dr. Rabinowitz."

"Hudson is a Harvard law grad who worked for a national law firm in Chicago for ten years until he figured out the plaintiff's side of the equation can be more profitable. He handles mostly product liability cases involving medical devices and drugs. He knows the drug's value to this company."

Murphy nodded. "I know Hudson. We went to law school together. He handles big cases and wins outrageous verdicts. He's smart and hard-nosed as hell."

"We're going to win this case," Van Doren said. "No ifs, ands, or buts about it. We're going to win, because we can't afford to lose. Michael and Alex, I won't tolerate anything less than absolute victory. Do you understand?" Van Doren shot Alex a glance that cut right through him.

"Charles, we won't let you down," Murphy said, taking the pressure off his young companion.

"Thank you, Michael, I know you'll do just fine, which is why you're representing me. Why don't you and Alex take the materials Wilson gave you back to your office and give them a thorough review. Let's set up an appointment in the next few weeks for a strategy conference. That should give you some time to formulate a game plan. Hudson's demand letter gives us until the end of the month to respond before he files the complaint. Come up with something good."

"You can count on that, Charles," Murphy responded and stood to exit. "We'll be in touch."

5

From the deck of his home, Mark McCall stared out at the orange sun peaking over the ocean's horizon. The colors glanced off the water straight into his mind to release memories he'd thought long forgotten. A natural death he could have handled, but a brutal double-murder; that was the sort of thing that happened to strangers.

They were gone, though, and Mark knew he couldn't do a thing to change that fact. No mom to remind him to be careful every time he flew off to some game; no dad to talk football with.

He finished his coffee and followed the trail to the beach. A creature of habit, he walked from his house to the open market in Atlantic Beach every Saturday morning during the off-season. Fresh fruits, vegetables, and seafood filled the myriad of wooden carts with prices written in black marker across the front, and vendors who seemed as interested in conversation as sales. He wasn't really in the mood to go this particular morning, but willed himself to get out of the house. Get back a normal routine and stop thinking about his loss.

Near the shore, a school of dolphin kept pace with him on his walk. Hands in pockets and head down against the crisp morning sea breeze, he meandered along the coastline, just beyond the water's reach.

Lost in thought, he didn't notice the man following about fifty paces behind him.

The outdoor market used up a half-mile of beachfront property and was marked by a wide, paved sidewalk that separated shops, restaurants, and storefronts from the beach. The sidewalk carved a popular path for rollerbladers, bicyclists, and skateboarders.

He traversed the bright sand the sun hadn't yet superheated. He stopped and turned toward the ocean. A couple strolled along holding hands with a little, ponytailed girl skipping along in front. He thought about his own daughter, Jessica. She would visit this weekend. He could use the company and they were close.

An older man and his dog found his vision. The little Terrier was bumping against his master's legs-barking up a storm at a man skipping shells. Seemingly oblivious to the racket, the young man ignored the older man and his aggressive dog.

He watched the older man say something to the younger man. The younger man didn't respond. Not even a look in the older man's direction. The older man walked off, pulling along his dog and shaking his head.

Thirty more paces and Mark was in the center of the market. A chill rushed up his spine. He turned to face the ocean again. The man skipping shells was gone. Nowhere in sight.

He struck up a conversation with a tomato vendor, bagged several items and moved on to the next stand. A half-dozen men stood near a sun-wrinkled shrimp vendor boasting about the size of his most recent catch. One of them recognized him as being the Jacksonville Jaguars' offensive coordinator and started talking football.

Suddenly, the vendor detected a new customer standing behind Mark. "Help you, sir?" he asked loudly. Mark rotated his head and found himself inches from the face of the man who was skipping shells. The man's face was expressionless. Eyes hidden behind sunglasses. But he stood close enough that his sport stick deodorant invaded Mark's senses.

"Sir?" the vendor asked again.

"No, thank you," the man responded.

Mark was accustomed to getting looks, more so from his playing days than now. This man was not a star-struck fan. After a few uncomfortable moments, the man turned away.

———

Mark exited his conversation with the locals and moved on. While weaving through the crowd, a sharp sting invaded his lower back, like a horsefly's bite. He reached around to swat away the culprit. He turned, but didn't see anything. The crowd continued casually transacting business. Nothing appeared out of place.

He scratched his irritated skin and wondered what had bitten him.

He couldn't possibly have known the answer.

He shrugged and continued from stand to stand, chatting as he passed through the market. After filling his bag, it was time to go.

He crossed the asphalt pavement and hit the sand, retracing his earlier steps. Home in sight, nausea engulfed his body. He fought the urge to vomit. "Just get home."

Sixty seconds later, his eyelids drooped. He had experienced many physical ailments while playing professional football, but nothing like this. Something was wrong. Seriously wrong.

With each step, a different symptom surfaced. His breath shortened and his vision blurred.

Finally home, he leaned his full weight on a wooden balustrade and struggled up the stairs. His heart raced. He gasped for air. Saliva funneled out of his mouth.

He barely made it, stumbling through the French doors leading inside. Through spotted vision, the telephone filled his sight. It stood on his glass coffee table. Legs numb, he lost balance and spilled onto the table's center.

The glass top was no match for his 230-pound frame. It shattered into bits on contact. A shard gouged his shoulder. Blood pulsed onto the floor.

The telephone bounced off the charger and skipped across the tile floor, out of reach.

Legs immobile, he crawled through the glass toward the phone. A trail of blood snaked behind him. He stretched his trembling hands

---

toward the phone. Before his fingers reached, a foot entered his vision and kicked the phone across the room. He rotated his head. The man from the marketplace stood directly over top of him.

"Just relax. Don't fight it," Lunden said, like a doctor soothing a child.

His brain screamed orders to grab Lunden's legs and topple him, but his strength was gone. He was paralyzed—couldn't speak. Lungs unable to pull air into his body. He was dying.

Lunden calmly watched him fade away. "Sleep well."

6

Alex wiped the sleep from his eyes and reloaded his mug with coffee. He had left the office at 2:45 A.M. after preparing for his strategy meeting with Murphy, and was back to work five hours later.

Murphy ordered him to research the claims asserted in Hudson's letter. He knew the Van Doren case was the most important project of his career. It could make or break his run for partnership at Parker Jones. He reviewed Hudson's demand letter countless times and contemplated every possible claim Hudson might assert. He painstakingly examined the contract for sale of the patent between VDP and Dr. Rabinowitz. He researched the law again and again. He even sat idle for hours, staring into space to mull over the case.

He entered the elegant conference room that provided a birds-eye view of the St. Johns River. Kyle Kirkpatrick, a partner in the firm's patent group, was also present for the meeting. Kirkpatrick was in his forties, but appeared ten years older. Life stressors, which included three divorces, had taken their toll. He carried a short, roly-poly build and had just a few strands of dirty gray on his dome.

Murphy entered the room and saved him from the requisite small talk. "Good morning gentlemen," Murphy said in his typical clipped tone. "Alex, I've asked Kyle to sit in on our meeting to lend some of his insight to potential patent issues."

Murphy directed his attention to Kirkpatrick. "Kyle, as I explained to you over the phone, VDP recently purchased all property and patent rights to a drug invented by a physician up in Chicago. We have a written agreement that indicates VDP paid the inventor, Dr. Rabinowitz, twenty million dollars for all such rights. A group of the doctor's former patients now claims that he acquired their DNA without informed consent to develop the drug eventually sold to VDP. These folks want a piece of the pie, a share of VDP's proceeds from the sale of the drug."

Kirkpatrick played with the tab of his Coke can while pondering Murphy's question. "Sorry Michael, but I haven't had a chance to study the issue in detail. What I can tell you is, to preserve any rights to a patent, people who claim ownership must record their interest with the patent office within three months of purchasing or discovering their interest. If these people who claim to have an interest fail to record ownership, anyone who buys the patent without notice of the conflicting ownership interests is the owner, free and clear." Kirkpatrick stopped talking. He pulled at the tab of his can, finally prying it loose.

Murphy leaned back and crossed his arms. "Alex, would you excuse us for a moment?"

He left the room, closed the door behind him, and waited in the hall. He heard Murphy lash into his partner. The thin walls didn't provide the necessary soundproofing.

Two long minutes later, the door cracked open, followed by Murphy's voice, "Jesus Christ, Kyle, if I wanted a shit answer, I would have gotten a summer clerk." The door closed again.

Despite the tension, he couldn't help but laugh at Murphy's tirade. After a bit more discussion, Kirkpatrick exited. His face was beet red. He passed Alex and never took his eyes off the floor.

"Alex, are you still out there?" Murphy asked.

"Yeah," he responded, not pleased at the prospect of entering the lion's den.

"Why don't you tell me your thoughts on the case," Murphy said, his eyes still narrowed.

He cleared his throat to release some tension. "While patent rights are an issue, they're secondary to the heart of Van Doren's controversy, which is whether a person has property rights to his or her DNA. If no such rights exist, then Rabinowitz's patients have no claim."

Murphy mulled over his analysis. "What's the legal landscape on patenting a person's DNA?"

Alex reviewed his notes. "The U.S. Supreme Court has held, in order to be patented, the subject of the patent must have a 'substantial utility' and 'confer a specific benefit in its currently available form.' Dr. Rabinowitz patented a drug. He did not patent or invent someone's DNA. The DNA he discovered, let's call it Mr. X's DNA, was merely a product of nature. Under federal patent law, discovering unique DNA in a human being is no different from a beachcomber finding an odd-shaped shell. In their discovered form, neither item has any worth to the public. Rabinowitz added the value through genetic engineering, without which we would have no drug. This case isn't about patent rights, because the class of plaintiffs has no proprietary rights to their DNA."

"Alex, what's Hudson, the Harvard law grad, going to say in response to your argument?"

"He's going to argue medical advancements, such as cloning and gene splicing, have changed the patent playing field. Mr. X's DNA has a special genetic code that when copied, does have substantial worth to the public. Therefore, Mr. X's DNA is clearly worth something. By analogy, it would be the equivalent of telling the Coca-Cola Company its secret syrup formula doesn't have value, because the drink is not complete until it's carbonated."

"Who wins the argument, Alex?"

"We do. The key fact in our favor—no one knows the identity of Mr. X. Hudson obviously doesn't know, because he's threatening a class action. He wouldn't need a class if he had the individual. Hudson hopes one of the plaintiffs he rounds up will have DNA matching the genetic sequence in Transviazine. He's also hoping we'll throw him a load of money to settle on the remote possibility he does. He's gambling, but who doesn't in this business?"

"Good points," Murphy nodded. "Van Doren asked us to come up with a game plan. What do you think about litigating this thing in Chicago? I have some very good contacts up there to use as local counsel. You can call them to get the conflict-checks started. I want a team in place ASAP."

"Wouldn't we be better off litigating here, in Florida? This isn't just a patent case. It's a simple contract case that begs the question—did VDP enter a valid contract with Rabinowitz? Hudson and his clients are challenging the validity of VDP's contract with Rabinowitz. We have the right to seek a declaratory ruling from a court right here in Jax."

Murphy's eyes lit up. "Yes. Good. Very good. We file a declaratory judgment action here and ask the Court to hold the contract as valid. We beat Hudson to the courthouse and make him fight on our home court. Excellent," Murphy said. "You've earned your pay today. I'll call Charles to give him an update. Why don't you prepare the Complaint and have a draft for me on Monday? We obviously want to get this thing filed ASAP before Hudson files his lawsuit."

"Should we call him to tell him we're considering his offer to buy some more time?"

"In a typical case that might be a good idea. Hudson's smart, though. He knows companies like Van Doren come out swinging when threatened. If we make a friendly call to tell him we're considering his obscene offer, we'll tip him off that we're up to something. No, the first thing he's going to see from us is a big fat lawsuit right here in sunny Florida. I think that about covers it for now. Let's get to work."

7

"You're looking better today," the nurse said while she checked Jessica McCall's vital signs. "You got banged up hard, so you're going to feel some pain over the next few weeks, but we'll give you something so it shouldn't be too bad."

The nurse made some notes on her chart. "Do you need anything?"

"No," she answered softly, groggy from the anesthetic.

"Doctor'll be in shortly." The nurse smiled and hung her chart on the door and left the room.

Before long a young, rail thin man dressed in scrubs entered. "Good morning. I'm Dr. Stanton. How're you feeling today?"

"Sore. All over."

"To be expected. Bad wreck. You suffered head trauma, which caused you some brain swelling, but we've looked at the MRI and don't believe you suffered any permanent damage. You may notice some foggy thinking, but that should clear up. You had internal bleeding that we had to correct surgically, so you'll be in here for a while. We'll need to observe you to make sure the head trauma isn't worse than we initially thought."

The doctor smiled, "You can look forward to lots of MRIs, needles, tubes, poking and prodding, and some really bad food. The good news is you're going to be fine. You're one tough lady. Most people wouldn't have walked away from that accident."

"Thank you, Doctor," she said.

"Try to get some rest and I'll come by later today with our best orthopedic guy to look at your ankle."

She forced a smile and the man left. She turned her head away from the door and cried. "Dear God, what's happening?"

The answer would come looking for her.

8

lex worked around the clock on Van Doren's complaint and motion for summary judgment so he and Murphy could file first thing in the morning. He hadn't slept more than three hours any night during the past week. Van Doren appeared happy with the way the case was being handled, and to Alex's surprise, Murphy let Van Doren know that he had come up with some good ideas.

The plan was to file the Complaint in federal court along with a motion to ask the Court to rule that Rabinowitz's former patients didn't have property rights to their DNA. If Van Doren prevailed on the motion, it would severely damage Hudson's case and go a long way to assure Van Doren it was the rightful owner of the drug.

"Shit," he said, checking his watch. It was 12:05 P.M. Murphy had left a message to join him at Noon for a quick lunch to touch base on another matter. He smelled another case. Another case to make him work even later into the night, but he knew he couldn't say no. He rushed down to the building's concourse to meet Murphy in the cafeteria.

Murphy was busy studying the various mystery meats behind the glass in the hot lunch section. He didn't seem to notice Alex was running late. "Make sure you tell them to hold the salmonella if you're going to order from here," he called out. "I'm going down the line for a turkey on wheat. Even these guys can't screw that up too bad."

Murphy had a serious look on his face as they sat down to eat. "You probably read in the paper Mark McCall died. Collapsed in his home. Totally unexpected."

Alex and everybody else who had access to a news source knew

---

about Mark McCall's death. "Yeah, I know. That's awful."

"Mark was a good friend to me, as well as the firm. We do all the Jaguars' legal work. Mark and I served on several charitable boards together. You don't even know the half of the tragedy his family's gone through in the past few months. His parents were murdered in their home by some thug, then Mark dies. And just last week his only daughter, Jessica, was in a serious car wreck."

"Good God."

"Jessica's a great young woman," Murphy said. "She's just like her dad—excels at everything she puts her mind to. She's in law school right now at Florida and, from what I hear, we'd be lucky to get her to work for us when she graduates."

"Anyway, Jess was driving home on I-95 and lost control of her car. She rolled her SUV a bunch of times. She's lucky to be alive. We're all grateful for that. Unfortunately, after everything she's been through, the person she hit is suing her for personal injuries he allegedly sustained in the accident."

"What happened to him?"

"Jessica crossed the median and sideswiped the trunk of the guy's car, which was stalled on the shoulder with a flat tire. She knocked off his bumper and spun his car around, but he wasn't in the car. He jumped out of the way or something when he saw her coming. No signs of physical injury, but he's claiming a back injury and severe emotional distress. This guy's a real piece of work. Ronnie Patel's his name. I had Jim Haney, our investigator, explore Patel's background. You know Jim, don't you?"

"Sure, I've used him on a few cases. He's good."

"Anyway, this Patel clown is a leach. Workers' Comp, slip-and–falls; you name it, he's filed it. He treats the court system like the state lottery."

"Where do I fit into the picture? Isn't her insurance company handling the case?"

"Should be, except Jess wasn't covered when she had the accident."

"Why not?"

"Parking tickets."

"Huh?"

"Parking tickets. She picked up a couple from the campus rent-a-cops last year and forgot to pay them. She moved to a new apartment and the DMV notices didn't get to the correct address. She's been driving on a suspended license for the past six months and she didn't even know it until now. Never came up. Her insurance policy bars coverage if she's driving on a suspended license. We may be able to argue she's still insured anyway, but the insurance company's refused to pay for her defense."

Alex saw where the conversation was headed.

"I raised this issue at the last partners' meeting and got the firm's full support to provide a legal defense for Jessica in this case . . . which brings me to you. The partners kicked around the names of litigation associates to handle this thing and I was pleased your name came up quite a few times. You've obviously impressed some people. Hell, you've impressed me, and that's hard to do." Murphy laid it on thick.

"What would you like me to do?"

"Be a lawyer, Alex. We want this asshole, Patel, chopped off at the ankles. He's throwing around outrageous settlement numbers and we want him dispatched."

"Who's his lawyer?"

"Just flip over your phone book."

"Buddy Adkins?"

"The one and only. That rotten son of a bitch spends more time littering accident scenes with his business cards than the Pope spends in church. He also represents deadbeats in Workers' Comp cases. Of course, I don't think he's ever used a licensed physician to support one of his claims. He gets back-crackers who'll say anything he wants for a

$50 fee. The partners would love to see you hang one on good ol' Mr. Atkins."

"Happy to help."

"Good. I'll ask Francis to get you the case file this afternoon. I know it's late notice, but I told Jess someone would meet with her this week. Our clock is ticking on getting an answer filed. She's still tender from the accident, but she tells me she can get around now. If you need to call her, she's in town for a while at her dad's house. Francis has her number."

"I'll take care of it."

"If you need anything, let me know. And I want you to keep me posted every step of the way."

"Absolutely."

9

"Hey, Weaver. Let's go man," Rob Foster said with his head popped in Alex's office. The tree tall Georgian won over most everyone his quick wit and Savannah-style story-telling. Foster was Alex's closest friend in the firm. Early in their careers, the two young lawyers were packaged and shipped to Philadelphia for an intensive document review that lasted six months.

Twelve-hour days reading the illegible medical records of more than 2,500 plaintiffs made the days unbearable. But two young single guys loose in a big city with a hefty per diem made the nights quite entertaining.

Alex glanced up from the papers scattered across his desk. "Where?"

"Sliders. I'm meeting some friends from law school around eight-thirty for supper and adult beverages. More importantly, Tiffany is the hostess on Thursday nights."

"Is that the stripper you and the guys have been telling me about?"

"Please, Alex, adult entertainer. Show some respect."

"Can't make it."

"Boy, you gotta eat. More importantly, you gotta drink. You've been working way too much. You're making the rest of us look bad. Now come on."

"Man, you know I'd love to, but Murphy's kicking my ass. I'm getting him prepped for a hearing next week and he has me in meetings every day. I'm not going to face that guy first thing in the morning with a hangover."

"Speaking of, you brown-noser, you sure are the talk of the firm."

"What's that supposed to mean?" He leaned back in his chair.

"Well, let me see . . . you've been working with Murphy a lot and haven't been fired yet. You're working on a great case with the firm's biggest client. Your name is di-rectly beneath Murphy's on the pleadings. And, oh yeah, you've completely pissed off the two biggest asshole associates, which I guess makes you my personal hero."

"Felton and Ritz? How did I piss them off?"

"Both of those pricks went to Murphy's office looking to horn in on your project with Van Doren."

"Yeah?"

"Oh-yeah," Foster said, clearly enjoying himself, "and you know what Murphy said? You're going to love this one."

"What?"

"He told them to ask you if you needed any help. He may as well have pissed in their shoes," Foster roared. "Can you imagine Murphy telling those guys to go ask you for work? A couple Ivy Leaguers working for a lowly Florida grad."

"How do you know what happened?"

"Henrietta. You know the big lady from the mailroom who always wears stretch pants? She was picking up something from Murphy's bitch of a secretary. She heard the whole thing. Felton told Murphy he'd prefer to work for him directly and Murphy told him, 'you might learn more from Alex,' and tossed him out of his office like a trespassing Jehovah's Witness."

"Isn't Henrietta the one Felton calls Aunt Jemima?"

"Yeah. Racist prick. She's overheard him say that, too. Anyway, you overworked hound, you deserve a round of drinks for adding some much needed drama around here and I've rounded up some willing buyers."

"I really have to take a rain check, Rob. Otherwise, Murphy may just rethink his decision to use me over Felton and Ritz."

"All right. Point taken, but I remain disappointed. I'm not wasting any more drinking time to convince you. You sure you don't want to go?"

"Yeah, I'm stuck here for a while. Say hi to Tiffany for me."

"You got it," Foster said, slapping the doorframe as he left.

He finished his coffee. "Time for a refill." He wasn't going home anytime soon.

10

The firm had all sizes of conference rooms. The room reserved for Alex was small, able to hold six, but only four comfortably. Alex wasn't a klutz. He earned a golf scholarship to the University of Florida. But he didn't show it today as he entered the small, square room with too much vigor and stumbled forward clumsily.

The stack of files in his hands spilled out on the floor. He kept his balance, but not a whole lot of his pride. "So much for a smooth entry," he thought. He half-reached for the loose papers when it dawned on him he'd better first introduce himself to his client.

"Hi, I'm Alex," he said, face burning. The woman seated at the table reached for her crutches and tried to stand up.

"Please, don't get up."

"I wasn't getting up as much as getting out of your way," she grinned. "I'm Jessica McCall and it's nice to meet you."

"Excuse me just a moment," he said, attempting to recover both his papers and his cool. "Okay," he thought, "silky brown hair—shoulder-length, brown eyes, olive skin, warm smile, doesn't need makeup . . . couldn't possibly pick a worse time to look like an idiot."

"I'm sorry to hear about your accident," he said as he picked up the last file. "How are you feeling?"

"Thanks. I'm actually doing a lot better. Should be able to get rid of these crutches and the knee brace by the end of the week."

"That's good to hear."

"My dad worked with several lawyers at your firm through the football team and he was close to Michael Murphy. He's been a good friend to our family and is kind of like an uncle to me. I know the firm is handling my case pro bono as a favor to us and I appreciate everything you and Parker Jones are doing."

"Ms. McCall, I can't tell you how sorry we all are about your family. I only wish there was more we could do."

"Please, call me Jessica or Jess. That's what my friends call me. And thank you."

He began to explain the case to his client. "I understand you're in law school, so I'm sure you have a pretty good idea of what this case is about. The plaintiff, Patel, claims he suffered physical and emotional damages because you hit his car after you lost control. He's represented by Buddy Adkins, who's on the back of the telephone book."

"Lovely. Do you think he has a case?"

"Well, you did hit his car. It's an old rust bucket, but on his injuries, he's overreaching by a mile. He's looking for a settlement. Nothing more. I phoned Buddy Adkins this morning. He knows who you are and thinks your family has money. He's trying to play hardball."

"How much does he want?" Jessica asked.

"He threw out five hundred thousand as an opening bid . . ."

Jessica cut him off, "Five hundred thousand . . ."

"Don't panic," he said, "he'll be lucky to get five hundred, let alone five hundred thousand."

"Why on earth is he asking so much?"

"That's just Buddy. Don't worry about it," he said. "Look, here's what we'll do. We'll schedule a bunch of depositions and bury Adkins in paper. These billboard lawyers don't make money by going to court. They want quick turnover. They'd rather spend ten minutes writing a demand letter to make five hundred dollars than litigate a case for a year to make five hundred thousand. Adkins runs an assembly line based on volume and turnover. We're going to stall the line. Once Buddy figures out he'll spend more in fees on this case than he'll receive in settlement, he'll drop it like a rock."

He placed a legal pad in front of him and took out a pen. "To get what we want, though, we have to beat up on Mr. Patel. I have to know all the facts, which is why we're meeting today."

He thumbed through a file, pulled out some papers, and peeled back his note pad to a fresh page. "I've seen the police report and I know some basics. Why don't you give me the details; what happened the night of the accident?"

Jessica played with a water glass as she spoke. "With everything that's happened in my family, I've been traveling a lot between Gainesville and Jacksonville. I withdrew from classes at Florida this spring semester to take some time off to spend with dad until next fall. I was driving back to Gainesville to pick up some things the night of my . . . umm . . . my accident."

"Before you get to the accident, give me the background leading up to it," he interrupted.

"I'd been staying at my dad's house since he died. That's where I was when I left for Gainesville that night. It was a Tuesday around eight o'clock, so the traffic was light. As I pulled out of the driveway, I checked my rearview mirror and saw a car sitting on the side of the road. The car's headlights turned on and it pulled out behind me."

"Was there anything unusual about the car? Why did it stand out to you?"

"One headlight was brighter than the other. The passenger-side light on the car was dim. It's also just unusual for cars to park on the road in our neighborhood. There isn't much of a shoulder and there's no good beach access. It didn't make sense for anyone to just pull over and stop there. It's not a gated community where you have security guards, so we've always paid attention to strange cars passing through. I guess that's why I noticed. Just habit."

"Anything else?"

"No, nothing unusual. Just an old pickup truck."

"What happened next?"

"For starters, I felt creeped out. I don't know why—I just did."

Alex listened as his client spoke.

"Once I left the beach," she said, "I didn't notice the truck following me anymore. Everything was fine when I merged onto I-95. I was playing with the radio dial." She paused. Her breath became shallow and fast. Her face was a bit pale. "I'm sorry," she said. "This is difficult."

"Sure. Just take your time, now. You were playing with the radio dial . . ."

"Thanks. I'll get through this, I promise," she said with a strained smile. "This guy . . . he came out of nowhere. I didn't see him until it was too late."

"Who came out of nowhere?"

"The man in the truck."

"I thought he was gone. You didn't see him again after leaving the beach."

"That's what I thought, too, but all of a sudden, I saw that dim headlight directly behind me. It was the same truck I saw pull out behind me as I left my dad's house. It was like he knew exactly where I was going."

"What happened next?"

She sighed. "He was tailing so close, I couldn't brake or he would have hit me, so I started to change lanes so he could pass. That's when he rammed the back of my car and I swerved."

"God, what happened next?"

"There was a grass median . . . I crossed it, and then as soon as I did, my car slid all over the place. When I came back on pavement on the opposite lane, I was driving into oncoming traffic. My tires grabbed the road and then the steering wheel jerked out of my hands. Somewhere in there, I must have hit Patel's car, but things were happening so fast . . . I'm afraid it's a blur."

"Do you remember anything after that?"

———

"Well, yes and no. I thought I was in a bad dream. The frame caved in around me. Glass shattered. It was awful. I thought I was going to die." She paused again and took a deep breath. "The next thing I remember—everything just stopped. My car was stuck upside down in the ditch across the highway."

She glanced down. "The door frame was crushed and I was trapped inside. My body was numb. My ears were ringing so loud. I'll never forget that ringing sound. Then I remember hearing something outside. I looked over toward the door and saw a pair of eyes peeking in through the small opening in the crushed frame. Whoever it was didn't say a word. Not even an 'Are you okay?'"

Her hands trembled. "I tried to ask for help, but I couldn't really talk. After a few seconds, the eyes disappeared and two hands came through the small gap in the window. The man reaching through must have been strong, because he pulled the metal apart with his bare hands to create space to reach in. I thought, 'Thank God, he's going to get me out of here.'"

She choked up. He slid a tissue box toward her. "Do you need a break?"

"No, I'd like to finish," she said. She grabbed a tissue and watched herself twist the ends in her hands. "The man forced his hands and part of his arms through the window opening toward my face. I tried to reach for the hands. All of a sudden, he grabbed my wrist. He grabbed so hard, I thought my bones were going to shatter."

She paused. "I couldn't scream. I tried, but couldn't make any noise. He tried to get his other hand through the opening in the door to pry apart more metal. I heard him grunting. He was struggling to get at me. Then I heard his voice," she looked up. "He said, 'Come here, Jessica.'"

"How did he know my name? How could he possibly know my name?"

At that, he looked up from his notes. "Should we stop?" He asked. "We can continue this another day."

She acted as if she didn't hear him. "It took everything I had to turn my body and push away from him so he couldn't grab more than my arm. It's bad enough to think you're going to die once in a given day. I thought I was going to die twice."

"Then I heard other people coming up to the car. That's when he let go. They were shouting to call for help. I could feel the car move from people walking around and touching it, looking for a place to get in. I don't remember anything else. I woke up in the hospital." She stared into his eyes, "I know it was him. I just know it."

"The person who ran you off the road?"

"Yes."

Not exactly the story he was expecting. He wondered whether the trauma caused her to hallucinate. "You know, you've been through an awful lot," he said. "I think I should let you rest. I will do everything I can to help you. I promise." He hesitated, not sure how to handle his client. Instinct told him to hold her. She needed to be held, that much was obvious, but . . . no.

"Do you need anything else from me right now?" She appeared as if she wanted to escape.

"I have enough for now. Before you go, let me give you my card." He quickly wrote his home and cell numbers on the back before handing it over. "If you think of anything else—anything—please give me a call. Anytime. Do you have any family or friends in town you can stay with for a while?"

"I have some friends around. Like I said, I'm staying at my dad's house. I'll be fine." She cut off any discussion of family.

"Don't let this lawsuit bother you. You have a lot more on your mind right now. And please, if you need to talk about anything, just call me. It's the least I can do for a fellow Gator." He gave a reassuring smile.

She grinned at the small diversion. "You went to Florida, too?"

"Yep."

She hooked her crutches with a wrist, and started to stand. He got up to help. "Thanks. It was very nice to meet you and I'm sorry I got away from myself there. I just . . ."

"Don't apologize. I understand."

She brightened. "I have to say, I was a bit concerned after watching your entrance. I guess I'll keep you as my attorney anyway—for now. Make sure you have that carpet checked out. I wouldn't want you to get hurt."

He laughed. "I'll be calling for an investigation. You can count on that." He walked her out of the office. He was definitely interested in his new client.

11

One of the tenured female guards nodded a hello to Alex as he approached the metal detector in the brand-new federal courthouse. The large rectangular building with a glass and metal back was a work of modern engineering to some and an eyesore to others. He didn't have an artistic bone in his body-an architectural agnostic on evaluating modern building designs. When the topic came up in legal circles, he just nodded and stayed quiet.

The guard's badge introduced her as Lydia Rodgers, but everyone knew her as The Grande Dame. She was one of the first mixed-race hires for the courthouse and the very first female guard. She'd seen more than her share of action in her thirty-plus years as a federal guard and she relished her new relaxed role of "greeter guard." "Like Wal-Mart with a gun," she liked to joke. The Grande Dame held up a basket for Alex. "Personal belongings in here and your briefcase on the conveyer. Then walk through." She pointed to the frame metal detector.

He followed instructions and emptied his pockets. "Oh, no," he said when his fingers found his cell phone.

"No cell phones," Lydia eyed him over the tops of her glasses. "You know that, son."

"Can you keep it behind the counter?"

"We're not allowed to take any personal possessions." She smiled at the angst on his face. "See that bush on the front steps?" she asked, pointing.

He followed her arm. "Yeah."

"It's a thick bush, you know. If your phone was in there, it wouldn't fall out. You know what else?" Her sly smile worked like a tonic on his anxiety.

"What?"

"You'll find about four or five other cell phones in there. The boys and I keep a close eye on that bush. Can't promise anything, but we haven't had any complaints about lost phones. Just make sure you grab the right one when you leave."

He released breath he didn't know he was holding. "Thank you so much."

Problem resolved, he cleared security and rode the elevator to the fifth floor. He exited left and stopped in front of the double doors that read "Courtroom 5, Honorable Franklin W. Shelton." He pushed through and got his first glimpse of the courthouse of the future.

Television monitors were mounted all over the room. The litigator podium had a built-in microphone and a video projector facing the witness box. The jury box had video monitors fronting each juror's seat. The days of handing documents to witnesses and jurors were over.

The administrative clerk, who sat at a desk directly below the judge's bench, operated a control panel directing images to any screen in the courtroom. The courtroom even featured a sound system funneling white noise, like the sound of a television that had lost transmission, so jurors and spectators couldn't hear sidebar conferences between the judge and attorneys.

He passed through the three-foot swinging gates that separate the spectators from the court players. He dropped off his briefcase on counsel's table and approached the judge's administrative assistant who was busy reviewing the court schedule.

"Hello, Alex, how have you been?"

"Great, Sharon. You?"

"Keeping busy, that's for sure. What do you think of our new courtroom?"

"I'm going to need a vocational class in audio-visual to figure this out."

Sharon laughed. "It's not as bad as it seems. I'm sure you won't have too much trouble. Are you here for the nine o'clock?"

"Yes."

"Are you representing Van Doren Pharmaceuticals?"

"Yep."

"Are you the only attorney for Van Doren or will someone else be joining you?"

"Michael Murphy'll also be here."

"Okay, then. I'll mark it down. Have a seat. Judge usually runs on time. Opposing counsel, Mr. Hudson, checked in and stepped out."

"Thanks."

The courtroom doors opened and a fortyish man with jet-black hair entered the room. Tall and slender, he sported a double-breasted suit. Unusual for a Jacksonville courtroom.

"Good morning, I'm Gary Hudson. Are you here on behalf of Van Doren?" Hudson's game face read "all business."

"Yes, Alex Weaver."

"Will you be handling this today or can I expect Mr. Murphy?"

"Mr. Murphy," he said, glancing at his watch.

"Looks like he's cutting it close." Hudson opted against small talk and took his seat.

Murphy was never late. "Where is he?" Alex wondered. He organized his papers and tried to pull his thoughts together in case Murphy didn't make it. His nerves flared.

A voice boomed across the courtroom from behind the judge's bench. "All rise," the burly courtroom deputy announced and opened the chamber doors behind the bench. A man in his late fifties with white hair and small rectangular reading glasses perched on his forehead appeared from behind the door, black robe flowing and files under his arm. He moved swiftly and possessed an air that commanded attention. The courtroom silenced. With a sweeping glance from his stoic face, he took the bench.

The deputy finished the traditional announcement. "The United States District Court is now in session. The Honorable Franklin Shelton presiding."

"Please be seated," Shelton said with a commanding bass tone that belied his smallish build. His precise manner announced he was a stickler for rules and protocol.

"Good morning. I've reviewed the pleadings and all briefs filed by both parties. It looks like we have a potential mess here. My clerks, as well, have looked through your briefs and researched additional case law. To the attorneys' credit, you presented them well in your respective papers."

Before Judge Shelton could go any further, Murphy rushed through the courtroom doors. The judge halted while Murphy sped to his table.

"Your Honor, please accept my sincerest apologies. A semi overturned on the highway and traffic was blocked for miles. There is absolutely no excuse for my tardiness, but I owe you an explanation. Again, my apologies."

"It's nice you could make it, Mr. Murphy. I'm sure these proceedings would have been sorely lacking without your presence. Let's get to it, shall we?" he continued. "Van Doren Pharmaceuticals filed this declaratory judgment action to obtain a ruling that the contract between it and a Dr. Rabinowitz is valid. It is my understanding VDP purchased the patent rights to a drug Rabinowitz invented. Am I right so far?"

Murphy stood. "Yes, Your Honor."

Shelton continued. "Shortly before VDP filed this lawsuit, Mr. Hudson wrote a demand letter to VDP alleging Rabinowitz did not have the right to sell the patent. Specifically, Mr. Hudson alleges on behalf of a few dozen John Doe plaintiffs, Rabinowitz used their DNA to invent the drug that is the subject of the VDP contract. As a result, his clients hold title to at least a portion of the patent VDP purchased. The contract, therefore, between VDP and Rabinowitz is invalid. Does that sound about right to you, Mr. Hudson?"

"Yes, Your Honor," Hudson said, also standing.

Shelton had a knack for stripping issues to their core. "Now, in this declaratory judgment action," he continued, "the parties have asked the Court to make certain legal rulings regarding a person's property rights to DNA. The parties have stipulated to certain core facts and, as a result, the Court may have enough to rule on the pending motions. Mr. Hudson, in your motion, you have asked the Court to rule individuals have a property right to their DNA and that you can't patent cells modeled after an individual's DNA without permission. Van Doren has asked I hold the opposite—that people do not have a property right to their DNA. Mr. Hudson, I will hear from you first."

Hudson rose and approached the podium with a slender notebook he flipped open to a marked page. "Thank you, Your Honor. First, let me say I haven't had the pleasure of practicing in this jurisdiction before today and I appreciate the opportunity. In your opening remarks, you were correct in stating the parties have presented you with novel and compelling issues. We are dealing today with the scope of a human being's right to decide what is done with his or her body. When considering the building blocks of our society, I believe the answer is clear that every person has a property right to his or her own body." Hudson's high-pitched voice pierced the air without needing amplification.

"The primary support to my argument can be found in the Fifth Amendment to our Constitution, which guarantees every citizen a right to privacy. We all have privacy rights to our medical history. Because of this right, no one can explore our medical histories without permission. With the advance of genetic research, our right to privacy becomes more threatened every day. Scientists can take a snapshot of genetic code merely by drawing a little blood. They can predict whether a patient will develop certain diseases with a reasonable degree of certainty, not to mention seeing any and all afflictions from which that patient may currently suffer."

"Ancillary support comes, in a broad way, from the Fourth Amendment, which protects against unreasonable search and seizure."

"This isn't a criminal case," Shelton interrupted, "Let's move on."

"Your Honor, it's only a matter of time before scientists can predict anticipated dates of death on the day people are born. As this Court is well aware, laws currently on the books bar insurance companies from conducting DNA profiles on prospective clients. The reason is obvious. If an insurance agent knows his client will die within the next two years of a heart attack, he won't write a policy."

Shelton stopped the argument once again. "Mr. Hudson, I can appreciate your position on the right to privacy. How do we get from right-to-privacy to the issue in this case: right-to-property."

"Yes, Your Honor, that's where I was headed. My clients allege Dr. Rabinowitz did not obtain informed consent to use their DNA in his genetic research. A physician has no right to provide treatment, or even draw blood, until a patient is first informed of the doctor's intentions and then grants permission. In this case, the evidence will show Dr. Rabinowitz took blood samples for what he claimed to be treatment purposes when, in fact, he used these samples to patent a drug and get rich. Indeed, Van Doren paid Dr. Rabinowitz millions for his patent."

"Critical policy issues are at stake. Our law must discourage medical researchers from deceiving patients. Patients have every right to know how their bodies are being used. We cannot condone the practice of calling patients back to their doctors' offices for treatment under false pretenses. People miss work for doctor appointments. They lose wages.

They lose time. They're poked, prodded, and inconvenienced."

"Clinical research studies pay volunteers to submit to this kind of testing. Your Honor, if you have a miracle cell in your body that might be used to cure cancer, you have every right to negotiate a fee with medical researchers to submit to testing. If you're brought in for treatment under false pretenses, you unfairly lose that bargaining right."

"Mr. Hudson, let me stop you right there. Before we go any further, I want to hear from VDP on this point." He looked over toward Murphy and Alex's table. "Do patients have a right to remuneration for having body parts removed for someone else's benefit?"

Murphy rose, buttoned his coat, and approached the podium. He placed his notes in front of him. "Thank you, Your Honor."

"Mr. Murphy, what are you doing?" Shelton asked.

"I don't understand, Your Honor. You asked me to give VDP's position."

"No. I didn't. I said I'd like to hear from VDP's attorney. When you're late to my courtroom, Mr. Murphy, you are no longer that attorney. Not today. If I excused every attorney who was late because he or she was held up in traffic, no one would ever show up on time in this city. You of all people, Mr. Murphy, should know I take matters of professionalism very, very seriously. When my order says nine, it means nine. Do I make myself clear?"

"Yes, Your Honor, but with all due respect, if I'm not permitted to speak today, then I would ask the issue be stayed until we get another hearing. This is too important, and my client has requested I take the lead."

Shelton was apoplectic. "Mr. Murphy, sit down before I hold you in contempt." His voice echoed over the courtroom. "We are not going to reschedule this hearing. How you explain this to your client is not my concern. If you don't want to continue this hearing, that's fine. I'll let Mr. Hudson finish his argument and then I'll decide. In fact, you can leave any time you like. Your presence here became irrelevant at 9:01.

Now, what's it going to be, Mr. Murphy? I can hear from Mr. Weaver or you can both go home. Your choice."

By now, several attorneys from Parker Jones had entered the courtroom to observe the argument. Heads ducked and hands covered grins as the stunned audience relished in the impromptu show. Shelton stared directly at Murphy who was unprepared for the lashing. Murphy scooped up his papers from the podium, "Your Honor, may it please the Court, Van Doren Pharmaceuticals would like the opportunity to respond to Mr. Hudson. Mr. Weaver will respond on VDP's behalf." Murphy headed back to his table with his tail between his legs.

"Good. Please approach the podium Mr. Weaver."

Alex looked at Murphy who waived him to the podium without saying a word. He straightened his tie and cleared his throat, still in shock from what he had just witnessed.

"Thank you, Your Honor," he studied the notes he scribbled down before the hearing started. "With all due respect to opposing counsel, he is arguing a different case than is before this Court," he said, relieved he found a way to start his argument.

"He wants to talk about privacy instead of property. He wants to transfer Dr. Rabinowitz's alleged misconduct to Van Doren Pharmaceuticals, which had nothing to do with treating Dr. Rabinowitz's patients. Before allowing Mr. Hudson to castigate Dr. Rabinowitz further, I would emphasize no evidence has been presented demonstrating patients of Dr. Rabinowitz lacked informed consent to any procedures or testing."

"VDP seeks a simple and basic legal ruling-that the patent it purchased from Dr. Rabinowitz is valid, nothing more. Van Doren bought a drug from Dr. Rabinowitz, not a blood sample as Mr. Hudson suggests. A patent right exists only for a tangible process that is useful, novel and non-obvious. Human cells in their raw form are none of these things. As held by the U.S. Supreme Court, a patent must confer a special benefit in its currently available form. A human cell in its raw form does not confer any special benefit. As far as the law is concerned, cells removed from Dr. Rabinowitz's patients were worthless. The value was added when Dr. Rabinowitz used his expertise to develop a drug."

"Let's consider another angle. What happens to excess blood or tissue samples physicians draw for routine tests? They're discarded under procedures established by state law. The state, not the patient, decides what is done with tissue samples. Frankly, most hospital patients have no interest in having their blood samples returned. I've known many people who go to the hospital for tests. Not once have I seen any of them come back with vials of their own blood. I had my tonsils out when I was twelve. After careful consideration, I let the hospital keep them." He smiled. He was in the zone now. No more nerves.

"Mr. Hudson cannot point to one case where a person has been paid for his or her body tissue or organs. In fact, the U.S. Congress decided, in passing the Uniform Anatomical Gift Act, it is unlawful to compensate people for donating their organs. Can you imagine the Pandora's Box of ethical problems associated with letting people sell their organs or tissue cells? If I can't make the rent this month, maybe I can hock my left eyeball—it's a very good eyeball." Muffled laughter sounded from the gallery. Even Judge Shelton suppressed a smile.

"Responding specifically to Mr. Hudson's argument, if a doctor requires a patient submit to medical tests under false pretenses, that patient can file a malpractice claim against the offending doctor. That patient can then seek recovery for lost time at work, inconvenience, as well as physical discomfort. What the patient cannot do, under any circumstance, is place a dollar value on the extracted blood and tissue. Indeed, they have no value. Again, in their raw form, they're worthless. More importantly, we want to encourage doctors in every possible way to cure disease. If the lure of money results in medical discoveries, so be it."

"And what about the impracticalities of Mr. Hudson's position? We cannot create a bureaucracy that requires a doctor to anticipate every possible use for a blood sample taken from patients. The worth of a cell may not be discovered until long after any single patient is treated and gone. What happens if the doctor cannot then find the patient to get informed consent? What if the patient withholds consent to research that could cure cancer? In this particular case, we're talking about a cure for AIDS. With the lives of so many at stake, to the extent we err, we must err on the side of providing doctors more freedom and less red tape."

"Finally, current law does not support Mr. Hudson's position. We cited Moore vs. Board of Regents, a California decision, where the precise arguments raised by Mr. Hudson were flatly rejected. There, a physician scheduled his patient for medical tests under false pretenses. The physician did not disclose he was conducting a research project using the patient's cell tissue and the tests performed were not medically necessary. Those tests resulted in a scientific discovery from which the treating physician profited."

"The plaintiff sued his physician under a number of legal theories. As Van Doren stresses here today, the plaintiff had every right to recover damages for being required to undergo unnecessary medical procedures under false pretenses. But, the Court refused to stretch the law so far as to hold the plaintiff had a property interest into the medical discoveries that resulted from his treatment. Though no Florida case law is directly on point, every other jurisdiction to consider the argument falls on the side of prohibiting the public from selling their live tissues and organs. They also fall on the side of encouraging doctors to find cures."

"Your Honor, we must allow the doctors to continue inventing, and let's pay them well for doing so. Van Doren purchased a valid patent. That's why we're here, and that's how this Court should hold."

He ran out of words.

"Do you have anything else, Mr. Weaver?" Shelton asked.

He glanced back at Murphy who shook his head. "Nothing else, Your Honor. Thank you."

He returned to counsels' table. The tension rushed out of his body. Murphy pursed his lips and gave an approving blink as he passed.

The judge turned his attention back to opposing counsel. "Mr. Hudson, isn't a claim for malpractice sufficient deterrent to prevent doctors from lying to patients about their treatment?" Hudson stood quickly and shuffled his notes.

"I think not, Your Honor. If I happen to strike oil in my backyard, the law allows me to profit from that. The same should hold true if I have a rare DNA component that can assist with the development of a profitable drug."

Judge Shelton did not appear convinced. "Mr. Hudson, oil has independent value. Your blood does not. I happen to agree with Mr. Weaver that our DNA in its raw form is worthless. The researcher must do something with it to make it valuable. My high school biology teacher kept her polyps in a jar and proudly displayed them to the class. She is the only person I have ever known who asked for the return of a removed body part. And Mr. Hudson—she was a nutcase."

With the exception of Hudson, the courtroom exploded in laughter. Hudson tried again to press his point. "Your Honor, if a doctor thinks he can make money from your DNA, you should be able to negotiate a price to contribute your DNA to his research. If you don't have any property right to your DNA, your doctor isn't going to have any incentive to be honest with you. His primary goal will be to get blood, tissue, or whatever else he needs, out of your body. Then he's free to do anything he likes. Our current system encourages doctors to lie."

"Mr. Hudson, do you really want the cure for cancer delayed because contract negotiations have stalled with Joe six-pack? Do you want every hospital patient to feel compelled to hire a lawyer to supervise a blood draw?" The judge paused. "Don't answer the last question. I almost forgot my audience."

"Look," Shelton continued, "not to make light of this very serious matter, the chances of having million dollar DNA are rare. I don't see doctors lying to their patients as a matter of course. I'd like to think the cannons of ethics mean something in both law and medicine. I won't render a legal decision on the flawed foundation that doctors can't be trusted."

"Your Honor . . ." Hudson tried to press the issue.

"Sit down, Mr. Hudson. I've heard enough and I'd like to wrap up this hearing." Shelton waited for Hudson to return to his seat.

"On the issue of patient property rights to their DNA, I rule in favor of Van Doren Pharmaceuticals. To the extent that Mr. Hudson's clients assert rights to Van Doren's patent based on testing Dr. Rabinowitz performed using their DNA, their claims are dismissed. This leaves one remaining issue-whether anyone had rights to Dr. Rabinowitz's drug, by reason other than participating in the testing Dr. Rabinowitz conducted. As the parties are aware, the plaintiffs have also asserted claims to the drug Transviazine based upon express or implied contracts. If Dr. Rabinowitz entered any contracts with his patients or any other third parties concerning a right to profit in the drug, then he would not have had the right to sell the patent. Even this argument, however, may not prevail since VDP claims to have purchased the patent without notice of any third party claims. I'm sure all the attorneys know if a patent interest is not recorded, then the purchaser takes the patent free and clear unless he knows through other means the patent is being challenged."

"I'll issue an order and set the case for trial to see if the plaintiffs have any evidence. If they don't, then I think you all know what I'm going to do. I like to move my docket, so plan to work quickly."

Shelton made some notes and looked up. "Is there anything else I need to address at this time?"

Alex rose first. "No, Your Honor."

Hudson stood. He worked his jaw, but he didn't speak. The judge looked up from his papers. "Mr. Hudson, your lips are moving, but nothing's coming out. Do you have anything else for me at this time?"

"Not at this time, Your Honor," he said, finally.

"Very well, Court is adjourned."

"All rise," the deputy's baritone filled the courtroom.

Judge Shelton quickly moved through the door behind the bench. Hudson packed his briefcase and marched out of the courtroom with only a slight nod to his adversaries.

"This was a big win," Murphy declared. "Let's get a private investigator up to Chicago ASAP. I want to know everything about Rabinowitz: what he ate for breakfast, who his friends were, what he did in his spare time-everything. I want to see every contract this guy entered, even if it was selling lemonade for a nickel out of his garage."

"Do you think Hudson has anything?"

"Hell no. If he did, we'd have seen it by now. But I don't want any surprises. Hudson isn't the only one I'm worried about-in these kinds of cases, I've seen all kinds of crackpots come out of the woodwork to make claims. Class actions are like light to moths. I want to make damn sure we're clean."

They packed their briefcases and greeted several Parker Jones attorneys in the gallery who observed the hearing. After a few moments, Murphy grabbed Alex to thrash out the case as they walked out of the courthouse. At the security checkpoint, the guard caught Alex's attention.

"You should be in good shape." The Grande Dame gave a slow nod and blinked at him.

"What's that all about?" Murphy asked.

He reddened. "Well, to make a long story short, my cell phone is in that bush." He pointed to the viburnum, walked to the shrub, reached in the center and pulled out his phone.

"Alex, do me a favor, would you?"

"Sure."

"Reach back in there about a foot to your right and get my phone too, would you?" Murphy's face carried a big grin. Alex reached his hand back in and pulled out another cell phone.

"That's it." Murphy reached for the phone. "You know, I don't think I could have argued that one any better. Maybe not even as well. Excellent job. I'll see you back at the office."

12

Wearing pajama bottoms and an old T-shirt, Jessica strolled to the end of the driveway where her newspaper sat in a puddle from the overnight rain. "Perfect throw," she said, shaking off the water. When she turned around, she noticed a man wearing blue work pants and a striped button-down shirt standing in the side yard with a clipboard. He seemed to be examining the pale wooden shingles on her father's house.

"Excuse me," she shouted. The man appeared caught off guard. "Hello," she shouted again, moving closer. She weaved through the scattered palm trees her father planted to add some character to the otherwise barren, long and slender yard.

"Hey, ma'am. How you doing this morning?" The man spoke with strong drawl and tipped his baseball cap.

"Hi. I don't mean to be rude, but may I ask what you're doing here?"

"Yes, ma'am. Annual inspection. Mr. McCall has the place checked out once a year before hurricane season. Are you a friend of Mr. McCall's?" The man's eyes hid behind sunglasses.

"I'm his daughter."

"Oh, well ma'am, it's nice to make your acquaintance. I'm Bill Calfee." He stepped forward and reached out. She approached cautiously. His limp handshake surprised her given his strong build.

"I tried knocking on your door earlier, ma'am, but got no answer. You must not have heard me."

"Who are you with?"

"First Coast Home Inspectors."

"Do you have a business card?"

"No, ma'am, I'm sorry I don't. I ran out the house this morning in a bit of a hurry. Is there a problem?"

"I just haven't heard my father ever talk about an annual inspection."

"Is he home, ma'am? I'm sure he could straighten out any misunderstanding."

"No, he's not here right now."

"We'll, ma'am, I don't need much of your time. If it's all right with you, I'll finish the outside inspection and then I'll need to look at the windows from the inside. I shouldn't be but a few more minutes."

"Do I know you from somewhere?" She studied Calfee. Intently.

"People ask me that a lot. I must have a look about me."

Out of the corner of her eye, she saw her next-door neighbor, Bernard Volkman, emerge from his front door holding a tennis racquet.

"Mr. Volkman," she yelled. "Excuse me for a moment, Mr. Calfee."

"Good morning Jess, how are you?" Volkman put his racquet on the hood of his car and started across the yard.

"Great. Do you mind stopping over for a second. I have some mail for you that came here by mistake." She glanced back at Calfee, whose stare made her skin crawl.

"Be right there Jess." Volkman appeared younger than his 66 years. Tennis three times a week at the club kept him in great shape.

"I'm sorry. I've been trying to catch up with him," she told her uninvited guest.

"Take your time, ma'am" he said, and returned to his work, jotting notes on his clipboard.

Volkman trekked around the back of his house where the fence stopped and made his way toward Jessica.

"I'm sorry to trouble you Mr. Volkman. I wanted to give the mail to you before I left for the day. It's inside."

"No trouble at all. I appreciate you letting me know," he said, moving past Calfee.

"Getting some work done, Jess?"

"Annual inspection."

She and Volkman marched to the front door and entered the house. She closed the door and hurried him into the kitchen. "Mr. Volkman, I'm so sorry. I don't have any mail for you."

He raised his bushy eyebrows.

"I need to ask you something. Did my father have an annual hurricane inspection? That man out there said dad had the home inspected every year before hurricane season."

"He never said anything to me about an inspection, but that doesn't mean he didn't have it done. What's going on Jess? You don't look right."

"I don't think that man is who he says he is."

"What?" Volkman glanced toward the front of the house.

"I can't explain it," she said. "I have a bad feeling about him. Something seems off."

Volkman's focus softened. "Let's see what we can do to figure this out. What's his name?"

"Bill Calfee. First Coast Home Inspectors."

"Did he give you a business card?"

She nodded. "He forgot it."

Volkman grabbed the telephone and opened a drawer. He was in Mark McCall's house so many times; he knew where to find the phone book. .

"Let's see here," he said, thumbing through the white pages, "First Coast Home Inspectors—here it is." He dialed the number. "Hello?" he said into the phone, "do you have a Bill Calfee who works there?" Volkman nodded and glanced at Jessica. "Is he there today? Out on assignment is he? Well, this is Mark McCall. Am I still on the schedule for today? Uh-huh. Okay. I see. Thank you very much." He hung up.

"Jess, he works there and he's on assignment this morning. Your dad, I mean this place, is on the list of stops today." He touched her elbow. "Are you all right? Do you need me to stay? I won't have you troubled. I'll cancel my tennis match this morning if you like."

"No, that's sweet. Go to your tennis match. Maybe sometime this week you can take me to dinner and spend some of your winnings. Dad warned me you were a hustler."

Volkman laughed. "Mark should have known better than to say such things about the old and decrepit. You sure you're all right now?"

"I'm fine. Now please, go play tennis." Volkman left.

She retraced her steps outside to find Calfee. She felt bad about the way she spoke to him earlier.

He wasn't there.

"Mr. Calfee?" She circled the house, but didn't see anyone. She scratched her head. "That's weird."

Back inside the house, she dropped the newspaper on the stairway. She headed to the laundry room off the kitchen and tossed a load in the washer. The twist of a knob had the machine spitting and churning. She headed back to the kitchen. When she turned the corner from the hall, she found the man seated at her kitchen table.

"Oh," she yelped and steadied herself on the wall.

"I'm sorry, ma'am. Didn't mean to frighten you," Calfee, said. Still wearing sunglasses, his gaze held her attention.

"What are you doing in here?" Her heart pounded.

"I thought I told you, ma'am, I need to see the inside. I had a look around and everything checks out."

He pushed back from the table and rose deliberately. The smile abandoned him. He laid his clipboard on the table and moved toward her.

"What are you doing?" she asked. "Don't come any closer."

He ignored her, took another step forward, and then the doorbell rang followed by a series of loud knocks. Her eyes darted toward front door and then back at the man standing nearly on top of her.

"Ma'am, there's somebody at the door," he said calmly. His forward progress stopped.

She slid along the wall like a ledge walker and kept her eyes on Calfee until she entered the hall. She charged the front door and jerked it open.

A scraggly young man in work clothes greeted her. "Good morning," he said, "I'm here for the inspection. My first appointment canceled, so I'm early. Hope that's all right." He also spoke with a slight drawl.

Her eyes widened. She looked back down the hallway, but saw no one. She turned to the man at the door.

"Are you all right?" he asked.

"I'm not sure. I don't . . . I don't know what I am. I may be losing my mind," she said. "Are you with Mr. Calfee?"

"Excuse me?"

"Are you with Bill, the man in my kitchen?" Her stomach was in knots.

"I am Bill," he answered. "Is this the McCall residence?"

"You're Bill?"

"Miss, I don't know what's going on, but I'm obviously here at a bad time. Maybe I should come back later."

"What's your name?" She demanded. "Tell me your name."

"Bill Calfee. I'm with First Coast Home Inspectors. Here's my card." The man produced his business card. "Like I said, I had an appointment to do an inspection at this address for McCall. I'm sorry I'm early." The man sorted through his work papers.

She grabbed his arm and jerked him out onto the porch. She jumped down to the front yard and put some distance between herself and the young man. "Why is there a man in my kitchen who claims to be you?" Her pitch grew with each word.

"What? Look, ma'am, I don't know what you're talking about," he said.

"Do you have an ID?"

The man's face was blank. He found his license, walked down the stairs toward her. She backed up quickly.

"Stop. Right there. Throw it to me."

"What the hell is going on here?"

"Just throw me your ID." She softened her voice. "Please, just do it."

The young man threw his license on the grass at her feet. Her eyes never left him as she bent to scoop it up. She swapped glances between the license and the new Calfee, the real Calfee, several times.

"I need your cell phone." She pointed to the phone attached to the man's pocket. She started toward him. "I need 911 right now."

"I'm just here for an inspection, Miss. I don't want to be mixed up with the law. This is a company phone. I don't want no trouble."

"Give me the goddamn phone." In two strides, she ripped the instrument from his belt. He didn't resist.

She dialed and jammed the phone to her ear. "I'd like to report an intruder in my home."

13

"We've searched the entire house, Ms. McCall. All clear. Whoever was in there is gone now," Sergeant Walker explained to Jessica who now sat on her porch swing. Walker was a round man with prematurely graying auburn hair he kept in a crew cut.

"What about him?" She pointed to the second Calfee speaking to several other police officers in her front yard.

"His name is Bill Calfee and he actually works for First Coast Home Inspectors," Walker said. "We called his office and his manager told us he was scheduled to be here at 9:30 this morning. His first appointment canceled, so he got here early. The appointment was made sometime last week."

"Last week?"

"That's what they said. Last week."

"Who scheduled the appointment?"

Walker flipped through the pages of his pocket-sized note pad. "Mmm, let's see here. Looks like the appointment was made by—Mark McCall."

"That's impossible. You know that. My dad's dead. He couldn't have made the appointment," she said.

"Anybody could have made the appointment. Look, we have no way to check where the call originated."

"Why would somebody impersonate Mr. Calfee?" she asked. "Could the person have been another employee of the company? Someone who wants to get him in trouble? Play a trick on him?"

"We checked whether any other employees may have been assigned to this house and they said no. It's a small shop. They only have four employees. Calfee was here, one guy's on vacation, and the others were on assignment with customers at the time you say this other Calfee was here. Whoever he was, he wasn't an employee of First Coast Home Inspectors. As for why someone would try to impersonate Mr. Calfee? We have no idea. He does have quite a rap sheet, though. Not exactly the kind of guy you'd want to impersonate."

"Do you think he and the other man set this whole thing up?" she asked.

He chewed over the possibilities.

"Calfee's telling us he doesn't know anything about this other man you described. His story checks out. He was responding to what he believed was a legitimate appointment."

"You mentioned Calfee's rap sheet. What's he done?"

"Ms. McCall, I'd rather not say."

"Please, Officer Walker, I'm in law school. I'll go online and look up the charges in the public court records. You could save me hours of fumbling."

Walker removed his sunglasses and wiped his forehead. "To name a few," he said, "attempted rape, sexual assault, battery, and attempted kidnapping. A few years back he tried to snatch a teenage girl from a mall parking lot after dark. Fortunately, he didn't get very far."

"How could a company hire a person like that for in-home inspections? That's outrageous. And what's he doing on the street? Shouldn't he be in jail?"

Walker sighed. "The Sheriff's office provides criminal background checks for companies on a regular basis. In my experience, most companies check all their employees' backgrounds, especially those who'll be in customers' homes. But a lot of mom-and-pop shops like First Coast don't do background checks. Maybe Calfee knows someone there who vouched for him. I don't know. I *can* tell you I've seen entirely too many in-home crimes by employees who are supposed to be there on business. It's pretty common, especially theft."

Walker glanced over at Calfee, now resting in the back of a police car with the door open. The officers standing next to him appeared finished with their interview. Walker turned his attention back to Jessica. "As far as why he's out of jail, our prisons are overcrowded. We have to make room for all the new criminals. The average murderer, you know, spends only 7 years behind bars. I guess Calfee did some time and now he's out on probation. Maybe one day after law school you'll be a prosecutor and change all that," he said with half a smile.

The cadre of officers were getting restless. She could tell Walker wanted to leave, too. "What can I do about this situation? What if that guy comes back?"

"Not much we can do. We have his description. You still need to come down to the station to look through mug shots. Even if we find the man we're looking for, the only thing we can do is charge him with trespassing or, at most, breaking and entering. This won't be a high priority downtown. We're up to our eyeballs in more serious crimes. If you feel uncomfortable, you may want to get a dog or some other kind of protection."

"There must be something else you can do."

"Tell you what, I'll have a patrol car do an extra run by your house for the next couple of weeks. That's as far as I can go. You have to understand we serve the entire community. Jacksonville's the largest land mass city in the U.S. That's a lot of ground to cover with very few officers and I can't justify the extra resources for a trespassing situation."

Walker's words registered. She knew there wasn't anything he could do.

"If you have any problems, give me a call. I'll be in touch."

"Thank you. I appreciate your offer. And sorry if I was rude earlier.

———————

I've been through a lot lately."

"We're all sorry about your dad. We're here to help. You have a good day, now."

14

"One more pitcher over here," Foster waved at the bartender. His deep voice cut through the noisy beach bar. The bartender nodded and filled another pitcher. Foster rounded up a willing group from the firm for drinks.

"Here you go," Foster said, filling up Alex's glass.

"You're killing me, Rob." He knew his limits and didn't like to stray beyond a mild buzz. With only bar pretzels in his stomach, he was already there.

"Shut up and drink, sissy boy," Foster said, gulping down half his glass. His large frame was built for sustained drinking.

"Alex, you gotta tell me about the look on Murphy's face when the judge told him to sit down and shut up. Jesus, I would have paid admission to see that."

"Shelton was in a bad mood. He lit into Murphy, but Murphy handled it fairly well. Wasn't much he could do."

"I'd like to know how he explained that one to the client."

"Carefully, I'm sure. By the way, Murphy invited me to dinner at Van Doren's house next weekend."

"Man, what next? Dinner at the White House? Where does ol' money-bags live anyway?"

"San Marco. 10,000-square-foot house on the river."

"I expected a double-wide. Figures he'd be in the old money, high-rent district," Foster said, then tossed back some kind of chaser. "Are you working on anything other than Van Doren's case?"

"Yeah, I have a few going. You remember the football coach who died—Mark McCall?"

"Yeah. Heart attack, wasn't it?"

"Right. Murphy asked me to represent his daughter, Jessica, in a car accident case filed by Buddy Adkins. The girl's had some rotten luck lately." He swigged his beer. "Not too long before her dad died, her grandparents were murdered."

"God, that's awful. But we don't do insurance defense. Why'd we take her case?"

"A favor. Her insurance coverage lapsed and she's not covered. Long story." Alex raised his glass.

"So? What's she like?" Foster asked. "Spoiled, underachieving, trust fund baby?"

"Law review and top 10 percent of her class."

"So, she's hideous," Foster joked.

"That's what I expected until I met her. This woman is beautiful."

"Do I need to remind you of your legal ethics and how we're not supposed to get involved with clients?" Foster teased.

Temporarily lost in thought, he let the comment slip right past him. "You know, Rob, there's something about her that's odd. She thinks somebody tried to run her off the road—even kill her. That's, uh, a little . . . I don't know . . ."

"Sounds like a nutcase. Remember, you're representing her in a lawsuit, nothing more. Don't get mixed up in all kinds of sordid personal affairs, and by that I mean *affairs*. The last thing you want is to wind up in the wrong place at the wrong time."

"I guess so. Speaking of sordid matters, are you still working on the McGregor Medical litigation?"

"Good gawdalmighty, yes. How many more years of my life am I going to have to devote to mass tort product liability? I'm up to my ass in info on medical devices for spinal surgery. Do you have any idea how difficult it is to defend a lawsuit where the plaintiffs allege they hurt more now than they did before the surgery? How can I prove they're lying? I deposed a guy today who said he could barely walk after his surgery and his pain on a scale of 1 to 10 is a max 10. Later, I asked him how he got to the deposition. You know what he said?" Foster slammed his hand on the table. "He rode his motorcycle. Fergodsake, the man lives 100 miles from our office and he rode his goddamned motorcycle to the deposition. How does a guy who claims he can't walk, carry groceries, bend, or lift, ride a fucking motorcycle a hundred miles? I used to have a motorcycle, my friend, and that thing wore me out riding across town." Foster's animation increased in proportion to drinks and audience.

The thought of Foster's outburst during the deposition when the witness told him about the motorcycle ride was nearly more than Alex could bear without choking on his drink. "What was his attorney's reaction?"

"She wasn't listening. Too busy picking zits off her face. I shit you not. She had a mirror and actually picked zits. I thought I was in The Twilight Zone. They sure as hell didn't teach me to expect that in law school."

"Did you put it on the record she was popping zits?" He could barely get his sentence out without doubling over.

"If that's not enough for you, I deposed a guy last week for *six hours* who told me at the end he didn't understand a single question I asked. He took three times the normal dosage of his pain medication. He also told me he was an alcoholic and, because of his affliction, he was forced to drink *two pints* of scotch before he showed up. I wasted six hours of my life on this guy. And guess what? It's the product's fault he's an alcoholic."

"Hey, that's not a waste of time. That's good, solid, billable work, my friend."

Foster's eyes shifted toward the bar's entrance.

"Incoming, Alex. Radar on your back. Three o'clock. She's armed.

She's dangerous. And she's coming for you."

He spun around and spotted Kerry Westfall gliding through the front entrance. "Help me get to the back door," he groaned.

"What are you, gay or something? Look at her. You need to take her home if for no other reason than to have something good to tell me Monday morning. How many law students do we get who look like that—especially from Jersey, man?"

"She's a summer clerk, for God sake."

"So what? She's 23. You're 29. She's made the whole world know she wants a piece of the Weaver. What's the big deal? You don't supervise her. You're not her mentor. The only thing you are is a consenting adult. And let's get one thing very clear: You're not taking advantage of her. Nobody takes advantage of that one."

"She makes me uncomfortable."

"Nothing a few shots of vodka won't cure." Foster picked up his glass and stood. "I'm going to go see if Jensen needs a partner at the pool tables. Catch you later."

He staggered off and Kerry approached. They spoke briefly before she turned toward Alex.

"Hi," she said with a broad smile and a slow hug. Her snug, faded jeans fit entirely too well, and her undersized camisole top exposed enough skin to radiate trouble.

"How are you?" He asked, unable to conjure up anything witty.

"I suppose congratulations are in order for your performance at the Van Doren hearing. You're quite the lawyer."

"Anyone would have handled it the same. I just got the opportunity." He pushed back and pulled on his draught.

"You're too modest. Murphy talks about you like you're his favorite son."

"All right, enough ego-pumping. Let's talk about you. How's clerk life so far?" He hadn't gotten the bartender's attention, so he reached down behind the bar and swiped a clean glass from a stack. He poured the last of his pitcher into the glass and handed it to Kerry. She smiled and tapped his glass.

"Doing just fine," she said. "Working on all kinds of projects—some interesting, some boring. Social activities have been fun, though. We've gone to functions at different attorneys' homes, a few ball games, dinners—you know the deal." She paused and smiled, not afraid to hold his eyes with her gaze. "Shoot some pool?" She tapped on his chest and let her finger slide down to his navel. "I'll need a partner."

"Sure." *Anything to get her off of him.* "Don't expect much. I'm on my fourth pitcher."

He developed quite a pool game tending bar during law school. Kerry held her own and appeared comfortable in the male-dominated area. Together, they ran the table most of the evening. Since table bets involved payoffs in alcohol, he flew well past his limit by the time the evening wound down. He handed his stick to Foster, who was no doubt embellishing a story to a blonde.

"Partner, I'm retiring," he said to Kerry.

"Not so fast." She pulled him back by his belt. "We need to celebrate our dominance. Follow me." She locked up his hand and pulled him to the bar. She leaned over the bar like only a woman can and motioned to the bartender. She had no trouble getting the guy's attention. "Two shots of Absolute and two lemon wedges," she shouted over the bar noise. He thought back to Foster's comment about vodka and laughed.

"What's so funny?" She asked.

"You don't want to know."

She looked him over and let the comment pass. "A toast to the hottest lawyer at Parker Jones." She passed him one of the shot glasses sitting on the bar.

"Is Ritz here?" he asked.

"Shut up and drink, smart-ass." She gulped the shot and bit the lemon. He reluctantly followed suit. There'd be hell to pay in the morning. And her long gaze spelled trouble.

"You seem a bit drunk. How'd you get here tonight?"

"Foster."

"From the looks of it, Mr. Foster may have traded you out for the bimbo with the big hair."

Alex peered toward the back of the bar at his friend, who was hard at work. "You might be right."

"I'd better drive you home."

"Kerry, I don't think . . ." Before he could finish his sentence, she placed a finger on his lips.

"Shhhhhh. Don't say anything," she said. "Just come with me." She grabbed his hand and led him through the crowd. He made eye contact with Foster, who smiled and saluted.

15

"Alex wheeled into a long drive, stopped by a black wrought iron gate flanked by dark brown brick columns. He lowered his window alongside a speaker built into the brick siding. Two surveillance cameras mounted on the columns rotated toward him. A man's voice sounded from the speaker.

"Good evening. Can I help you?"

"Alex Weaver," he announced. The humidity seeped in his window.

"We've been expecting you. Please drive past the gate and pull up to the circle."

A row of small in-ground lights along the driveway guided him to the massive Tudor home perched on the river. A small, balding man wearing a sport coat and tie greeted him.

"Good evening, I'm Henry," he said, shaking his hand. "If you wouldn't mind, please pull your car forward, just a bit, next to the others." Henry pointed ahead to several other cars, which included Murphy's Mercedes.

Alex wore typical business casual: blue blazer, button-down shirt, and khaki pants.

Henry led him through a large ornate oak door into the foyer. He marveled at the heavy dark wood staircase that angled up 20 feet to the second floor.

The two men passed the formal dining area, which was perfectly prepped for dinner. The table was draped in a white cloth and adorned with orchids. An elaborate crystal chandelier hung over the table. They meandered into a conservatory that offered a picturesque view of the

St. Johns River through its seamless floor-to-ceiling windows. Henry opened the door to the brick patio that ran the length of the house.

Van Doren leaned against the 3-foot thick brick wall that protected the patio. Next to him, Murphy and Wilson Gates each had one hand in pocket; the other on a clear drink with a lime squashed to the bottom.

Three women seemed lost in rapid conversation at a table at the rear of the patio. His entry stalled the various conversations and all eyes shifted their focus.

"Good evening," he announced with a quick wave.

"Alex, good you could make it. Come, join us," Van Doren said. "What would you like to drink?"

"Beer would be fine, Mr. Van Doren. Thank you."

"Henry, please bring our guest a Heineken?"

Henry nodded and disappeared.

Van Doren turned for introductions. "You know Michael and Wilson. Let me introduce you to the ladies." He and Van Doren crossed the brick patio.

"This is my wife, Cheryl. Next to her are Emily Wilson and Pamela Murphy."

Though Van Doren was the oldest man present, he had the youngest wife. Cheryl Van Doren could pass for late thirties. Dark tan and long, wavy bleach-blonde hair. Heavy makeup and short skirt announced she was trying too hard to pass for late twenties. The two other women, casually elegant, dressed their age; around fifty.

"We've heard a lot of good things about you," Pamela Murphy said, giving him her full attention.

He exchanged polite conversation for a moment before Van Doren pulled him away. Henry returned with the beer.

"Alex, I want to thank you in person for all the hard work you've done on my case. Michael tells me you stood in for him at the oral argument and performed admirably. This means a great deal to me."

Van Doren sipped his red wine and let his eyes inspect the young man.

"Thank you, Mr. Van Doren, but Mr. Murphy deserves the credit for preparation and strategy. He is the best."

"What a crock of shit," Murphy threw back his head and joined Van Doren in the joke of the night.

"You've trained this young man well," Van Doren said.

Like everyone else, Gates matched the uninspired casual attire, but he looked worn. His eyes were dark and sported large bags. No spark. He laughed politely and nodded where appropriate, but his mind seemed elsewhere. As the men talked, he sipped his drink and listened, never adding much in conversation.

Henry announced dinner, which was an extravagant affair. Van Doren hired a chef to prepare a five-course meal complete with complementing wines. Snifters of Grande Fin Champagne cognac followed a fresh fruit Crème Brûlée.

"This is such a beautiful home you have, Cheryl," Murphy said.

"Thank you. If you, Alex, and the ladies are interested, I'd be happy to show you around."

"Yes, by all means, darling," Van Doren agreed, "give them the tour. I need a few minutes with Wilson anyway. We have to finish some business."

"Good. If everyone will follow me down the hall," Cheryl said, moving slowly out of the dining room. She began describing some paintings on the wall.

Alex didn't want to be rude, but his bladder was full and he needed relief. He excused himself and said he'd catch up in a few minutes. When he returned to his starting point, everyone was gone. Except Henry.

"Where'd they go?" He asked.

"Study." Henry pointed down the long hallway to his left. A red Oriental rug covered the wood flooring down the long corridor.

He passed several rooms on his route, unsure which was the study. He peaked into several rooms, but each was empty. Farther down the hall, he heard voices. They belonged to Van Doren and Gates.

Feeling foolish, he debated whether to ask Van Doren for directions or attempt to find the group on his own. But they wouldn't know, would they?

Plotting his next move, he overheard a conversation.

"Are we sure the agreement will never be found?" Van Doren spoke in a low growl.

"Yes, Charles. Everything was destroyed. The contract died with Rabinowitz," Gates snapped back.

"That had better be the case. We can't afford any screw-ups. This drug is too important. Where do we stand on the corporate transaction?"

"Taken care of. We've used the European accounts and created some new shells. No way to trace it back."

"What about the police, what have they found?"

"Nothing. Absolutely nothing."

"Good. Let's make sure it stays that way."

Alex felt sick to his stomach. He light-footed his way back down the hall. But after a few steps, his foot found a creaky floorboard. The voices in the study stopped.

Footsteps closed.

He froze, then he spun toward the study and started a normal pace toward the room he just left. Van Doren and Gates met him head-on.

His heart raced.

"Hey," he said, forcing a smile, "I lost the tour group and Henry told me they went this way. Have you seen them?"

Van Doren and Gates shot glances at each other and then back at him. "No, we haven't," Van Doren said. His eyes, unblinking, contradicted his casual tone. "I suggest you look upstairs." Van Doren pointed down the hall.

"Thanks. I guess I'll see you two shortly. I hope I haven't missed too much." He turned and started back down the hall. Van Doren and Gates watched him.

"Do you think he heard anything?"

"I don't know," Gates said. "I don't know."

He found the others and ran through the motions of touring Van Doren's estate. He couldn't get the conversation out of his mind. He struggled to make small talk and act normal the rest of the night. He was dying to tell Murphy what he heard, but he wouldn't dare try now.

The evening wound down around ten. Gates and his wife were the first to leave. Michael and Pam Murphy followed shortly after.

Alex said his goodbyes and intended to follow Murphy out the door. He nearly made it out when Van Doren called him back.

"Alex, may I speak with you?"

"Sure." Butterflies flew in formation in his belly.

"I want to show you something." Van Doren put his arm across his back and led him through the basement into a dimly lit hallway and approached a large oaken door with an oval window at eye level.

"There's something in here that might interest you, Alex. Go ahead." Van Doren pushed open the door to a pitch-black room and extended his arm. Following behind, Van Doren reached for a switch and turned on the light. Inside was a cavernous wine cellar.

"My favorite room in the house," Van Doren said, proudly scanning the massive wine cellar lined with several thousand bottles of premium wines.

"This is incredible," he said, wondering whether Van Doren could hear his heart beat.

"I want to show my appreciation for your dedication and figured you might appreciate this." Van Doren pulled a dusty bottle off one of the wooden racks. He handed it to Alex. "Château Margaux. I think you'll enjoy it."

"Mr. Van Doren, this isn't . . ."

"Please, I'll be insulted if you don't accept. It's the least I can do. Just promise you'll save it for a special lady. A fine wine like this should not be wasted on mere concubines," Van Doren leered.

"Thank you, this is—this is very kind of you."

Van Doren escorted him out of the wine cellar, up the stairs to the front door.

"Thank you again for the wine and the invitation to your home." He was anxious to leave. He turned, but Van Doren grabbed his shoulder firmly and stopped him in his tracks.

"Alex, I can expect your unwavering support as my attorney, can't I?" Van Doren kept a tight grip. Even painful.

"Yes, of course."

"Can you think of any reason why I wouldn't be able to count on your loyalty?"

"No."

"You'd tell me if there was a reason, wouldn't you?"

"Of course. Is there a problem, Mr. Van Doren? I don't . . . I don't understand."

"You have a promising career, Alex. I take very good care of my friends and right now I consider *you* a friend."

He didn't know how to respond. Fortunately, he didn't have to.

"Please drive safely," Van Doren said. "I wouldn't want you to have *an accident*—especially since we're friends." Van Doren released his grip.

"Good night, Mr. Van Doren, and thank you again for the wine."

16

Two police cruisers raced past Lunden with their lights flashing on the north side of Jacksonville. The Northside always kept police busy. The streets were speckled with black teens in tattered clothing. "Fucking animals," he blurted.

He pulled into a closed-down convenience store with barred-up windows and doors. He parked at the end of the lot, stepped out, and approached a beat-up pay phone that stood in total darkness. The place was dumpy with oversized weeds growing from every one of the thousand cracks in the asphalt. Weeds even sprouted out of the rusty and degraded gas pumps that hadn't seen action for years. Not the sort of place a Yuppie would feel comfortable.

But it didn't phase Lunden. He had seen much worse. Places the government sent him to apply his special skills, where death was part of everyday life. Places the government would steadfastly deny he had ever been.

Those days were long gone. Nobody could stay on Uncle Sam's payroll as an assassin for long. These special soldiers had limited life spans and he was no exception.

Too stressful. Only a matter of time before the alcohol and drugs would shift from a diversion to a need. Something to kill the pain of the kill.

Like those who came before and those who followed, he was replaced. New lives would be destroyed, on both ends of the soldiers' pinpoint sights. From the government's standpoint, an acceptable cost of doing business.

He shoved two coins in the slot and strained to see the numbers. After several rings, a voice answered.

"Hello?"

"I hit a bit of a snag and couldn't complete the job."

"I don't understand. I thought I was clear this needed to be resolved promptly," a male voice snapped back.

"We have time. I'll take care of it before the deadline. A contingency arose outside my control. A neighbor showed up. Then our pigeon appeared an hour early. A real cluster-fuck. But I'll take care of it soon."

"You blow this thing and you won't see another dime. Do you understand me?"

Two black teens leaned against the wall of the convenience store. They appeared out of nowhere and distracted him.

"Calm down," he said. "I'll honor the terms of our agreement and I trust you'll do the same." He glanced back at the men who were now stalking him. "I have to go. I'll be in touch."

He hung up the phone and headed back toward his car. The men bolted toward him and blocked his path. The apparent leader, heavy-set, wore jeans and an untucked Cowboys jersey. The other had a slender, muscular build and wore stained warm-up pants with only tattoos covering his top.

"Hey, man, you ought to know better than to get outta your car up here," the large man said. He pulled a long drag off a cigarette. Tattoo-man stayed quiet.

He studied them while they circled.

"You lost, boy?" The large man continued to close in.

"Whatever I am is none of your business," he responded in a low tone that should have signaled a warning.

"No shit? You hear the shit this fucking cracker is talking?" The large man said to his buddy, clearly pleased with himself.

Tattoo-guy was silent.

"Well you know, boy, you owe toll for driving through here," the large man said.

"You and your friend are making a mistake. You'd best move on."

"Fuckin-A. You a cop? You don't look like no cop. You're too decked to be a cop up here. No one looks like your punk-ass. Now reach into your pockets and show me what you got."

The larger man raised his right hand in the air and pressed the release on a switchblade. The blade snapped open. He moved close enough for the stench of alcohol and cigarettes to offend Lunden's senses. Tattoo-man walked directly behind him, out of sight.

"Did you hear me, boy? Empty them pockets," the large man said, jutting his knife toward Lunden's face. "I ain't gonna ask you again."

Lunden smiled. "This might hurt." Without a blink, his foot connected with the heavy-set man's groin. With that one doubled-over, he spun around into tattoo-man. He thrust the open palm of his hand into tattoo-man's nose, crushed the cartilage and sent a stream of blood shooting into the air.

Tattoo-man hit the ground and clutched his face. Lunden turned to the larger man, still bent over, and grabbed his right hand. He twisted and yanked it behind the man's back. Tendons and small bones crackled. The large man's screams filled the sticky night air.

The knife fell to the ground. Lunden drove his heel into the man's leg, sending him to his knees. He spun again and kicked his target squarely in the face.

He turned back toward tattoo-man, who was still holding his nose and mopping blood from his face. The man struggled to his feet and swung wildly. Easily dodging punches, Lunden launched another open-fist blow, and sent tattoo-man down for the last time.

The two men lay motionless.

He rummaged through their pockets, pulled out several wads of cash and a dozen colorful pills stuffed in sandwich bags. He emptied the bags on the ground and put the cash in his pocket. "Fucking animals."

17

Alex handed his keys to the valet who gave him a ticket in exchange. "Welcome to The Surf Grill," the young man said. "Enjoy your dinner."

"Thanks," he responded with a quick glance at his watch. Running late, he hurried inside the overpriced restaurant that fell somewhere on the moderate end of the dining spectrum. Good seafood, average steaks. No more than three stars. Not by a long shot. The selling point was location. Smack dab on the beach. It was only a matter of time before the condo developers bought it and knocked it down. They were buying everything south and east of town.

Inside, two older couples blocked the hostess stand. The foursome was locked in a philosophical debate about whether a twenty-minute wait was too long. One of the men demanded a menu to ascertain whether the meals were too pricey. They didn't seem to notice the line growing behind them.

The hostess noticed Alex. "Excuse me for a moment," she said to the group and looked toward him. "Can I help you?"

"Yes, I'm meeting someone and I'm not sure whether she's here."

"What's her name?"

"Jessica McCall."

"She's at the bar." The hostess pointed at two saloon doors that opened up into the lounge. A table should be available shortly."

"Thank you."

He walked past the bickering couples and rolled his eyes to the hostess. She tilted her head to hide her grin before chasing down a menu.

Jessica sat at a bar stool with a glass of white wine. He remembered she was attractive, but didn't quite recall how beautiful she was. This time she didn't have crutches, bruises or other blemishes. She wore a black sundress that fell to just above her knees. The kind that would hug and slide across her athletic frame when she walked—just enough to make a man wonder what lay beneath. She needed no make-up and didn't wear much. He couldn't take his eyes off her.

She gave him a warm smile. "Hi, Alex," she said, offering her hand. "Thank you so much for meeting me."

"No problem. Sorry about running late. I got held up at work."

Flashes of red announced that their table was ready. "Perfect timing. I hope you don't mind, but I asked to sit on the ocean deck. It's always chilly in here and I love the breeze."

"Sounds good."

The hostess seated them and the waitress was close behind with a pair of menus. The sky showed scattered clouds and various shades of red off the shoreline.

A perfect night, warm and just a slight breeze.

The seating wasn't fancy. Tables you'd find at any outdoor wedding and chairs that seem to all have one leg that couldn't find a flat spot. But the view made up for it.

"So, how have you been?" he asked.

"Better, thanks. I'm getting back into a normal routine. You'll probably think I'm crazy, but I'm looking forward to getting back to school."

"That's not crazy. I wish now I never left school. Especially my third year—no Friday classes."

"Weren't you sick of studying?"

"At the time, yeah. Looking back, it's different. Now, I'm driven by the billable hour. Or, should I say, 2000 hours each year. That's 40 billing hours a week, fifty weeks a year. Of course, you can't bill for every hour you're in the office. You have other important tasks; surfing the Internet for fantasy football scores for example." His animation ramped up when she smiled.

"I know what you're thinking—well, at least he gets two weeks vacation. But wait, I forgot to add continuing legal education, sick days, holidays, and especially those difficult clients who ask you to dinner."

She laughed. "You really love being an attorney, Alex. I'm inspired. Maybe you should come down to Florida and give that speech on career day. I'm sure it would really boost your firm's recruiting. 'Hello, my name is Alex and I work in a sweat shop. I'd love for you to slave away in the office next to me and lose any semblance of a life. We offer comprehensive benefits that include an employee assistance program, which happens to be very popular.'" She giggled, "You'll have 'em eating out of the palm of your hand."

The two got along like long-lost friends. The only breaks in conversation came when the waitress interrupted. During dinner, he caught himself gazing at her a few times and she definitely noticed.

She just smiled. If she minded the attention, she didn't let it show.

The waitress lifted the empty plates from the table. "Can I get you something else?" she asked. He looked at Jessica, who shook her head.

"Not right now, thanks," he said.

The waitress cleared the plates and left.

"I'm sorry, Alex. I asked you to get together to talk about my case and we've talked about everything except the case."

"I'm not disappointed."

The waitress returned. "Do you want your check?"

He glanced at his companion to gauge her reaction. "Mmm . . ." She probably wanted to talk some more, but was too polite to suggest he stay longer.

"I'm up for another drink if you are," he offered.

"Okay," she answered quickly, leaving no doubt she was happy.

He ordered a Red Stripe and a chardonnay. "So, what in particular would you like to discuss?" he asked.

She tilted her head to the night sky as if to gather her thoughts. "I think the man who caused my accident is still after me."

She told Alex the story about the two Calfees.

"Did the police figure out who he was?"

"No. And they told me it won't be a high priority case, either. The only thing the guy could be charged with is trespassing. I don't trust they put much time into it after coming to the house. I looked through mug shots, but didn't see anyone who matched."

"Has anything else happened?"

"Other than having all the locks in the house changed, no."

"Why you?"

"I don't' know. But I wonder whether this man had something to do with the deaths in my family."

"What makes you think that?"

She seemed determined to convince him. "I've given it a lot of thought. The man who came to my house impersonated a worker at the inspection company who had a criminal history for attacking women. He may have intended to kill me and frame the real Calfee. I can't think of any other reason to choose Calfee's identity. When I think about my grandparents, it makes sense. According to police reports, the man who supposedly killed them was drunk at the time— over twice the legal limit. Yet, he was able to kill two people, steal their jewelry, then run a half mile down the beach to his car. I have a hard time believing a drunk could be so efficient."

"As for my father, he was healthy as an ox. His side of the family doesn't have a history of heart disease. It's ludicrous he would just drop dead of a heart attack in his forties."

Alex rubbed his forehead like he was stumped on a test. "Why would someone go to so much trouble, Jess? I've done criminal pro bono work. These people are not rocket scientists. They don't do complicated. It's unlikely your typical criminal could concoct what you're suggesting."

"I'm not saying this is a typical criminal . . ."

He interrupted, "To give you an idea of what I'm saying, a friend of mine who practices law in Michigan had a criminal case this winter where his client was arrested for armed robbery. The guy robbed a doughnut shop. Do you know how the police caught him?"

"No."

"They followed fresh footprints in the snow from the doughnut shop to the house next door where he lived. If the footprints weren't enough, during the robbery, he said 'Hello' to several employees and asked that they bag him a double chocolate doughnut along with the money. The chocolate doughnut happened to be the same thing he ordered every morning for the previous six months. One employee even said 'Hi, Charley' when he strolled in the door, thinking he was wearing a ski mask to stay warm."

"Why should I expect you to believe me? No one else does."

In a split second, all the goodwill he gained over the evening seemed lost.

"Jessica, don't be upset. I'm trying to say there's a reasonable explanation for all of this. It doesn't make sense someone would try to kill you and all the members of your family."

"I'm not crazy," she said. "I know what I've been through. Someone *was* following me when I had my accident. Someone hit the back end of my car. Someone stuck his hands in my car window and tried to hurt me. Someone came to my house impersonating a convict. My grandparents and father died within a short time of each other and under strange circumstances. I find it hard to believe this is just bad luck or coincidence."

She'd make an excellent attorney. Quite convincing.

"When you put it like that, it's hard to argue with you." He picked the right response this time as he could see the tension drip from her shoulders.

"I know it sounds far-fetched," she said. "Believe me. Sometimes, I think I'm crazy. I want an explanation for what's happened. And I want to stop feeling anxious." She sighed and shook her head. "I'm really worried."

He reached across the table and covered her hand. "I'd like to help you."

"How?"

"By getting you an explanation. I'm using a private investigator on a couple of matters, including your case. His name is Jim Haney. He's a former FBI agent and all-around good guy. He can get information that isn't public. I'm not sure what he might find, but it's a start."

"Would you do that?"

"Yes. I would and I will."

She squeezed his hand. "Thank you so much. It means a lot."

He changed the subject to lighten the mood. He and Jessica swapped stories about their law school experiences. After finishing their drinks, he signaled the waitress over and handed her a credit card. Jessica tried to stop him.

"Please, Alex. Let me pay. It's the least I can do."

"I was given strict instructions that you don't pay for anything. You wouldn't want me to lose my job now, would you?"

The waitress overheard the conversation. "I'd let him pay. He looks like he can afford it," she said, winking at him.

By the time he paid the bill and walked her out, it was midnight.

"It's late. Would you like me to follow you home and walk through your house?" He asked.

"I couldn't ask you to do that."

"Please. I insist. It's on my way home."

"You sure?"

"Yes, I'm sure. Come on."

"I didn't think they made guys like you anymore."

He grinned. "Something tells me you don't have trouble getting guys to offer assistance."

She blushed. The valet sped up with her car and held the door open. She waited for Alex to pull up behind her.

Her smile told him she felt safe.

18

"Have a seat, Alex. What's on your mind?" Murphy pointed with his open hand to a chair in front of his desk.

His office was immaculate. The busiest litigator in the firm and yet only one file sat on his polished desk. It was whatever file that demanded his current attention. The rest of his papers were no doubt within arms reach.

Alex marveled at how Murphy did it. Every other litigator's office was cluttered with stacks and stacks of paper. Not Murphy. He could have made more money organizing people's files than practicing law if he ever decided to give away his secret. He never did.

"Mr. Murphy, Something's been bothering me since the dinner at Charles Van Doren's house."

"What's that?"

"I overhead the tail-end of a conversation between Van Doren and Wilson Gates. They were in the study discussing what sounded like business."

Murphy didn't say anything. He waited for him to continue.

"I can't recall the exact words, but they were talking about Dr. Rabinowitz. Van Doren asked Gates whether the contract could be found. Gates said everything had been destroyed. He also referenced using European accounts to legitimize some kind of corporate transaction. It sounded dark."

Murphy tented his hands against his mouth. "Do Van Doren and Gates know you overheard the conversation?"

"I don't believe so, no."

"Good. Let's keep it that way."

He couldn't hide his concern. Murphy tried to appease him.

"Look, if we discover damaging evidence in this case, we'll deal with it at the appropriate time. So far, we have no evidence to suggest Van Doren has done anything unlawful or inappropriate. He claims to have told us everything. If we tell him we're suspicious of a conversation *you weren't supposed to hear*, we're basically calling him a liar. He'll then fire the firm and we'll lose millions in legal fees. Let's not go down that road unless we have a damn good reason—something concrete."

"In other words," Alex thought, "don't mess with the cash cow."

"The comments you overheard could mean anything. Van Doren has lots of contracts that could be the subject of conversation between CEO and General Counsel. Large companies use off-shore accounts, and we already know Dr. Rabinowitz's practice was destroyed. If something else turns up, we'll deal with it. Otherwise, just forget that conversation."

Murphy was right, he thought. There had to be a reasonable explanation for what he overheard. Sinister plots were for the movies, not his life.

"How are things going with Jessica?" Murphy asked.

I hesitate to tell you for fear you'll think I'm a crackpot."

"I don't follow."

"She thinks her life is in danger and someone is trying to kill her, and the same person is responsible for the deaths of her father and grandparents."

"What?" Murphy's head tilted to the side. "I don't understand. Why in God's name would she think something like that?"

"I don't have all the details, but some things that happened to her seem suspicious." He started to explain, but Murphy cut him off.

"The stress on her in the past weeks has been enormous. Frankly, I don't know how anyone could handle what she's been through without suffering side-effects. I'm not surprised her mind is playing tricks."

"I don't know that it's her mind playing tricks. Like I said, strange things have happened."

"Listen, Alex. Your role is limited to handling her legal issues. I don't want you playing psychologist or criminal investigator. Let's leave that to the trained professionals. From what I know, the authorities found the man who killed Jessica's grandparents, and the autopsy report on her father didn't turn up anything suspicious, either. She's having a hard time dealing with everything and it's not surprising she's having some delusions about what really happened. The worst thing you can do is agree with her. You'll fuel her fire. I'm telling you, stay out of it." Murphy's tone told him not to argue.

"I'm honestly concerned about her. If at all possible, I'd like to put her at ease."

"What do you have in mind?"

"We have Jim Haney investigating the Van Doren case. I'd like him to investigate Jessica's case. If nothing else, he could reassure her that nothing unusual is going on."

"Fair enough," Murphy said. "She deserves as much. You can ask Jim to look into it, but let's not spend a lot of time on this. Remember, it's a pro bono matter. The firm is covering Jim's expenses." Murphy stood and gave him a pat on the shoulder. "Speaking of Jim, he's waiting for us in the conference room. We should get going."

19

Jim Haney stood by the window peering down at the river. From the twenty-fourth floor, the boats traveling north and south on the St. Johns resembled toys.

Haney was in his early fifties, but his exercise regimen masked the aging process. He stood about six feet tall and wore the same crew cut the Marine Corps gave him 30 years earlier when he enlisted. "Once a Marine, always a Marine," he loved to tell people.

Anytime a big case at Parker Jones required a private investigator, Haney got the call. He had a wealth of experience. Military police and then FBI. He was well connected with law enforcement and always found answers that nobody else could. Most of his clients didn't ask how. They were happy with the results. People expect private investigators to bend the rules when it really matters and attorneys are people too.

Haney turned at the sound of the conference room door opening.

"Jim, how the hell are you?" Murphy asked, extending his hand.

"Great, Michael. And you?" Haney's voice was thunderous.

"Good. You know Alex Weaver, don't you?"

"Sure do."

Haney offered his hand. His grip felt like a bear trap.

"Please, Jim, have a seat." Murphy said. "Do you need anything to drink?"

"Bourbon and water," he said with a smile. "Actually, Michael, I'm fine."

"How was the Chicago trip?" Murphy asked.

"It rained sideways for two straight days, but I was there to work, so it didn't bother me. At least I got some information on Rabinowitz and his medical practice."

Haney pulled a notepad filled with scribbles from the folder in front of him on the table.

"Let's see now," he said, sorting through his papers. "I'll start with some background information on Rabinowitz. No real family to speak of. Never married. Parents died years ago. No siblings. Apparently, his work was his life." Haney paused and raised his eyebrows. "I believe he lived what some might call an *alternative* life style."

"Do you mean what I think you mean?" Murphy asked.

"Yep. He had a significant other who died of AIDS about twenty years back. After that, Rabinowitz dedicated his life to finding a cure for the virus. From what you guys tell me, I'll be damned if he didn't do it."

"Now for the sixty-four thousand dollar question, Jim," Murphy said. "Did you find out anything more on the identity of the patient, or patients as the case may be, that led to Rabinowitz's discovery?"

"Sorry, Michael, I didn't. Rabinowitz's office was burned to the ground. Nothing left. His computers melted. The hard drives were destroyed. His patient lists are nowhere to be found. I got the names of some patients treated during the past few years, but that probably won't help much if the donor we're looking for was a patient ten or more years back."

"What about employees?" Alex asked.

"No luck there, either. In the past ten years, the staff must have changed over a dozen times. The employment records were destroyed along with everything else. I'd have to petition the IRS for W-2 forms to find these people, and my request would probably be denied. Even if we did find the records, I don't think the employees would know much. I talked to the current staff and, with their help, tracked down a few former employees. I have a list of others I haven't gotten around to yet. The consensus is Rabinowitz was tight-lipped with his research. He didn't give the staff access to his research materials. I'll keep checking this angle, but I'm not sure it will be productive."

Alex followed up. "Well, if we can't find Rabinowitz's patients, how did Hudson?"

Haney opened a folder resting in front of him, removed several sheets of paper, and slid them across the table. They were copies of block advertisements placed in Chicago newspapers last year. Murphy picked up the papers and Alex looked on.

If you or a loved one received treatment for HIV or AIDS in the greater-Chicago metropolitan area, you may not have been informed about the purposes for which your DNA was used. In providing any medical treatment, health care providers must fully disclose the nature and purpose of all treatment their patients receive. We are currently representing a class of people who were not informed their DNA was used for experimental purposes. If you have been treated or tested for HIV and/or AIDS, you may be eligible to join our class. Please contact the number listed below to speak with one of our legal experts for a free consultation.

"I've seen this before" Murphy rumbled. "Not surprising."

"The ads aren't everything, guys."

Haney lifted his oversized briefcase from the floor to his lap. He pulled back the tattered flap, reached inside and lifted a VHS tape.

"Hudson put out television ads to complement the print versions. If you're interested in watching the videos, here you go." He slid the tape across the table. "By the way, don't these kinds of ads violate some rule of ethics?"

Alex and Murphy both rolled their eyes. "Unless it's stealing money from a client or murder, the bar association doesn't care," Murphy said matter-of-fact. "I served on the bar disciplinary committee, and I can tell you that the process is a joke. An oral or written reprimand isn't going to stop some-one from using questionable means to sign clients. And frankly, repri-mands are rare. It's still a good-ol'-boy's network out there."

Alex got the conversation back on track. "What about Rabinowitz's home? Did he have anything there?"

Haney leaned forward, "You know, the thought crossed my mind," he said. "I happened to be in Rabinowitz's neighborhood and stopped by one afternoon. One thing led to another and, the next thing you know, I was standing in his living room."

"Jim, I'll assume for purposes of this conversation you had an invi-tation," Murphy said. "I don't want to know anything else about how you got in there. Please continue."

"His house had a really strange feel to it. Rabinowitz was meticu-lous. Not a dirty dish in the sink. Beds made. Bathrooms clean. A clas-sic neat-freak. Very organized. Home office has a filing cabinet that's just as organized as the rest of the house. Hundreds of labeled folders in alphabetical order with papers inside, including bank statements, mortgage statements, and even instruction manuals for appliances and electronic devices. This guy was a pack rat."

"Funny thing is, there was no folder with Van Doren's name on it. No contract or anything else to prove a business transaction between VDP and Rabinowitz." Haney ran his hand across his head. "Something else struck me. The filing cabinet drawers were labeled to show what letters were contained in each drawer, so if Rabinowitz had an 'Alfa' file, he would have obviously kept it in the 'A' cabinet. The strange thing was the letter 'H' had its own file drawer. When I opened the drawer, only about a third of the file space was utilized. Every other drawer was crammed full. Why give 'H' its own space if you don't have anything to put in there?"

Alex scribbled frantically to keep up with Haney. When he lifted the page to fold it back and start another, Murphy reached over, ripped it off, and hurled it in the trashcan.

"What gives?" he asked.

"Goddamn. Do you really think it's a good idea to make a record of this conversation?" Murphy asked.

He got the point.

"I want to show you guys something," Haney said. He lifted a device that looked like an Ipod.

"Whatcha' got there?" Murphy asked.

"An ingenious little device, Michael. This little bugger will copy the hard drive off of a personal computer in minutes."

"FBI issue?" Alex was curious.

"Radio Shack." Haney smirked and placed the device on the table. "It's a little burner unit we call a ghost. You can get these at most electronics shops. Great little gadget. I thought you might be interested in looking at Rabinowitz's computer files." Haney reached again into his briefcase and pulled out two encased compact disks. He slid them across the table to Murphy. "Two copies of his hard drives."

"Have you looked through them?" Murphy asked.

"I scanned them and found something of interest. There was one file folder that contained only binary digits—you know, computer gibberish. Numbers and symbols only computers can read."

"I'm not sure I follow." Murphy said, scrunching his eyebrows.

"Computers have their glitches. When I looked at Rabinowitz's files, one file was reformatted from words to binary digits, which you can't read."

Haney's comment drew blank stares.

"Guys, you obviously have the computer skills of my eighty-year-old mother. Listen, the computer's file structure has to be degraded for this to happen. One way to degrade a file is to continually write over it. Another way is to plant a bug in the computer to destroy the file."

"Tell me why I should care," Murphy asked.

"I'm not sure you should care, Michael. I'm just telling you this is an unusual happening that could be evidence of tampering." Haney's tone told Murphy he didn't appreciate the last question.

"Sorry, Jim, didn't mean to sound crass. How would you know whether the computer problems were the result of tampering or a simple malfunction?" Murphy asked.

"I wouldn't know for sure, but Rabinowitz's computer was fairly new. Not likely the degraded file would have been written over enough times to cause a malfunction. It takes years to overwrite a file enough times to erase data. Also, if it were an overwriting problem, more than the one file would have been damaged. It's possible someone wanted a particular file from Rabinowitz's computer destroyed."

"Maybe Rabinowitz destroyed the file," Alex offered.

"Possible," Haney responded, "but unlikely."

"Why?" Alex asked.

"Well, first off, you need to have some specialized computer skills to do this sort of thing. It's not something your average Joe knows how to do. If I asked you to create a computer virus to destroy a particular file and leave everything else untouched, would you be able to do it? I had to sit through a bunch of training classes at the FBI and that's the only reason I know about this stuff. I didn't see any books, magazines, or other papers in Rabinowitz's house to suggest he was a computer wiz or that computers were even of interest to him. So, I'm not sure he had the technical know-how. I suppose he could have asked someone else to do it, but I don't think that happened, either. Super-organized people, like Rabinowitz, don't destroy papers or files. They save virtually everything for that dreaded rainy day."

"We have no idea what the file was, do we?" Murphy asked. "It may not be relevant to anything we're doing. Perhaps pictures of hippos mating."

"We do know something about the file," Haney said. "The name of the destroyed file started with the letter H. We know that, because whoever destroyed the insides of the file forgot to destroy the out-side—the file heading. Rabinowitz kept his computer files just like his paper files, in lettered folders and files. Just as the H file was missing

---

in his file cabinet, it was missing on his computer."

"H," Murphy repeated. "Does that mean anything to you?" he asked his associate.

"Not off the top of my head."

"How about you, Jim?" Murphy followed up.

"Nope."

"This is all very interesting, but it sounds like we're hitting a lot of dead-ends. What's the status on Rabinowitz's murder investigation?" Murphy asked. "Any arrests?"

"They brought in a few suspects for questioning, but no arrests. According to police reports, Rabinowitz got popped in the parking lot. A witness saw someone who looked like a skinhead standing over his body. Details were sketchy. The slug pulled out of the good doctor came from a .25-caliber pistol, probably a Saturday Night Special. It's the hardest to trace, because ballistics can't find grooves from the barrel. Police theorize the killer took Rabinowitz's keys, dragged him into the lab, then torched the place. No prints. A professional job."

"Why burn down the medical practice?" Alex asked.

"If you follow the police hate-group theory, I suppose they wanted to destroy all the work Rabinowitz had done to treat AIDS patients."

"Do you have your own theory?" Alex asked.

"I'm not investigating the murder. It was an odd crime. No murder weapon. No real clues, and no solid leads. Hate crimes are usually poorly planned and sloppy. Even with the witness, the police can't find the killer. Doesn't add up. Could be a set-up job. One thing's for sure, the killer knew what he was doing and I'm guessing he's not someone whose path you want to cross."

"We'll leave the criminal matter to the authorities," Murphy said. "That's not our concern and we needn't waste any more of your time, Jim, discussing criminal theories. The good news for our client is, if you didn't find anything, Hudson probably isn't going to find anything. We're pretty sure none of Hudson's clients generated the DNA that led to Transviazine. If he had the right patient, he wouldn't need all the others. He's either buying time to find the right person, or hoping for a settlement." Murphy checked his watch. "I have a conference call, so I'll excuse myself. Alex, you can finish up."

"Sure," he said.

Murphy started out of the room. "Oh, one more thing, Alex," Murphy turned, "Van Doren sent over all the documents we asked for in response to Hudson's discovery requests. I'm having them sent to the war room— all twenty-five banker boxes. Lots of scientific documents and financial records. We'll need to go through them carefully to evaluate which documents correspond to any of Hudson's hundred document requests and, of course, whether any documents are privileged. We'll also need to go through the patient records Hudson sent us. And Alex, when I way 'we', you know I mean 'you'," Murphy smiled and winked at Haney.

"Mr. Murphy, there's nothing I'd rather spend my weekend doing than looking through medical and financial documents," he offered with a twinge of sarcasm.

"Yes, I'm sure," Murphy said and left.

Alex flipped through his notes. "Jim, what do you still need to do on the Van Doren case?"

"I'm working on getting a listing of financial transactions, property distributions, criminal history, and anything else I can find. I'm waiting to hear back from some people. As soon as I do, I'll let you know."

"Sounds good." Alex put his Van Doren files away and pulled Jessica's file. "Jim, I also wanted to touch base with you on the other case we talked about before, Patel vs. McCall."

"Okay."

"Mr. Murphy gave the green light to have you look into the issues we discussed yesterday. I brought a copy of the file, the pleadings, police reports, and my notes. Jessica is convinced somebody tried to run her off the road. I'd appreciate your help on this one." He handed the papers to Haney.

"Be happy to." Haney stood and gathered the rest of his things. He stacked his papers into neatly labeled folders.

Meanwhile, Alex crammed his papers into a single file folder with no regard for order. There was a reason his office looked as if his ceiling had been removed during a ticker tape parade.

Haney shut his briefcase and started toward the door. He shook hands with Alex. Another crushing grip. "I'll talk to you soon."

"Let me ask you one question before you go."

"Sure. What is it?" Haney released the door handle and leaned against the door.

"You remember talking about getting into Rabinowitz's house?"

"Yeah."

"How does a person get inside a stranger's house in the middle of the day without being noticed? Off-the-record, of course."

Haney smiled. "Simple, Alex—act like you're supposed to be there."

"How?"

"Show up in a uniform. Utilities, pest control, cable television, anything that appears ordinary. People aren't suspicious of ordinary. Even if they see you, they won't be able to describe you. Only the uniform. Works like a charm."

Alex had the look of a man diagnosed with a tumor.

"Are you all right?"

"Uh, yeah. Fine."

Haney watched him for a moment before accepting his answer. "Okay. You take care of yourself."

"Jim, if possible, I'd like to have your input on the McCall case sooner than later."

20

Jessica pulled her shiny brown hair up in a ponytail to keep it out of her face while she read the cases and articles scattered across her living room floor. She lay on her stomach holding a yellow highlighter in one hand and a case printed off Westlaw in the other.

She finished her first year of law school ranked second in her class. Only a B in criminal law kept her from the top spot. She made Law Review, which carried with it the responsibility of drafting a detailed article on an innovative legal topic. In her case—the Supreme Court's recent decisions on Affirmative Action. Her first draft weighed in at fifty pages.

Given her recent tragedy, Jack Farmer, her exacting editor-in-chief, granted her an extension.

She was lost in the details of her work when the doorbell rang. She checked her watch and sprung from the ground. "Oh, crap," she said and rushed toward the front door. Stopping in the hallway, she gave her appearance the once-over in the glass from a hanging picture. "Coming" she called.

"Who is it?" she asked before opening the door.

"Alex," a voice she recognized said.

"Good evening, madam," he bowed as she opened the door. He held a large pizza and a six-pack of Red Stripe like an offering. "I hope you didn't eat already."

"Hi," she smiled. "No, I haven't."

"Green peppers okay?"

"Mushrooms would have been better, but they'll do," she joked and led him to the kitchen.

From behind, he couldn't help but notice how well she fit into her old, faded jeans.

She grabbed the beer and pointed to the deck off the kitchen. "This is a nice surprise. Why don't you take the pizza outside and I'll get some plates and glasses."

He unlocked the sliding glass door and the screen. She wasn't taking any chances.

"You can leave 'em open," she called out.

For early summer, the air was lighter and cooler than normal. A tropical storm passed offshore, carrying through a high-pressure cell that brought a comfortable fall-like evening. He couldn't resist glancing in her direction. A more pleasant sight than even a sunset.

She poured the beer too quickly. Foam rush. She stuck her head down and tried to catch the excess with her mouth before it escaped.

"Tilt the glass," he shouted from the deck.

"You weren't supposed to see that," she yelled. She conquered the second glass and signaled thumbs-up, then joined him.

"What was it like growing up with a famous dad?" he asked while they ate.

"He was always just Dad," Jessica said. "He wouldn't let me think of him as someone famous." The ocean breeze blew a loose strand of hair back and forth across her face.

"Did you go to his games?"

She nodded. "I loved watching him play, even in the cold Chicago winters. My eyes followed him the entire game. Didn't matter what he was doing. Running for a touchdown or sitting on the bench, I was watching. I was amazed how such a gentle man off the field could be so violent for three hours every Sunday. I used to joke I deserved the credit for his success by getting him so frustrated during the week he was ready to explode by game day," she said, laughing.

"What about your mom? Where is she?"

"I couldn't tell you," she answered solemnly. "She took off when I was three."

"Sorry."

"Don't be. You didn't know. Plus, that's the one loss in my life I'm over."

"Did your dad remarry?"

"No. He dated, but I don't think he ever got over my mom. He never said so, but I could see it in his face when he talked about her."

She stared out over the ocean for a moment before returning attention to her guest. "What about you? Tell me about your family."

"Are you out of sleeping pills?" he asked.

"If you must know, I grew up in Columbus, Ohio. I have a younger brother, John, who still lives there. My parents retired to Amelia Island a few years ago."

"What does your brother do?"

"He's in med school at Ohio State."

"And your parents? Tell me about them."

"Dad ran a little printing business for thirty years. He sold it after he and mom decided to retire and start traveling more. Mom stayed at home while we were growing up, but the woman never sat still. In addition to raising John and me—no easy task I might add—she volunteered for every philanthropic committee and social cause that came along. She worked harder than everyone else and she did it free. Funny how that works."

She pushed her plate away. "I'm stuffed. Not another bite for me," she said, holding her stomach.

"Okay, Alex," she continued, "thank you for the pizza and allowing me a diversion. I suppose we have to talk about my case, since that's why you're here. I don't want to make you stay any later than you planned."

"Lately I've been eating every meal at my desk, so I should thank you for getting me out of my hole. But you're right. We should talk about the case."

He explained the litigation process from filing the complaint through trial. Her first year in law school supplied the foundation to understand the basics, but the real-world practice of law differs from book law. She seemed interested to hear him explain how the concepts she learned in school were actually applied.

"You're taking Patel's deposition next week?" she asked.

"Friday morning."

"What's your plan?

"Well," he answered, "it's a personal injury case, so the meat of it is Patel's alleged injuries. We've subpoenaed his medical records, which contain more pages than War and Peace. This guy is a real piece of work. He's spent more time on Workers' Comp leave than he has working—back trouble, elbow, knee, joint pain, headaches, you name it. He's no stranger to litigation either. He sued two previous employers for retaliation and wrongful discharge, both related to his absences. One employer settled cheap to get rid of the nuisance. The other fought it and the case was thrown out. He filed for Social Security benefits last year alleging he was totally disabled."

"What a slime-ball," she said. "Can we use those other lawsuits and claims to show he's sue-happy?"

"Yes and no," he answered. "We can't use the other lawsuits to show he's litigious, but his medical history and any recovery he received for his prior pain and suffering is relevant. So, we can back-door the prior litigation into the case."

"How do we prove I didn't hurt him?"

"One of the hardest cases to defend is one based on subjective feelings. That's the problem with Workers' Comp. Even doctors have a hard time diagnosing fakers. The trick is to use Patel's prior injuries against him. Going through this guy's medical history will remind you of that circus act where the clowns keep pouring out of the Volkswagen Beatle. After a while, it gets ridiculous. We'll expose him for what he is—a scoundrel who takes advantage of the system and has already received way more than he deserves."

"Works for me," she said. "What about the man who caused my accident?"

"What do you mean?"

"Do you think Patel might have seen him? Can you ask him whether he did?"

"Oh, yeah, of course. I'll ask Patel to describe everything he saw that night. Hopefully, he'll have some answers."

She and Alex finished their conversation. He gathered his papers and she escorted him to the door.

"Thank you again for all your help, Alex."

"You're welcome."

The two became locked in an awkward gaze while standing in the foyer.

"Well . . . uh . . . I'd better get going," he sputtered.

She slipped her arms around his waist and squeezed. He had imagined how she'd feel. This was better.

She followed up the hug with a kiss on the cheek. "Goodnight," she said softly. She rested a hand on his chest and let it linger.

He opened the door. "Make sure you lock up behind me," he reminded her.

Windows rolled down, cool ocean air rushed across his face. The Van Doren case consumed his thoughts, day and night. On this night, it didn't enter his mind. He was thinking about a girl.

21

"Another Wild Turkey," Ronnie Patel shouted in the bartender's direction inside the run-down bar on an inlet near the Navy base. Drinks were cheap and trouble was never far away. A distorted jukebox oozed out the Rolling Stones in the back corner. A cloud of smoke and hard drinkers filled the room.

Patel dug for a pack of Camels in the pocket of his ragged, green flannel shirt. The weathered bartender nodded and broke off his conversation with two sailors.

"That'll be three dollars, Ronnie," the bartender said, pushing the drink to Patel.

"You took all my money for the last four drinks, Harvey. Just put it on my tab." Patel grabbed the glass, but before it touched his lips, the sinewy bartender clamped onto Patel's forearm with a vice-like grip and slammed it down on the table. Half the drink splashed on the bar.

"Bullshit, Ronnie. You still owe me twenty bucks from last week. I ain't running a bank."

"Come on, Harvey, I'm good for it. I got some money coming in a lawsuit. I know you seen that lawyer on TV. Buddy Adkins is gonna get me a nice chunk of change," he said.

"Then have your lawyer come up here and pay the bill," Harvey scowled. He released Patel's arm and repossessed the drink.

"I'll buy the man a drink. And get me a Bud while you're at it." A man standing behind Patel threw a twenty on the bar.

Harvey shrugged his shoulders, picked up the money, and returned Patel's drink, minus the booze that escaped during the tussle. Patel turned to acknowledge the gracious patron. He looked up at a man at least six inches taller. He wore a baseball cap, an old tee shirt, and Wrangler jeans. His eyes were covered by dirty wire-rimmed glasses and his mouth was outlined by a goatee.

"Thanks, man. Do I know you from somewhere?" Patel's glazed eyes confirmed his buzz. "You look familiar."

"Name's Jack Thompson." He held out his hand and gave Patel a firm shake. "I don't believe we've met. I just happened to overhear your problem with the bartender and thought I'd help. I hate to see a Navy man go thirsty. I'm at the table over there." He pointed to the back wall of the tavern. "You're welcome to join me for a drink." He turned and started back toward his table.

"Sure thing, Jack." Patel wasn't about to pass up free drinks.

"How'd you know I used to be in the Navy? Did we serve together?" Patel asked.

Thompson smiled. "Folks in this place are fishermen, Navy men, or rich pricks waiting for the ferry next door to take them to Ponte Vedra. I can tell by shaking your hand, you ain't no angler. Them boys' hands feel like sandpaper. If you ain't got three bucks for a drink, you sure as hell ain't no rich boy. So, I guessed Navy. Served ten years myself."

Harvey reappeared with a Budweiser bottle, which he set on the table along with change from the twenty. Thompson scooped up the beer and took a swig. Patel followed suit and finished his drink with one gulp.

"Could I trouble you for another drink? I'll pay you back later." Patel's speech was slurred.

"Damn, boy." He waived to Harvey. The two men threw back their drinks.

"You from south Georgia?" Patel asked.

"Yep. Born and reared in Waycross. How'd you know?"

"Recognize the accent. You ain't the only one who knows how to read folks." Patel straightened up, as if he were proud of his knowledge.

"I guess not," Thompson said, taking a drink. "I couldn't help overhearing you got yourself a legal case. I got me some legal issues myself. Your lawyer any good?"

"Yeah, he's all over the TV. Buddy Adkins. He's gotta have money to run so many commercials, so I know he's good. He's gonna get me a shitload of money with my case."

"What's it about, if you don't mind my asking?"

"I got me a deposition coming up, so my lawyer said it's all gonna be public record anyway."

Patel appeared to revel in the fact someone was interested in what he had to say. "I was broke down with a flat tire on I-95, heading south, near downtown. As I was fixing my tire, I heard some shit from the other lane, like metal on metal, hitting pretty hard. Then I saw this SUV go out of control and come flying across the median, like right at me. Freaked me out, man." He paused for another drink.

"What happened?"

"She came up on me like lightning. Thought I was dead. I hit the ground and covered my head. The truck fish-tailed in the grass and hit the back-end of my car, but by the grace of God, missed me." He gave a cross gesture with his right hand across his chest. "Lucky, the crash just knocked off my bumper and didn't hurt nothing else. After the truck shot past me, I could hear the tires squeal when they came off the grass and hit the pavement. The rubber grabbed the road and that's when all hell broke loose. That SUV flipped up in the air like a kingfish and started twisting and turning. Rolled five times when it finally stopped in the ditch. The lady driving was messed up pretty bad, but she lived, and my lawyer tells me she's okay. Hard to believe she made it."

"Thank God." Thompson cocked his head. "Wait a minute," he said, oozing disbelief, "if the truck only knocked off your bumper, what's your lawsuit about? How's your attorney supposed to get you a lot of money for that? You drive a Porsche?"

"Hell no. I ain't got no fancy car or nothing, but it really don't matter none," he proclaimed with his chest out.

Thompson lifted his hat and scratched his head.

"You see," Patel continued, "them lawyers get all the accident reports and call all the people involved. I must have gotten twenty letters from lawyers about that accident 'cause the police took my name and put it on a report somewhere. Buddy Adkins is my Workers' Comp attorney, so I called him."

"That's great," Thompson interrupted, "but that doesn't explain what you're suing for."

"I'm getting there. Just hold your shirt," he couldn't wait to explain. "I told Buddy what happened, and he said I didn't need much damage to have a claim. He said being close to an accident caused me what lawyers call, emotional distress. Buddy told me when I jumped to the ground, I re-injured my back, which means I may not be able to come off Workers' Comp. He says, if you can't work, you can get some pretty good damages. And get this—the lady from the accident is Mark McCall's daughter. You know, the football coach, or at least he was. I heard he died somehow. Heart attack or some such. It don't matter none. I figure he left some nice money for his little princess, and I'm gonna get mine. Buddy got me a chiropractor who's going to testify I'm disabled and can't work. So, I'm in good shape to get a lot of money."

"You don't look disabled."

Patel rotated his head as if he was concerned about being overheard. He leaned closer. "I ain't. That doctor'll say anything Buddy tells him. Buddy says, so long as a doctor testifies I'm hurt bad, my case is worth a lot of money. That's why I'm telling you, Buddy is a hell of a lawyer. On my Workers' Comp case, he's got me out of work for the past six months. He thinks we can get disability pay, so I can get a paycheck every month without doing squat. I'm tellin' you, if you got a legal problem, you need to see Buddy."

Thompson ignored Patel's monologue on attorney ethics. "What happened after the accident? Did you go over to the truck?"

"No way, man. Not to see that lady's guts splattered all over the place. I ain't no doctor or nothing. I hung back and checked out the scene. It was only a few seconds before a car came up and stopped."

"Somebody came to help?"

Patel shook his head. "Yeah, that was weird, man. When that lady's truck stopped rolling, I got up to look around. I saw some old pickup hit the breaks on the other lane and come ripping across the median like a bat out of hell. Remember I told you before that lady come across the median I heard some metal on metal? I'm wonderin' whether that truck might have tried to run that lady off the road. Maybe a pissed off boyfriend."

"Anyway," he continued, "that pickup went flying over to the SUV and some big dude got out and ran down to her car. He was messing around, I guess trying to help. I don't know. I couldn't really see when he went down to down there, 'cause it was at the bottom of the ditch. When some cars came up and pulled over to help, he just took off. It was like he was there one minute, and gone the next. Like I said, it was weird, man."

"That is weird," Thompson agreed. "Did you get a look at him?"

"I got a fair look at him, yeah." Patel turned to his right to accept the drink Harvey brought over. He raised it like a toast and inhaled two-thirds with one swallow.

"What did he look like?" Thompson pressed.

Patel laughed. "Hell, he looked a bit like you, Jack."

Thompson leaned back in his chair, stone-faced. The smile ran away from Patel's mouth. Thompson erupted in laughter. "I confess. It was me. Ha!" Thompson's outburst put Patel back at ease. "Did anyone else get a look at this guy?" Thompson asked.

"Nah, I don't think so. He was gone in a flash."

"Did you tell the police what you saw?"

"I told 'em about the accident. But they ain't ask me nothing about folks coming up to help out." Patel finished his drink and stared at Thompson for a moment. "Jack, you sure ask a lot of questions. You ain't working for that lady's attorney, are you?"

Thompson shook his head and held up his hand. "Just making conversation. Sorry if I'm bothering you."

"No. You ain't bothering me. I'm just not used to folks asking so many questions."

"Tell you what. No more questions. Just drinks. I gotta get out of here or my wife is gonna kill me. Let me buy you a drink for the road."

Patel nodded, grinning ear to ear. "You're one hell of a guy. One for the road it is."

Thompson signaled the bartender yet again and this time, he ordered Patel a whiskey chaser.

"Nice talking to you," Thompson said, holding out his hand. "I'd better get going."

"Good meeting you, Jack. Thanks for the drinks." Patel tried standing to shake Thompson's hand, but the booze in his system wouldn't allow it. He lost balance and fell back to his seat.

"You okay to drive?" Thompson asked.

"Well, I better be, 'cause I'm too drunk to walk." He slurred. "I'll be fine, Jack, just fine."

"Okay, then. See you around." Thompson threw some bills on the bar and exited.

Harvey brought Patel his drink. "This is the last one for you and you ain't in any kinda shape to drive. You better get a ride or you're gonna kill yourself or, worse yet, somebody else," Harvey warned.

"I'm just fine. You can get your ass back behind that bar and mind your own damn business." His head bobbed as he spoke.

Harvey shook his head and returned to his spot behind the bar. Patel nursed his drink like a baby. After finishing, he struggled to stand, clutching chairs and tables, anything he could get his hands on, for balance. Weaving through the bar proved difficult.

Once outside, he fell forward to the porch rail. He held tight, waited, and took several deep breaths.

"Navy men are supposed to be able to hold their liquor," a voice announced. Patel swung his head around to see Thompson laughing at him from the parking lot. He released the rail and tried to imitate a Navy man standing at attention. He looked more like a rail thin pine in a strong breeze.

"I'm just fine. Hell, I'm just getting' warmed up," he said while tugging at his belt.

"Glad to hear it."

Thompson approached Patel from the gravel lot. "Say, I've got some car trouble," pointing out to several cars that sat side-by-side.

"Damn battery died again. Bad alternator. Could I trouble you for a ride? I live just a couple miles down the road. I'll get my wife to take me back in the morning for the car. I'm not about to call her at this hour, if you know what I mean."

"No problem, Jack. Least I can do."

He stumbled forward off the porch and fumbled around in his pockets.

"You okay to drive?" Thompson asked. "I'm happy to take the wheel if you like."

"Why the fuck is everyone so concerned about my driving? I'll be just fine."

"Calm down. Just asking."

"I'm over here." Patel pointed to an old, gray '65 Chevy Impala Super Sport with a rusted front quarter-panel. Twenty paces away.

"I see you haven't replaced the missing bumper," Thompson said, pointing.

"Nah, not yet. Waiting for that lawsuit money."

Patel needed three tries to get the key in the door. Thompson pulled out a flask inside. "You said you were just getting warmed up. Can I offer you another swig?" He handed Patel the container.

"Hell-yeah, man. You're all right, Jack." Patel cranked the engine. Despite the car's ragged appearance, the 396 cubic inches under the hood packed a punch. He jammed it in drive and stepped on the gas, spitting gravel all over the lot.

"The old beater's got some spunk, don't she?" Thompson asked.

"Rebuilt the motor myself. Wanna see what she'll do?" He raised the flask yet again.

"Shit-yeah, man. Let's see what she'll do."

Patel punched the pedal and employed all four hundred horses under the hood. The force of acceleration pinned the two men against the back of the seat.

"Hell-yeah," Patel yelled, one hand on the wheel and the other clutching the flask. The smell of burnt rubber billowed through the open window.

Thompson watched the speedometer needle shoot past seventy. Patel hugged the centerline around a curve and found the straightaway. Up ahead, Thompson saw a drawbridge that lifted the road over the St. Johns River.

"Hey, Ronnie," Thompson shouted over the wind and engine roar.

"What?"

"You mind if I try her out? I'd love to see what she'll do."

"No problem."

He hit the brakes and skidded to a Dukes-of-Hazard stop off the two-lane road into the grass.

"I'll walk around. You can just slide over behind the wheel."

"Would you do a favor for me and pop the hood?" Thompson asked. "I wanna see what you got under there."

"Pure muscle," he answered and popped the release under the dash. Patel reached through the front grill to release the latch and raised the hood. He pointed proudly to various engine components. Patel didn't notice Thompson seemed disinterested.

Thompson's head was on a swivel, scanning his surroundings. No one was around.

"You got magnum cylinder heads?" Thompson asked, pointing.

"Oh, yeah, man. Pure performance," he stretched forward under the hood and used the bottom of his shirt to protect his right hand from being burned as he played with the smoldering block.

Thompson took one last look around. He and Patel were alone.

He grabbed the hood and slammed it down with all his might, ramming Patel's head into the heated metal. He raised the hood and watched Patel slide to the ground, unconscious. He lifted Patel by his hair and pulled him around to the driver's side door. After stuffing Patel into the driver's seat, he entered the passenger side, started the car, and put it in drive. The car eased forward, still on the side of the road, the idle speed sufficient to move it forward without pressing the accelerator.

Lunden opened the passenger door and jumped out. He watched the car roll past and disappear over the thirty-foot drop into the choppy water and rocks below.

A gust of warm wind hit Lunden's face. He peered over the hill at the scene below. The trunk of Patel's car stuck straight up in the air. The water wasn't deep enough to swallow the entire vehicle, but it covered up the passenger compartment where Patel sat.

Lunden dusted himself off. "Shame your lawyer couldn't be here to join you, you piece of shit."

22

"Wilson Gates to see you, sir."

"Send him in," Charles Van Doren said, pressing the intercom. 5:30 P.M. Gates was always on time, regardless of the occasion. Three knocks sounded on the solid cherry doors that protected Van Doren's office- an office the size of an upscale studio apartment.

"Come in, Wilson," Van Doren said. He pushed aside papers cluttering his classic Edwardian desk. Gates entered the room and closed the door.

"Good evening, Charles," Gates said, and walked across the large Oriental rug that covered the heartwood pine flooring.

"Drink?" Van Doren moved around his desk toward the bookshelves that overtook the east wall of his office.

"No, thanks. I still have work to do this evening." Gates sat in one of the two chairs in front of Van Doren's desk.

"One drink won't kill you, Wilson. Scotch?" he insisted.

"Oh, very well. Scotch it is," Gates said, forcing a slight smile.

Van Doren tugged on a red book that stuck out slightly from the others sitting next to it. The shelving turned 180 degrees and a bar appeared. He chose a bottle of single malt Glenmorangie from the shelf and poured two drinks.

He leaned back in his chair and eyed Gates. Gates swallowed a large drink, wincing from the quick warmth at the back of his throat.

"Wilson, I've noticed a change in your behavior the past few months. Frankly, I'm a bit concerned. You seem distracted. Is there anything you need to say?" Van Doren spoke like a school teacher to child.

"I hope you don't mind if I speak freely," Gates responded.

"By all means, speak. We're not in the military, Wilson. What's on your mind?"

Gates swirled his drink, searching for words. "I'm not sure I can live with myself knowing what we've done." He threw back the rest of his drink. "Do you mind?" he asked, pointing to the bar.

"Help yourself."

Gates hit the bar and poured a strong one. His hands trembled. "My wife and children don't know me anymore," he said, retaking his seat. "I haven't laughed in six months. I feel sick to my stomach every night when I lay down to sleep. It takes every bit of energy I have to act normal, and it gets harder and harder every day."

He ran his hand through his graying hair while staring at the floor. "I went to my son Mark's baseball game last Saturday," he continued. "Regional finals. He pitched a two-hit shut-out. A great game. When it was over, I couldn't remember one single pitch. I didn't even know his team won until I saw his face when he came out of the locker room. He asked me what I thought about this pitch and that pitch. I faked the whole conversation. Couldn't remember anything."

"My mind is consumed with what we've done. All day, every day. I can't shake it. I thought I could, but I can't. I need to get out of here. Leave this place. I don't care about the money anymore." He refocused his gaze from the floor into Van Doren's eyes. He brushed away a lone tear that peaked from the corner of his eye.

Van Doren's return stare was anything but sympathetic. "There's nothing you can do to change what's been done."

He gulped his drink. "Sit down, Wilson."

"I prefer to stand."

"Sit the fuck down," his face pulsed red. After a brief staring contest,

Gates sat. Van Doren circled the desk and sat next to him.

He softened his tone. "Wilson, how many times have we talked about this? We have acquired the most incredible medical invention of our time. With our resources, we can get the drug to market faster than Rabinowitz ever could have. At the rate he was going, his clinical trials would have taken years to get FDA approval. We can do it inside a year."

Van Doren paused, measuring Gates' reaction. "Wilson, my friend, we can save thousands of lives—thousands. I suggest you let that thought resonate for a while. Rabinowitz made his own bed. He could have accepted our initial offers and retire a rich, rich, man. He could have saved lives. But he didn't. His hatred and distrust of corporate America interfered with logic and reason. His life was a necessary expenditure."

"Charles, you and I don't have the right to decide the worth of Rabinowitz's life. Only God does. And while I appreciate lives might be saved, we'd both be lying to ourselves without acknowledging that the lives at stake are secondary to the prospect of our own personal wealth. It wasn't altruism that killed Rabinowitz. It was greed." He stood tall and set his glass on the bookcase. "This is my last week. I'm resigning."

Van Doren exploded. "Like hell you are," he jumped up and charged around his desk. He hastily grabbed a calendar from the pile of papers. "We need just a little more time to see this thing through. You started this with me, goddamn it, and you're going to finish it. Then you can do whatever the fuck you want."

"I'm sorry, Charles. I'm not staying. I can't." He kept his eyes focused on Van Doren.

Van Doren let his eyes wander and ran his hand across his mouth. "There's something I need to show you. I hoped it wouldn't come to this." He opened a drawer and lifted an envelope. He threw it across the desk. "Go ahead. Open it. I got these from our friend," he pointed.

Gates picked up the plain, white envelope. The fold wasn't sealed. He bent the flap and emptied the contents. Shock shifted to rage.

"You motherfucker," he growled. "You as much as come near my family and, I swear, I'll kill you with my bare hands." He crumpled the three pictures in his hand. One of his wife shopping for groceries, the second of his fifteen-year-old son at baseball practice, and the last of his twelve-year-old daughter on her school playground.

"Calm down." Van Doren waved his arms. "Nothing is going to happen to your family. I just need your word you'll see this thing through for the next thirty days. Then you can resign a wealthy man and do whatever you want."

"And if I refuse?"

Van Doren poured another drink. "I don't think either one of us want to think about that. Just a few more weeks, Wilson. That's all. Then you're a rich, free man who will never have to work again. You'll never have to see me or this place again."

Gates stepped back from the desk and grabbed the back of a chair. The blood rushed out of his face.

Van Doren slowly passed him and opened one of his office doors. "If you'll excuse me, Wilson. I'm scheduled for a conference call."

As Gates exited, Van Doren grabbed his arm. "Do we have an understanding?" he asked.

Gates jerked his arm out of Van Doren's grip and marched off.

Van Doren closed the door and went for the telephone. He dialed a series of numbers and waited. "It's me," he said. "Mr. Gates has become a problem."

23

Alex wheeled into his parking space in the cold, dark office garage, opened his door, and climbed out. His feet hit the concrete. Something didn't feel right. His eyes shifted down and saw socks, but no shoes. Worse yet, they were white tube socks, no chance of matching his traditional blue suit. "What in the hell is going on," he mumbled.

Several co-workers appeared out of nowhere and invited him to stroll with them into the office. He stood frozen. His co-workers didn't wait. They smiled and marched off. They didn't seem to notice his fashion problems or care whether he joined them.

After a moment, he ran to catch his officemates, but they were long gone. His legs were heavy. He could barely move. Halfway out of the garage, he decided to go home to get his shoes. When he returned to his parking space, his car had vanished. The entire garage was empty. All the dozens of cars present earlier had vanished.

He rushed to the edge of the garage and studied the street below. No activity. No traffic. No people. The city was empty.

Suddenly, a ringing sound caught his attention. The sound stopped and then repeated. The emergency alarm in the garage. He ran toward the stairwell, and rolled directly onto his bedroom floor.

Awake now, he knelt in front of his side-table and slapped clumsily at the snooze on his alarm clock. Nothing happened. The ringing continued. "Shit," he said. The telephone.

"Hello," he said, clearing his throat.

"Mr. Weaver?" A muffled male voice asked.

"Yeah."

"The girl is in a lot of danger."

"Who is this? What girl?"

"You know the girl I'm talking about. Just listen to me. You don't have much time. Get her out of her house. She's a sitting duck. Take her somewhere safe. She has to vanish for the next thirty days."

"Is this some kind of joke?"

"I can assure you I'm not joking."

"What are you talking about?"

"Just do it," the caller demanded. "In thirty days, it'll all be over. She'll be safe then."

"Can we meet? Is there a number I can reach you? I'd like to talk more about this."

"If we need to talk, I'll contact you. And if you have any doubts about what I'm telling you, just watch the local news in the morning. You'll know the story when you see it."

"What are you talking about? What story?" he asked.

Dial tone. No more caller.

"Shit. What in the hell is going on?"

He powered his nightstand light, rubbed his eyes, and checked his Caller ID. UNKNOWN CALLER. He threw on a pair of old jeans and a tee shirt, splashed water on his face, and headed for the door.

24

"Here," Jessica handed Alex a mug of coffee. The fresh brew scented the air.

"Thanks."

"You didn't recognize his voice?"

"No. Sounded like he had something over his mouth. To be honest, I was half asleep, which made things more difficult." He carefully sipped the hot coffee.

Jessica wore the oversized T-shirt she slept in. "What do you make of the news story comment? Do you think he was talking about me?"

"Didn't get that impression. I'm guessing, whatever the news story is, something already happened. He warned me to get you out of danger, so I assumed you weren't the story. If he's legit, we'll know what he was talking about soon enough." He clicked on the small television perched on her kitchen counter.

"What are we going to do? Call the police?"

"Wouldn't do any good. You haven't been threatened by anyone."

"What about the guy who called you? Couldn't the police do something about that?"

"No. He didn't mention names. He didn't even say what would happen. He really didn't say anything. The police would have nothing."

"So, I'm a sitting duck."

"I didn't say that. You're going somewhere safe. Somewhere no one can find you. I'm going to call Jim Haney to help us sort through this."

"It's on," Jessica pointed to the television. The bad music for the local news floated into the room. "Get the remote. Turn it up."

The lead story covered a dispute involving the planning for a new courthouse, followed by a sports and weather preview. About ten minutes into the program, something caught their attention. A young, male reporter stood at the scene overlooking the St. Johns River north of town.

A Mayport man is dead this morning after driving his car over a thirty-foot embankment into the St. Johns River. The accident occurred early this morning on Hecksher Drive near the Mayport ferry. The deceased is believed to be Ronald J. Patel, a Mayport resident and former Navy enlisted man. Police indicated alcohol may have played a role in the accident. Preliminary tests show Patel's blood-alcohol level at over twice the legal limit. Eyewitness News will have more details as they develop.

"That's the guy suing me," she said, wide eyed. "How did the person who called you know about this? Do you think he had something to do with the accident?"

"Doubtful. Why would Patel's death have anything to do with you?"

She tugged his shirt. "What if it's him, Alex? The man who reached into my car window after my accident and tried to grab me."

"You think Patel tried to grab you?"

"No. I think Patel may have seen the guy who grabbed me at my accident scene, and maybe he didn't want any witnesses who might recognize him."

"I don't know. That seems a bit far-fetched, doesn't it? I mean, the news report said Patel was drunk as a skunk."

"Then why the call?"

"I don't know," he said. "Let's focus on the comment about hiding you for 30 days. Do you know of anything that's going to happen in the next 30 days involving you or your family? Why would someone want to kill you now, but not 30 days from now?"

"No idea."

"Well, keep thinking," he said. "If the guy who called me is for real, that's a clue."

She breathed deep and rested a hand on her chest.

He wrapped his arms around her. "We're going to get through this. Trust me. I won't let anything happen to you."

"What are we going to do?"

"First thing, get you someplace safe. Go pack a bag."

"Alex, I'm scared."

"You're going to be all right. I promise."

"Where are you taking me?"

"Someplace no one would expect." He rinsed his empty mug and set in the dishwasher. "Let's get you out of here."

25

Morning rush hour traffic was heavy on Butler Boulevard, a four-lane highway leading from the beach to the interstate. Lots of stopping and starting. Jessica watched Alex rotate his view from mirror to mirror, twisting his head in every direction.

"You think someone is following us?"

"I don't know, but I'm not taking any chances. Hold on." He jerked hard right and cut across two lanes of traffic. He shot down an exit ramp and accelerated to the traffic light, which turned yellow just as he reached the intersection. He raced through the light and cut left onto the shoulder, barely missing a minivan.

"Look back behind. Do you see anyone coming down off the ramp?"

"No," she said, clinging to the door handle.

He mashed the accelerator through a series of back roads and side streets until he found the Interstate. They sped along in silence for twenty minutes.

She finally spoke up. "Are you going to tell me where we're going?"

"Ortega Boat Yard. Up around the corner."

He eased in the lot and found the parking spot closest to the water. "Wait here," he told her. He exited and scanned his surroundings.

Two shirtless men working on the hull of a sailboat. An older man wearing a wide-brimmed hat and Bermuda shorts was climbing off his trawler. Everything looked normal.

He grabbed her bag from the back seat and hot-footed her down A-dock past a dozen boats tied into their slips.

Just before the 100-yard dock ended, he stopped and dropped Jessica's bag. He climbed out on the arm of a slip and hopped aboard the cockpit of a fifty-foot Bénéteau sailboat named "Summer Wind." The sloop was pure white with a single, blue line along the hull that stretched bow to stern. He reached under one of the two wheel covers and, after a bit of groping, found the key. She followed him aboard.

He slid open the thick, wooden slats leading below and they climbed down. The white leather cushions in the settee created a dramatic contrast with the majestic teak wood that covered the floors, walls and cabinetry.

He worked the knobs on a control panel as she explored the cabins. "Why don't you unpack? The V-birth is where you'll sleep. There's space in there for your clothes, too." He pointed toward the forward cabin. "Make yourself comfortable and I'll get everything working."

She unpacked and returned to the salon where he continued to check equipment. "Everything looks good," he said. "You have refrigeration, air conditioning, running water, television, stereo with CD player, shower, a communications system set to the Coast Guard channel, stove, microwave, and most importantly, a coffee maker," he said with a cock-eyed smile.

"Would you like to tell me whose boat this is? Is the owner going to show up later today and wonder what I'm doing here?"

"A client of mine, Steve Tanner, owns a yacht business. This boat belongs to a guy from Boston who's looking to get out of the charter business. Steve brought the boat up from the Bahamas. He's going to do some work on it and list it for sale. No worries. Steve is okay with it. He won't bother you."

"How do you know so much about sailboats? Didn't you tell me you were from Ohio?"

"I am, and I don't. Steve insists we go sailing a couple times a year and, since he's a pretty good client, I say yes. Last Spring, we did a weekend trip to St. Augustine and back. Believe it or not, turning the power and lights on isn't that hard."

"I never thought of a sailboat as a safe hideout. Are you sure I'll be all right here?"

"Let me show you something." He pulled the cover back over the entry and dropped the slats in place. He pulled down the latch and locked the entry from the inside. "See this?" He asked, pointing toward the exit.

"Yes."

"It's the only way into the boat. You'd need an axe to get in here without a key." He walked to the beam and pointed toward the cabin windows. "A person can't fit through there." He dropped the shades over all of the windows. "No one can look into the boat to see where you are."

"Do I have to sit here by myself for the next month?"

"Let's hope we figure everything out before then. But in the meantime, I'll make sure you don't go hungry or thirsty. I checked the fridge. Still a few snacks and drinks in there. That should get you through the day. I'll stop back tonight with supplies. There's a grocery store right around the corner."

"I can't thank you enough for everything you're doing."

"You're going to be okay. I promise." He unlocked the latch and opened the cabin. "You have a cell phone, right?"

"Yeah."

"You have my number. If anything comes up, call me. Remember, we don't know what's going on here. Don't tell anyone who you are or what you're doing here. If someone asks, make up a name and tell them you're from Connecticut. Your boyfriend owns the boat. You're staying on it for a few weeks until he finishes some business and comes down here to sail you to the Bahamas."

"Who's going to talk to me?"

He chuckled. "About half the boats down here are live-aboards. They'll find you if you come out of the cabin. But don't worry. They're as nice a group of people as you'll find anywhere—free-spirit types with a live-and-let-live mentality."

He tossed her the keys. "Lock up behind me. You're okay to go outside on the dock. Nobody knows you here. Just make sure you keep it that way. Wear your hair up and keep a hat and sunglasses on." He climbed up the steps into the cockpit.

"I'll see you later tonight." He closed the cabin behind him, and jumped over the lifelines onto the dock. He checked his watch and jogged back to his car. He had a lot of work to do.

26

"Have a seat, Alex," Haney pointed to the booth opposite him in the small diner across the street from his dungy, brick-faced office building. Haney wasn't wealthy by any stretch and rental space was cheap near the courthouse and jail. His office sat just blocks from the St. Johns River, which had developers salivating. The condos and town homes were coming. Plans were already in the works and the developers were throwing unprecedented sums of money at the property owners. The city even agreed to move the court-house and jail. No reason at all to waste a river view on dope pushers waiting for trial. A renovation project, they called it. Lots of folks said it was good for the city. Haney wasn't one of them.

He studied a pad filled with notes. "Let's get down to business. I've been on the phone all morning trying to get more detail on Mr. Patel's untimely demise. My contacts at the Sheriff's office tell me they won't know any more until after the autopsy, but preliminary reports indi-cate Patel left a Mayport bar about three o'clock this morning and he was drunk as a skunk. Three times the legal limit, not two like the news said. Police found an open container of booze in the front seat of his torpedoed car."

The waitress came by to pour coffee. Haney waited for her to leave before continuing.

"I got the name of the bartender and spoke to him by phone. His story was consistent with what he told the police."

"Was Patel drinking with anyone at the bar?"

"That's affirmative." Haney glanced down at his notes. "He

apparently latched onto another customer who bought him drinks most of the night."

"Do we have a name or description on the guy Patel was drinking with?"

"No name. The bartender hadn't seen the guy before. He was about 6' 2", ball cap, glasses and looked to be in pretty good shape. That description fits about half the service."

"Did they leave together . . . Patel and the other guy?"

"Negative. According to the barkeep, the man buying drinks left about a half-hour earlier."

"How many drinks did Patel have?"

"Could have been 10 or 12, some of them doubles. The bartender warned Patel against driving, but he didn't listen."

"Any witnesses to the accident?"

"None. Not too many people out and about at 3:00 A.M. on a Thursday." Haney mangled a sugar packet as he spoke.

"You're saying it was an accident? How do you explain the phone call I got?"

"I'm not telling you it was an accident, I'm reporting to you the results of my investigation. As for the phone call, I find it suspicious. Look, Alex, I'm starting to believe you may have yourself quite a mess with this McCall case. I've looked into the McCall family deaths and, to be honest, it's all suspect."

He sat up. "What do you mean, Jim? What in the hell is going on?"

"I can't tell you what's going on. I don't know what's going on. Unfortunately, I don't have a crystal ball. I learned early on, both with the FBI and military intelligence, report facts, not conclusions."

"Let's cut to the chase. Just tell me what you found." He wasn't in the mood for a lecture.

Haney got the point. "Let's start at the beginning of this mess with Jessica's grandparents, Thomas and Joanne McCall." Haney sifted through his notes. "They were murdered in their beachfront house in the middle of the night. According to the police theory, Thomas stumbled across the burglar who threw him down a flight of stairs. He broke his neck. Joanne McCall took a bullet to the brain in her bedroom, apparently trying to call for help. When the police arrived at the scene, they didn't have to work hard to find the killer. They pinned the crime on a three-time loser, Lance Granger, who, lo and behold, was dead at the scene."

Haney continued, "According to the police, Granger killed and robbed the McCalls, ran down to his car, which was parked behind a dune off of the highway. In a rush to leave the scene, he hit the road without checking traffic and got himself broadsided. Deader than Julius Ceasar. The truck split his car in half." Haney paused to let him finish the notes he was writing.

"Granger," he continued, "gift-wrapped the crime. Post-mortem, of course. They found the gun that shot Mrs. McCall on the floor of his car and jewelry from the McCall's house scattered all over his smashed-up car. A crime couldn't be easier to solve. Almost too easy."

"What do you mean, too easy?"

"I mean crimes aren't usually so neatly gift-wrapped. When you dig deeper into Granger's criminal history, some questions come up about what happened and whether he had an accomplice or someone else was involved."

"Go on," he gagged on the stale coffee the waitress poured him, but he forced it down, more for the caffeine than his taste buds.

"I should have warned you about the coffee here. Anyway, I looked up Granger's rap sheet. The guy was an accomplished cat-burglar. Former Navy. Specialized in electronics, to be precise. He had the skill to shut down just about any alarm and used his talent on high-rent homes. Here's the strange part—the guy's last conviction was nearly ten years ago. He did a year and a half of hard time. According to his parole officer, he started a carpentry business and turned his life around. No arrests or convictions since getting out. Here's something else," he said scanning his notes, "the guy didn't have a history of violence. Other than a few days in the cooler for fighting in a bar twenty years ago, the guy hadn't displayed any violent tendencies. The times he was busted for burglary, the police didn't find any weapons. Looking at Granger's past history, the crime doesn't fit."

"Did the police consider the fact the crime didn't fit Granger's MO?"

"They considered it, then promptly dismissed it. Too much evidence pointing to his guilt. They surmised Granger didn't intend to hurt anyone, but was forced into a scuffle when Mr. McCall caught him during the break-in. After tossing the old boy down the steps, police believe Granger panicked and shot the wife to stop her from calling the police. The phone was in her hand when they found her body."

"Sounds plausible," he responded.

"Well, if that's all I knew about the case, I'd probably agree. But there's more." Haney reached into the briefcase sitting on the booth seat and lifted another note pad.

"The night of the killings, several witnesses placed Granger in a dive bar in Neptune Beach, just up the road from Ponte Vedra. He was a regular. I spoke to the bartender who closed the place the night of the murders. He recognized Granger on the night in question. He mentioned something that didn't mean a whole lot to me until this incident with Patel came up."

"What's that?"

"Granger was hanging with a couple of regulars most of the night, but after the regulars left, some other guy the bartender hadn't seen before ended up buying Granger drinks."

"Did you get a description?"

"Oh, yeah. Over six feet tall with dark hair and wore a ball cap. Sound familiar?"

"No shit," he shot back.

"There's one more thing," Haney said.

"What?"

"The guy left about fifteen to twenty minutes before Granger and, according to the bartender, when Granger left, he was drunk and alone."

"I'll be damned. Same as Patel. Any leads on this man who likes to buy people drinks."

"Not a one. The guy vanished into thin air."

"What about Jessica's dad? Did you look into his death?"

"Yeah." Haney flipped again through his notes. "According to the autopsy report, Mark McCall just dropped dead of a heart attack in his home. Strange thing is, he had no history of heart trouble, and it didn't run in his family."

"What do you make of it?"

"Don't know. There're lots of drugs and chemicals that can kill and make it look like a heart attack. Unless the coroner knew exactly what to look for, he wouldn't have found it."

"Any way to know for sure?"

"Nope. Too late now. I'm just speculating."

"What now?"

"Good question. Something tells me we aren't going to find the killer without help. I'm guessing the person who called you this morning is getting a conscience. Let's hope he'll surface again. Was there a return number on your Caller ID?"

"No. Blocked call."

"Usually means cell phones. I'll make some calls to my contacts at the phone company to see what I can find out."

"Jim, speaking of the caller, what do you make of the guy telling me to hide Jessica for the next thirty days?"

"Impossible to say. Given everything that's happened, I'd take him seriously and keep the girl out of sight. And make damn sure you don't tell anyone where you're keeping her. Until we know what's going on, we don't know who to trust."

"Thanks for all of your help on this."

"Just be careful. It's possible there's a crazy man out there somewhere and, if so, you don't want any part of him." Haney threw a five down on the table. "I got this one," he said, gathering his papers. "If anything comes up, you have my number."

"Something tells me we'll be talking soon, Jim."

"I think you're right."

27

Wednesday afternoon was busier than usual at the Duval County Courthouse. Built in 1958, the old, rectangular structure was on life support and every year it survived was one year too many for the judges and lawyers who made a living there. Plans were in place for a new building, but budget overruns halted the project in its tracks.

Alex sat on a wooden bench outside the row of courtrooms on the second floor. To his right, a heavyset man with his right arm covered in tattoos wearing torn jeans and a T-shirt crowed to his lawyer about a restraining order just entered against him. The lawyer worked hard to calm down his client. To his left, several attorneys lined up at the bailiff's desk to check in for a hearing. After a few minutes, Rob Foster caught his attention rounding the corner.

"Hey, Rob. Thanks for coming."

Foster dropped his weight on the bench next to his friend. "What in the hell is going on?"

Alex scanned the hall to see if he recognized anyone before answering. "You remember the girl I told you about? Jessica McCall?"

"Yeah, what about her?"

"She's in trouble. Serious trouble. I think someone's trying to kill her."

"What?" Foster spat. The attorneys at the bailiff's desk turned to look before returning to their business.

"Quiet down," Alex said. "I don't have time to explain everything right now. I'm still trying to digest it myself. People related to, or involved with, Jessica are winding up dead. I got a call from someone this morning who warned me to move Jessica to a hideaway, or else." He could see Foster's brain churning probabilities. "Rob, I need to see Jessica and I can't risk being followed. That's why I called you."

"What makes you think you're being followed?"

"I don't know if I am or not. But I'm not taking any chances."

"This is ridiculous. Go to the police."

"Wouldn't do any good. They already investigated everything and closed their files. The deaths could have been set-ups. The problem is, I can't prove it right now. I need more evidence."

"Are you listening to yourself? You're talking about murders, conspiracies, and set-ups. You sound whacked."

"Trust me. I know it sounds crazy. And I hope like hell I'm wrong. But, in case I'm not, I can't take any chances. Jessica's life may be at stake. Mine too, for that matter."

"I don't know what you've gotten yourself into, but it's not good." Foster reached into his pocket and handed over his keys. "I'm on level three across the street."

"I owe you, big time." He stood and grabbed the briefcase at his feet.

"Hey, wait a minute, Slick," Foster grabbed his arm.

"What?"

"I'm not walking home."

"Oh, yeah. Sorry." He reached for his keys and tossed them to Foster. "I'm in the back lot. Do me a favor and hang out here for a bit before you leave. The briefcase'll be in the stairwell on the fifth floor. And thanks again."

He left Foster sitting on the bench, scratching his head. He hustled to a stairwell and ran up three flights of stairs, skipping a stair with each step. He found a bathroom in a quiet corner of the courthouse. He entered the restroom in a suit and tie. He walked out a few minutes later wearing old jeans, a T-shirt, and a ball cap.

He left the courthouse opposite the side he entered, slid on a pair of sunglasses, and loped across the street to the parking garage where Foster's car was waiting. He entered the courthouse as an attorney and left a pedestrian. He hoped nobody noticed.

28

Jessica vision was blurred from scanning all the documents related to her father's estate. She put off the administrative work associated with probate long enough. Being cooped-up on the boat took away all the excuses she used to put it off any longer.

Alex returned as promised around seven with a half-dozen thin, plastic bags filled with groceries he picked up from the supermarket near the boat yard. He unwrapped two deli sandwiches, turkey on rye, and popped the cap off two beers. Over the light dinner he recapped the conversation with Haney and confirmed her suspicion that she might be in danger.

"What now?" she asked.

"We keep you hidden. We also try to find the guy who called me. He has the answer."

"Would you . . . would you mind staying here tonight? I don't want to be alone."

"I was going to suggest that. Hope you don't mind, but I asked Jim Haney to stay with you during the day when I'm not here. He'll be here tomorrow morning. I don't want you alone, either."

"I'd like that."

Bread crumbs flaked off his sandwich and landed on legal papers scattered across the settee. He brushed off the mess. "What's all that?" he asked, eyes panned down.

"It's all from the package Michael sent me that relate to dad's Will and estate. I reviewed it, but the legalese is maddening. I haven't taken Wills and Estates yet in school. You mind helping." She gave a coy smile that he couldn't refuse.

"Sure, I can help."

He swallowed the last of his meal and popped open another beer. He scooped up the messy pages and placed them on the dining table where he began his study.

She picked up around the cabin to give him some space while he worked. Her smooth, firm legs distracted him a few times as she passed by in her soft, cotton shorts that didn't leave much to the imagination.

She finished picking up and decided to take a shower. The hot water streamed across her face and body while she rested her head against the shower wall. The tension oozed from her neck and shoulders. As she dried off, he interrupted her reverie.

"Jessica, come here," he called. His tone told her not to dally.

She returned to the main cabin wearing a white robe. "What is it?"

"I may have found something." He stared at the papers.

"What?"

She plopped down next to him. Fresh. Clean. Her wet hair carried a scent of apricot. He was temporarily distracted.

"According to the Will, your dad distributed his estate among five beneficiaries. Looking through this, he left the majority of his estate to you. In the event you died before your grandparents, they would get the estate. I guess he didn't get around to having the Will changed after your grandparents died, because they're still listed as beneficiaries." He pointed to the language.

"Other beneficiaries include two local charities. Your dad served on the board of directors. He set up a few trusts in their names, which I have here." He pointed to a separate stack of papers on the side of the table with the Trust Agreements.

"Dad was always involved with charities. That's not unusual."

"Here the Will references a third trust named Trust Agreement of Mark McCall, but this Trust isn't attached to the Will and it's not with

the papers you received with your dad's documents. Do you know anything about this Trust?"

"No. Never heard of it. Is it important?"

"Well, take a look at this." He turned to the fifth page of the Will and
found the section captioned SURVIVORSHIP. He picked up the page
and read the paragraph underneath the caption:

If any devisee under this Will and I should die simultane-
ously or in circumstances that make it difficult to determine
which of us died first, I direct such devisee be deemed to have
predeceased me for purposes of this Will. I further direct the provisions of this Will shall be construed upon that assumption. To
assure my wishes are carried out, only those devisees who may
survive me by 120 days from the date of my death shall be considered to have survived me for purposes of interpreting this
instrument.

"A hundred and twenty days . . ." She said. "That's weird."

"It's a survivorship clause. Some people put these in their Wills to
avoid confusion in cases where a beneficiary dies at or near the same
time the Testator dies. The order of death can also have tax conse-
quences. What this means to you is, you have to survive your dad by at
least one hundred-twenty days to collect under the Will. If you don't
live that long, you get nothing." He could see her wheels turning.
"When did your dad die?"

"March 17."

"One hundred-twenty days is four months. You have to live until
July 17 to collect under the Will. I got the call to hide you for thirty
days on June 19 . . . ."

"Which is about thirty days before July 17 . . . are you saying someone wants me dead before dad's estate passes to me?"

"I'm not saying anything for sure. I'm just pointing this out as something we need to investigate. Now take a look at this . . ." He fingered one of the lower paragraphs on the page titled NO LIVING DEVISEES.

In the event no living devisees survive me, I give, bequeath, and devise unto the Trustee of the Trust Agreement of Mark McCall all of the rest, residue, and remainder of my estate. Real, personal, or mixed, of whatever kind and character, and wherever so situated of which I die, seized or possessed, or to which I may be in any way entitled an interest, including all property over which I have a power to appoint. Said Trustee shall distribute said property under the terms and conditions set forth in the Trust Agreement.

She bit at her thumb as he read. "Jessica, if you and your grandparents are not alive on July 17, your dad's property all goes into the Trust. We have to review that Trust Agreement. It may have some answers."

"How do we get it?"

"Parker Jones drafted your dad's Will, right?"

"Yeah, Michael's been the legal contact for the football team for as long as I can remember. He and dad go back to the team's start ten years ago. He's been very supportive."

He glanced at his watch. Past nine o'clock. "He's not at the office now. I'll try him at home."

"Who?"

"Murphy." He had the firm lawyers' home phone numbers programmed into his cell phone. He dialed and waited. She huddled beside him and tried listening.

"Hello?" Murphy answered.

"Mr. Murphy, it's Alex Weaver."

"Isn't it a bit late, Alex? What can I do for you?"

"It's about Jessica McCall."

"Yes, what about Jessica?" Murphy's tone shifted upward a note. He seemed more interested in the conversation. "How is she?"

"I think she's in trouble."

"What now, Alex? I thought we'd been through this before."

"We've discovered evidence that suggests someone is trying to murder Jessica, and we believe it's related to her father's Will." His words brought dead air.

"Sir?"

"Still here. You'll have to excuse me. You caught me a bit off-guard. What are you saying?"

"Jessica asked me to look over her father's probate documents and a Trust Agreement is missing. We believe it may be linked to the death of Jessica's grandparents as well as her father. We also believe someone may be trying to kill Jessica, because of what's in this Trust."

"What Trust Agreement?"

"It's called the Trust Agreement of Mark McCall."

"Wasn't that Agreement in the package I sent her?"

"No, it wasn't."

"That was an oversight." Murphy sighed. "Hold on just a minute," he said. After a brief delay, his voice returned. "Listen, my calendar is open in the morning. Stop by my office when you get in and we'll discuss this matter further. I'll ask Francis to get another copy of the Trust Agreement for you to review. I seriously doubt it's going to point you in the direction of a murder conspiracy. It's a charitable trust, nothing more."

"What's the Trust about?"

"It's something Mark set up to provide health care for people who can't afford it—a very worthy cause."

"Thank you, Mr. Murphy. I'll see you first thing in the morning." Murphy's words smacked him right between the eyes. An overreaction?

"You must be exhausted," he said. "Why don't you try to get some sleep?"

She wasn't the only one. His lids were heavy and his mind over-loaded. Sleep would recharge him.

He followed her into the forward cabin and pulled a cover over her. "I'll be right out here," he pointed at the settee.

"Thank you," she said softly. She drifted off to sleep almost instantly. He returned to the cabin and unrolled the pillow and blanket she set out. He reclined on the settee and scrunched the pillow under his head. A part of him wanted to believe Murphy was right—that Jessica's circumstances were just a big misunderstanding. Hopefully, the morning would produce some answers.

29

lex left the marina at dawn, shortly after Haney arrived. He rushed home for a shower, gathered some personal belongings, and slipped into a fresh suit. His condo was close to work, so the stop didn't cost him much time.

He arrived at the office shortly after eight and headed straight for Murphy's office. Murphy's secretary hadn't yet arrived. He pushed open the door and knocked on the frame.

Murphy was immersed in a telephone conversation. He spotted Alex and abruptly cut it short. "I'll have to call you back."

He hung up the phone.

"Good morning," he said. "Please, come in," he motioned to a chair. "Why don't you tell me what's on your mind."

"I know we've been through this several times, but I truly think someone might be trying to kill Jessica McCall."

"Yes, I gathered as much from your call last night," Murphy pulled the wire glasses from his face and ran a cloth handkerchief over the lenses. "I thought we went through all of this. This is a case of a distraught young woman's mind running wild. You, however, are a different matter. I'm surprised you bought into her wild theories." Murphy put his glasses back on and peered at him, sizing him up.

"With all due respect, I don't think Jessica's theories are wild. I think she might be in danger. There's evidence to support it."

"Like what?"

He reached into his briefcase and pulled out Mark McCall's Will. He showed Murphy the survivorship clause and the reference to the Trust

Agreement of Mark McCall, which was missing from the documents Jessica received. He then recounted the discussions he had with Haney about the murders of Thomas and Joanne McCall by Lance Granger, as well as Patel's drunken driving accident, and how an unidentified man was buying drinks for both Granger and Patel. Finally, he described the anonymous telephone call he received, which warned him to hide Jessica for the next thirty days. He finished his presentation and waited for a reaction.

"You've put a great deal of thought into this and I understand your concerns, but . . . Listen, with respect to Jessica's grandparents, the police caught the killer at the scene. A career criminal who had the McCall's jewelry and personal possessions scattered all over his car. He even had the murder weapon."

"According to the ME, Mark died of a heart attack. No traces of drugs or poisons in his system. No signs of foul play. Nothing. And, Patel, he's a scoundrel. Got drunk, drove his car over an embankment, and died. Witnesses saw him in the bar, slobbering drunk and warned him not to drive. Does that about sum it up? Or am I missing something?"

"You're overlooking the man who appeared at Jessica's house posing as a home inspector and the man fitting the same description buying drinks for both Granger and Patel the night they died. And how do you explain the anonymous call I received?"

"I'm sure each of those events has a reasonable explanation that doesn't lead to a murder conspiracy. The man who called you is probably a nut-job. My wife and I got an unlisted number years ago, because of strange calls from idiots who failed to identify themselves. Unfortunately, people on the opposite side of our cases don't like us. They can get pretty nasty. That's part of the business. I wouldn't lend much credibility to your anonymous caller."

Murphy continued, "As for people drinking alcohol with Patel and Granger, that fact shouldn't come as a surprise. They were both a couple of cretins who drank themselves into oblivion every chance they had, especially if someone else was buying. As for the man at Jessica's house, if you haven't noticed, she's an attractive young woman. People do crazy things when they're infatuated with a pretty girl. He could be a stalker. Maybe some guy saw her on the beach or at the grocery store and went nuts. Happens every day."

"What about the Trust?" He asked. "Do you have a copy for me?"

"Yes, the Trust." Murphy picked up the lone document on his desk. "Here you go." He handed it over.

"Can you tell me about it?"

"Sure. A few years back, Mark asked me to sit on the board of a charitable organization. The charity was founded to provide health care to the underprivileged. He made some provisions for the charity in his Will. And, by chance, if he had no survivors in his family, his estate would pass on to the charity. It's all in there," Murphy pointed to the document. Alex studied the Trust Agreement as Murphy looked on.

"What's the name of the charity?"

"Horizon. Alex, if someone has it out for the McCall family," Murphy said, "it's not because of this Trust. But don't take my word for it. Read it yourself."

"Thanks for your time this morning, Mr. Murphy. I appreciate you giving me a copy of the Agreement."

"No problem. I hope it helps. And make sure you keep the contents confidential. Mark was a good client, and we don't want his personal laundry showing up in the newspapers."

"Absolutely." He stood to leave, but Murphy stopped him.

"I want to make sure you're prepared for the Van Doren trial coming up. I can't stress enough the trial's importance. And you know Shelton. We need to have all our ducks in a row."

"Yes, sir. Working on it."

"Do I need to be concerned your attention is being diverted

elsewhere? I can find someone to take your spot—perhaps Felton or Ritz."

Murphy knew how to push his buttons.

"That won't be necessary. I'll be ready."

"Good. Now, get to work."

He started out of the office, but when he reached the door, Murphy stopped him again.

"Alex."

"Sir?"

"Please give my warmest regards to Jessica."

"Sure."

"You mentioned moving her from her house after getting that anonymous call. Where is she?"

"Ortega Boat Yard. A friend of mine loaned me the use of his boat. Even if I'm totally wrong about her, I think she'll feel safer there for a while, at least for the next few weeks. I'd appreciate your keeping her whereabouts confidential."

"Of course. Just curious. You know, my old neighbor used to keep his trawler down at Ortega. Been down there a few times with him. Have they upgraded that old, wooden dock?"

"Nope. Still standing."

"I'm surprised that place has survived the storms we've had," Murphy said. "Anyway, I won't hold you any longer. You can go."

30

The morning sun already lifted the temperature to eighty-six degrees. Beads of sweat trickled down Murphy's forehead as he stepped up to the first tee at Avondale Country Club. He didn't want to play golf with all the work piled up on his desk, but Van Doren insisted. As he rustled around in his golf bag, Van Doren pulled up in his golf cart with Wilson Gates tagging along.

"Charles, congratulations on picking the hottest day of the year to play golf," he said while toweling off his face.

"You'll have to earn your fee today, Michael. You wanted to talk business, so I know your meter is going to start running very soon, if it hasn't already. At least the golf makes talking to a lawyer tolerable." Van Doren chuckled.

"How are you, Wilson?" Murphy asked.

"Fine, Michael." Gates wasn't convincing.

The three men plodded along, alone on the perfectly manicured private golf course. Van Doren's club had less than one hundred members. It was exclusive not only because of its exorbitant membership fees, but also because of its exclusionary admission policy. The running joke around town was the only way an African-American, Jewish, or Hispanic citizen could see the inside of the club was through the service entrance.

"So, Michael, tell me about the case. Are we going to prevail at the trial?" Van Doren asked. He scanned the ninth green before putting.

"Yes. Hudson won't present any evidence at the trial to establish a third party has a priority interest over your company in the patent rights to Transviazine."

"And will that end the case?"

"Yes."

"What does that mean for future challenges toward our patent?"

"It means your patent will be bulletproof. Hudson made his complaint as broad as he possibly could, included everyone affiliated with Rabinowitz as a potential plaintiff. As a result, a ruling in your favor would have preclusive effect on any future third party claims. This would fall under a legal doctrine known as *res judicata*, which means: a thing already decided. If anyone else tries to sue you in the future, you waive this judgment in the air and say, 'Sorry, been there and done that,' and it's over."

"Good, Michael. Good." Van Doren stroked his putt and watched it dink over the right side of the hole.

"Yes." He pumped his fist.

Murphy followed with an ugly putt that missed the hole by four feet.

Van Doren picked up Murphy's ball and handed it to him. "I'll give you that one. I couldn't bear to watch you putt it again."

"So, what'd you wanted to discuss, Michael?" Van Doren asked as the men walked from the green back to the cart.

"I have a few concerns."

"What?" Van Doren stopped and gave his full attention.

"My first concern is the girl."

"What about her?"

"She's convinced somebody is trying to kill her and she's moved locations. She's hiding."

"Well, goddamn. That's no good. No good at all," Van Doren howled. "We need to find her."

"Don't worry, Charles. I know where she is."

"Where are you getting your information?"

"Alex Weaver."

"Please, tell me you haven't brought him in on our plan."

"Absolutely not. He's working on the girl's case and trusts me. He tells me everything. The problem is, Jessica is convincing him the deaths in her family are related, and he's investigating her story. I'm doing everything possible to put him off, but it's not been easy." He paused for a moment. "Charles, he asked for the Trust Agreement."

"Did you give it to him?"

"Had to."

"What in the hell for?" Van Doren barked. He slammed his putter into his golf bag.

"Because it would have raised too much suspicion if I didn't. Plus, the document itself won't tell him anything. Don't worry."

"Don't worry? If this kid starts up with questions, there's no telling what he might dig up. He's no idiot. I don't like this at all, Michael. Not at all. I'm afraid Mr. Weaver might be getting too close. We may have to do something about this."

"Charles, I don't want to see anything happen to Alex. I can control him," Murphy pleaded.

Gates chimed into the conversation. "Please, Charles. Listen to Michael on this one."

"And what do you think Mr. Weaver is going to do when the girl winds up missing—or dead? Isn't that going to confirm his suspicions? Isn't he going to start snooping around more?"

Van Doren's questions were difficult to answer. "Charles, I can control Alex. Trust me."

"I trusted you when you told me you would put a snot-nosed kid on our case who wasn't smart enough to put the pieces together. It seems that your pigeon has more talent than you gave him credit for."

Van Doren walked behind the golf carts. His metal spikes clicked against the cart path.

"I'll give it some thought." He jumped in his cart and smashed his open hand on the wheel. He started driving, but stopped. "Was there anything else you wanted to talk about, Michael? We may as well clear up everything right now while we're on the subject."

"There was one more thing."

"What is it?"

"Someone telephoned Alex to warn him the girl was in danger."

"Beg your pardon?"

"Alex received an anonymous message telling him to move the girl. The call was nondescript. Not sure what to make of it. I've asked Alex to keep me apprised if he receives any additional calls."

Van Doren rubbed his chin. "Do you know anything about this?" he asked Gates.

"Not a thing." Gates toweled off the back of his neck.

"Uh-huh," Van Doren responded. "Very well, Michael. I'll take it under advisement."

Other than the occasional "nice shot," the three men barely spoke for the rest of the round. The tension was thicker than the humidity. After the 18th hole, Van Doren pulled Murphy to the side when Gates walked back to pick up a club he left on the apron of the green.

"I need to know I have your complete support on this project."

"Of course, Charles."

"There's a lot at stake for you," Van Doren said.

"I'm aware of that."

"I've already made arrangements for your daughter. For your sake, I don't want her situation jeopardized."

"Nor I, Charles. You have my unconditional support."

"Good. I need to make some difficult decisions going forward and I can't have people around me wavering. He stared in Gates' direction.

"Is something going on with Wilson? He doesn't seem right."

"It's nothing that can't be remedied." Van Doren held out his hand. "It's been a pleasure playing today. I need to get going. I have some late business to attend. Please, excuse me." He shook Van Doren's hand

and a caddie ran up to clean the clubs. Van Doren handed the teenager a twenty. "This is for all the bags."

"Thank you, Mr. Van Doren," the young man said, busily wiping. "I'll store your bag in the locker room, sir."

"That's fine, Gregory. Thank you."

He turned to Murphy. "Again, my apologies. I'll speak to you soon. We have some work to do for the trial."

Van Doren approached Gates and said a brief goodbye. Then he left.

"Wilson, it's been a pleasure," Murphy said, holding out his hand. Gates ignored the gesture.

"Is everything all right, Wilson?"

"No, everything is not all right. In fact, it's all wrong. All of this is wrong."

"What do you mean?"

"If you can't figure it out, then it's not worth explaining."

Gates turned to leave, but stopped. "You're not God, Michael," he said, "neither is Charles."

31

Alex brought several copies of the Trust Agreement back to the boat, where he, Jessica, and Haney each scanned a copy. They huddled around the u-shaped dinette.

"Do you lawyers just make up your own language?" Haney asked, squinting at the document. "Wherefore, heretofore, designee, testator, administrator . . . good grief, I'm glad I don't write this crap for a living."

Alex had reviewed the document earlier in the day. He referred to some notes on the margins of his copy as he discussed the Trust's contents.

"This document doesn't tell us much of anything," he said. "It's a very basic Trust Agreement that names Michael Murphy as the Trust Administrator and identifies its purpose as raising funds for a non-profit organization named Horizon. Murphy has broad discretion how to administer the Trust."

"Why would Michael be the administrator instead of my father?" Jessica asked.

"Probably tax implications. If the person setting up the Trust has control of it, then money going into the Trust is counted as income. The tax benefits come when the person setting up the Trust gives up control. I'm not a tax attorney, but I think that's why."

"I don't see any tight controls over how the money is supposed to be used other than simply for the benefit of Horizon." Haney said. "Is that normal?"

"It's not abnormal. A Trust is just a one-sided contract. You can write Wills, Trusts and related documents to say and do anything you want. Some people include lots of controls to keep the administrator honest.

Some take the opposite approach. The more you trust the administrator, the more discretion you leave in his hands."

"What about this non-profit organization, Horizon?" Haney followed up.

"Not sure what you're asking?"

"Do you know what it is? Did Michael tell you?"

"He said it was founded to advance medical research and he was on the board. He didn't get specific."

"You want me to investigate?" Haney asked.

"We're at a dead end here. Murphy isn't part of a murder conspiracy. And truthfully, I'm not willing to put my career on the line by directing you to investigate Horizon. If you start snooping or asking questions, it's probably going to get back to Murphy, and I'll wind up on the street."

Jessica snapped, "we don't have anything else to go on. I think we should look into this. Last night, you were pretty certain the Trust might be linked to someone trying to kill me. The fact Michael serves on the board doesn't mean he knows everything going on behind the scenes. He's a full-time attorney. Things could be happening he doesn't know about."

"Look," he said, "the Trust Agreement is the wrong angle, that's all. I'm not saying someone hasn't been after you. I'm just not ready to cop to a conspiracy theory. We have nothing to go on other than hunches and speculation. As far as we know, the guy who showed up at your house is a stalker or random screwball. Let's hope you never see him again so we can put everything behind us."

She lapsed into a silent pout.

Haney checked his watch. "It's late. I need to get going." He gathered his belongings, including a laptop computer, cell phone, note pads, and some extra clothes.

Alex and Jessica followed him out of the cabin to the cockpit and watched him leave the marina.

"Can we sit out here for a bit and get some fresh air? The breeze feels nice, and I'm getting cabin fever," she said.

He spied the marina. Nothing out of place. "Sure. We can hang out here for a bit."

"Do you think I'm crazy?" she asked.

"No, of course not. Why?"

"I got the impression after you talked to Michael and saw the Trust, you thought I was just making up everything." She spoke quietly, as if the life had drained out of her body.

"Jessica, when the Trust Agreement didn't produce the answers I wanted, I felt good, because it increased the chance you're not in danger. There are reasonable explanations for all the bad things that have happened to you."

"What now? Do I go back to my normal life? I can't ask you to keep babysitting me, but I'm nervous to go home. I can't live like this forever."

He put his arms around her and she leaned her head on his shoulder. "Let's take it one day at a time for now. Jim and I are going to investigate a few things. Just in case the man who called me was right about hiding you for thirty days, I think you should stay here for the next few weeks and just lay low. Give it a little more time, and we'll probably figure it all out."

They soaked up the cool night breeze in the roomy Bénéteau cockpit for another hour before returning to the cabin. She retreated to the forward cabin. He unpacked his carrying bag. Milling through the contents, he realized he was missing something.

"Crap," he said.

"What is it?"

"Forgot my tie. I have court tomorrow morning. I need one."

She returned to the main cabin. "Do you need to run home?"

"No. I can pick it up in the morning. I just hope Jim gets here early."

"Go," she insisted. "It won't take you long. You live close by, don't you?"

"Yeah, but I shouldn't . . ." The buzz from a cell phone stopped him in mid-sentence. "I think that's mine," he said. He lifted a few blankets on the settee and snatched up his phone.

"Hello?"

"Alex? It's Michael Murphy."

Murphy never called him outside of work before. "What can I do for you?"

"I'm glad I found you. I hate to ask you this, but I need a big favor."

"What is it?"

"I'm at the Mayor's fundraiser tonight and I can't get away. I have a pleading that needs to go in the Federal Express late pickup at the office. It's an answer to a pending complaint that has to be filed tomorrow in the Northern District. An attorney has to sign it and make sure it gets out. Francis stayed late to make the final edits and left them on my desk. The case is Friedman versus Wells Construction. Would you go over to the office and do a spot check on the edits, sign it for me, and stick it in the Fed Ex box? The envelope should already be prepared."

"Oh, this really isn't a good time. Are you sure no one else is available?" He didn't want this project, especially under the circumstances.

"I'm sorry, but I don't have the luxury of spending the next thirty minutes trying to track down another person. I'm afraid I'm going to have to insist you do this." Murphy listened to dead air.

"Okay. I'll take care of it," he conceded. He flipped closed his phone and threw it down. "Shit."

"What happened? Was that Michael?"

"Yeah."

"What did he want?"

"I have to run to the office before eleven tonight. Murphy needs something filed and I have to make sure it gets in the last Fed Ex run." He released a long breath.

"Well, it's not all bad," she offered. "You could stop by your place on the way back and get your tie."

"Yeah, I guess, but you should come with me."

"I'll be fine," she insisted. "You won't be gone long, and I'll lock up behind you. Really. It'll be fine."

"Are you sure?"

"Yes. Now go already so you can get back here faster."

He grabbed his keys and climbed out of the boat. He checked the lock before jumping down to the wooden dock. The wind had picked up. Boats swayed in their slips. As he approached his car, he took a long look around the marina. All was quiet.

32

Alex's trip to the office didn't take long. He made it downtown in about fifteen minutes. The papers were precisely where Murphy said they'd be. He spot checked the pleading, signed it, and stuffed it in the Federal Express box with ten minutes to spare before the last pickup. So far, so good. Next stop: condo.

After his third year of practicing law, he gave up renting and bought a two-bedroom condominium in San Marco. His unit was on the twelfth floor with a roomy balcony that got frequent use. Given the escalating real estate prices, he often joked he couldn't afford his own condo if he had to buy it now.

He flipped on the kitchen light and noticed the message light flashing. He hit the speaker option and hurried back to his bedroom to locate a tie for the morning. "You have one message," a digital female voice announced.

"Alex, I'm calling about the girl."

His heart jumped. He recognized the muffled voice and ran back into the kitchen. "Listen carefully: they know where she is. Get her off the boat. Now."

A dial tone followed.

"Jesus Christ. What in the hell is going on?" He tossed the phone and charged out the door.

33

Jessica felt the boat rock like a cradle from the whipping wind. She tried to stay awake until Alex got back, but her eyes were heavy. After washing her face, she crawled into bed and curled up under the covers. She took a few deep breaths to relax. Getting to sleep wasn't easy and, over the past few months, she tried every ploy from counting sheep to drinking warm milk. Some nights were better than others.

Just as she got comfortable, a strange sound found her ears. Every two or three seconds, a sharp clanging noise sounded.

She sat up and listened. It was outside. She peeked through the hatch above her bed, but couldn't see anything. The porthole in the main cabin didn't help either. She still couldn't see anything.

Clunk, clunk, clunk. The sound continued.

She elected to ignore it and go back to sleep.

It didn't work, especially now. She was thinking about it. Focused on it. She sat up again, but this time, pushed open the hatch and poked her head through. A cool, damp wind—the kind that sweeps through just before a storm—raced through the narrow opening and whipped her hair across her face.

She saw the culprit. There it was. The halyard line had come loose. It banged against the mast.

From the hatch, the marina appeared lifeless. She pulled on some shorts and climbed up into the cockpit. Taking careful steps along the boat's rail, she grabbed the lifelines for support, scooted along the outer rail and climbed to the mast.

"Gotcha," she said, grabbing the swinging line. She noticed a hook at the bottom of the mast where she could attach the halyard, but there wasn't enough slack in the line to reach.

"Crap." She followed the halyard back to the cockpit to find the release. The lines were difficult to distinguish in the dark. After fumbling around, she elected to released all of the lines. One of them had to be the halyard.

She carefully retraced her steps to the mast, hugging the rail, and climbed up to secure the noisy line. She jerked it hard and snapped it on the hook.

"Yes."

She climbed below and decided to call Alex to ask how long he would be and brag about her newfound seamanship. "Where is it? I could have sworn I put it here," she said, scanning the galley. Her phone was nowhere in sight. She gave up the search.

She retreated to her cabin, shut the door, and climbed into the soft sheets.

The noise stopped. She could relax.

Her eyes glanced up in the dark. She noticed something unusual. The hatch was closed. "That's weird," she thought. She was sure she left it open when she popped her head through earlier. She stood on her knees for a closer look. The handles to the hatch were missing; broken off.

"What?"

Her eyes searched the dark cabin. The handles weren't there. A creaking sound escaped from the closet in her small quarters. The closet door was cracked open, but only black showed through the crack. Just like the hatch, she was sure she had closed the closet door before going to bed earlier.

Her heart pounded against her chest. She became a statue. Perfectly still. Thoughts raced through her overloaded mind. Deep breath.

She reached for the hatch and strained with all her might to open it.

Without handles, she couldn't gain any leverage. "Come on, come on," she begged, pushing and pressing with her whole body. It wouldn't budge. If she wanted off the boat, she had to go through the main cabin.

She reached down along the floor, searching for any object she could find to defend herself.

Nothing.

Another creak filtered out from the closet. She froze on the bed for a moment and thought about what to do. "You gotta get out of here," she told herself. She slid off the bed, kicked the closet door as hard as she could to slam it shut. She flung open the door to the main cabin and ran headfirst into what felt like a brick wall. She crashed down and hit her head on the table's edge during the fall.

A large man dressed in black and wearing gloves stood over top of her.

"Help," she screamed. "Help."

The man reached down and backhanded her face, leaving her dazed. "That's enough shouting," he said.

"Who are you? What are you doing here?" Tears stung her eyes.

"Do you realize how much trouble you've been?" Anger filled his voice.

"What do you want?" Blood trailed down her face from the cut on her forehead.

"Get up," he nudged her with his foot.

She met his eyes. "I've seen you before."

"You have, and I'm disappointed in your manners, Jessica. When I was in your house, you never even offered me a drink," Lunden sneered.

"You killed my father, didn't you?"

"He was a lot easier than you," he said, "but don't worry, dear. He didn't suffer long." His blue eyes were all business.

"And my grandparents? Did you kill them too?" She shook with rage.

"They went quickly," he said matter-of-fact. "The old ones always do."

"You son-of-a-bitch. How could you do this?"

"Keep your mouth shut. I planned to make this painless, but if you keep talking, I may change my mind. Now, for the last time, get your fucking ass up off the ground," he kicked her ribs and watched her curl in pain.

"Get the fuck up," he yelled again.

Her eyes scanned the floor for anything to grab to defend herself. A pencil. Under the table.

"Looking for this?" he asked, holding her cell phone in his hand. "I'd prefer you didn't make any calls right now."

His lips curled into a smile.

She grabbed the pencil and hid it in the palm of her hand. He jerked her to her feet. "Don't worry. It'll be over quickly," he said and wrapped his arm around her neck from behind, his grip a makeshift vice.

Her brain shouted the command to scream, but she couldn't. Her air supply disappeared.

"Don't fight it. Struggling will just make you more uncomfortable," he said, cutting off her oxygen.

Using all the strength she had, she plunged her make-shift weapon into his thigh.

He let out a wail. "You fucking bitch." By reflex, he let go of her, doubled over, and clutched his leg. She turned and kicked him in the groin as hard as she could. He fell to the ground. She ran to the galley and jiggled opened the top cabinet.

He pulled the pencil out of his leg and stood, grimacing. "You shouldn't have done that," he said, limping toward her.

She grabbed the flare gun out of the cabinet and pointed it at him. "Stop right there."

He did as she asked. "You don't want to do that, Jessica."

"Give me my phone," she demanded.

"What? This?" He held it up in the air like kids do playing keep away.

"Don't move. Just toss it from there."

"As you wish."

He hurled the phone and lunged toward her. The hard object collided with her face and knocked her to the ground.

He slapped the gun from her hand and piled on top of her. His face was purple with rage. "I'm done playing games, bitch," his hands covered her neck and squeezed.

Pinned down, she couldn't move or breathe. There was nothing left to do but die. Just as she began to fade out, the hatch door flew open.

Alex hurled himself on top of Lunden and knocked him away from her. They hit the ground hard and began wrestling. Lunden gained the advantage and landed blow after blow to Alex's head.

"Run, Jessica! Run," he howled, absorbing damage.

Lunden halted his attack and jumped up to make another run at her. A flash lit up the cabin. The flare ripped through Lunden's clothes and buried itself into his body.

"Ahhhhh!" he shrieked as layers of skin melted off and smoke filled the cabin. He fell to the ground and struggled to remove the object.

Alex ran to Jessica. He grabbed the empty gun and threw it aside. "Let's get the hell out of here," he yelled and pushed her up through the hatch.

She bounded up the stairs with Alex close behind. Just as Alex made the last step, a pair of hands grabbed him from below and jerked him back down. Lunden was back on top of him with his hands wrapped around his throat.

"Alex," Jessica screamed. "Help. Somebody . . ."

He freed his right arm from under Lunden's knee and punched him squarely on his chin. The blow dazed Lunden, and gave him a chance to break away. He struck Lunden again in the head and pushed him off to the side.

"Jessica, get the hell out of here. Goddamn it, go."

Both men jumped back to their feet.

"You're in over your head, boy," Lunden said, grabbing Alex's arm and twisting it behind his back. He ran him into the wall, face first, and watched him fall.

"Get up, punk," Lunden ordered.

He pushed himself away from the ground, but Lunden struck him hard in the side and followed with a shot to the face, sending him down yet again.

"We're just getting started, boy. Now get the fuck up."

Alex tasted the blood running from his nose into his mouth. He couldn't win the fight, but he could buy enough time for Jessica to get safely away. He stood again and threw a wild punch Lunden easily dodged.

Lunden grabbed him and threw him across the galley where he collided with the sink. "The fun's about over," Lunden announced. "Say your prayers, boy."

Lunden started forward and Alex kicked backwards. His foot caught the same spot the flare had embedded.

Lunden grunted and doubled over.

Alex ripped open the galley drawer and reached for a knife. With Lunden on the ground, he charged forward and stuck the knife in his chest.

Lunden fell to his knees and pulled the bloody instrument out of his damaged body. Alex backed up and watched him release the knife from his grip and fall forward on his face. He lay on the ground, motionless. A blood trail seeped from under his lifeless body.

Alex hurdled the body and climbed out of the boat. He jumped to the dock and ran as fast as he could toward the parking lot.

"Alex," a voice shouted. Jessica waited by the road with an older couple she flagged down. She ran to him and wrapped her arms around him.

"Are you all right?" he asked.

"Yeah, I'm okay," she said. "What about you? Are you okay?"

"I'm okay."

"What about him?" she asked, turning her head toward the dock.

Flashing lights and sirens poured into the marina.

"It's over, Jessica."

34

"That's it," Alex said, pointing at Summer Wind. He led a group of police to the boat. Jessica stayed back to receive treatment with the Fire and Rescue squad.

"Wait here," a hefty police officer ordered. He and four other cops drew their sidearms and surrounded the slip. Two climbed aboard and straddled the hatch, while the others held their positions.

"Police," one of the officers shouted into the cabin. "Is anyone inside?" No response.

"If you're inside this boat, you need to come out so we can see you with your hands in the air." The officer waited for a moment and then signaled his partner. His partner nodded and both men charged down into the cabin. Two other officers jumped aboard to provide cover.

Alex moved closer to hear what was going on. A thin trail of smoke oozed from the cabin. It smelled like a fireworks show.

"Everything all right down there?" one of the cops asked, peering into the cabin.

"Looks like a damn war zone. There's blood everywhere," a cop inside responded.

Alex ran past the officer standing next to him and jumped aboard. The two police officers standing in the cockpit stopped him.

"Wait a minute, son. This is a crime scene. You're not supposed to be here," the older officer said.

"Where's the body?" he asked, bobbing his head to see past the men holding him back.

"There is no body," one of the officers responded.

Alex was stunned into silence.

"Whoever it was you stuck with the knife didn't stay down long."

"How is that possible?"

The officer released his arm and shined his flashlight around the cockpit. "This is how it's possible," he said pointing to the water over the side of the boat. "Look at the trail he left."

The officer aimed the flashlight along a path of blood that ran from the main hatch to the side of the boat. He climbed up on the deck and shined the light out into the water. The choppy river showed nothing.

"You think he survived?" Alex asked.

"Hard to say. From the looks of things, he lost a lot of blood, so I don't like his chances."

"What happens now? How are you going to find this guy?"

"We're going to look for prints and anything he may have left behind. We'll get the dredging crew out here first thing in the morning to drag the river. We have his blood, so if we find him, we'll be able to do a DNA match. I'll also need you and Ms. McCall to come down to the station so we can get your statements and you can check the mug books."

"If you don't find him, what am I supposed to do? This guy is trying to kill her."

"Mr. Weaver, all I can do is investigate the crime and try to apprehend the suspect. We don't provide personal security. I'm sorry, but you'll have to look elsewhere for that."

The officer's words were anything but reassuring. "What would you do if you were me?" he asked.

The officer hesitated for a moment. "Hope a body washes ashore."

35

"Please, have a seat," Detective Ferenz said, standing half out of his seat and pointing to two wooden chairs in front of his desk. Ferenz's gray polyester shirt had seen better days and his thick tie wasn't long enough to reach his belt buckle. A man of average height, he carried a heavy build. A sour look covered his face, the same look that infected most career cops. He wore a crew cut and chewed an unlit cigar.

Pictures, certificates and commendations filled the wood-paneled walls in his office, tracing his history in law enforcement. The dated pictures showed a man much younger and thinner. The years had taken their toll.

"I heard you didn't have much luck looking through the mug books," Ferenz said.

"No, we didn't," Alex answered.

"How are you holding up, Ms. McCall?" Ferenz asked.

"Not well," she answered with a hint of attitude. "I've been telling you people all along my father's death wasn't an accident, but no one believed me. The same guy who killed my grandparents and father tried to kill me two different times and the police have done nothing to stop it."

"Well, I guess we're not having a tea party," Ferenz said and straightened up in his chair. "What is it you wanted to see me about?"

"We would like you to re-open the investigation into the deaths of Thomas and Joanne McCall, as well as Mark McCall," Alex responded. "You're the lead investigator and it's my understanding you can re-open the cases."

"Why should I re-open those investigations?"

"Because the man who tried to kill Jessica and me confessed he was involved," he half-shouted.

"Did you hear this confession?"

"I didn't, but she did."

"Uh-huh," Ferenz mumbled. "Are you here on behalf of Ms. McCall? Officially, that is."

"What do you mean?"

"You're a lawyer, aren't you?"

"Yes."

"Do you represent Ms. McCall?"

"Yes, I do, but . . ."

"Well, I guess I'd better watch just what I say," Ferenz said. "But, since you asked," he continued, "we caught the man who killed Thomas and Joanne McCall red-handed with the McCall's jewelry and personal items in his car. Did I mention we also found the murder weapon on the man and he had gunpowder traces on his hand? That means he shot the gun, in case you were wondering."

Ferenz looked at Jessica. "We've been through all this before, Ms. McCall. We can't just disregard evidence. As for your dad, I got a coroner's report that says he died of a heart attack. No foul play. No motive. No enemies." He leaned back in his chair. "Now, take a look around this office," he said, pointing to the stacks of paper littered all over the dingy room. "These are hundreds of open case-files that need to be investigated. My phone rings off the damn hook all day every day with different people calling about these cases. The Sheriff and the DA are constantly on my ass about making arrests. The families want arrests, and the witnesses—when we can find them—don't want to get involved. Now you're demanding I re-open a couple cases where we got evidence stacked to Mount Everest showing they've been solved."

Ferenz grabbed a file off the ground at the side of his desk and opened it. "Why don't I just call Mrs. Jensen and tell her we've got to put off finding her missing ten-year-old daughter, who's presumed to be murdered." He grabbed another file. "And then I'll call Thelma Bender and tell her we've got to stop looking for her estranged husband, the man who killed her two children and who's loose somewhere in the city with an arsenal of weapons. Is that what you want?"

"What we want, Detective, is for you to do your job," Alex shot back. "We're telling you a man admitted to killing Jessica's father and grandparents. This is the same man who tried to kill Jessica and me. Now, you may not want to re-open this case, but you had sure as hell better find this maniac. I can promise you the nutbag I'm talking about makes the killers you described look like a couple stooges. He's probably left a trail of bodies that stretch from here to California."

"Listen," Ferenz said, "the fact of the matter is, we don't know who in the hell the man was who attacked you two on that boat. He's obviously a sick twist. I can't put a lot of weight into what some crackpot may have told Ms. McCall during a struggle. He may have been wired up on PCP or some other drug. I've had drugged-up freaks tell me they're Jesus Christ our Lord and Savior. That don't make it so."

Ferenz rubbed his forehead. "Look, we're going to try to find this guy. From the sounds of things, he's probably imitating a log at the bottom of the river right now, so I'm not sure it matters much. But we're looking, and we're going to keep looking. You have to understand, though, you're not the only people in the city who want me to solve a crime."

"What do we do in the meantime?" Alex asked. "I tried to hide Jessica before and this guy managed to find her."

"I can't help you there. Some of our officers provide security services when they're off duty. I can give you some names if you like."

"Thanks, but I already have somebody in mind," he said. "Come on, Jessica. Let's get you out of here."

36

"Matt," Murphy said, holding the phone to his ear on the rear deck of his home. A warm, evening breeze swept across his face. "How's she doing?"

"It's been a rough week. Her T-cell count is hovering around 50. She spent most of the day in bed."

"Are the cocktails still making her sick?"

"Sometimes, yeah. She won't let on how bad she feels though. You know how stubborn she is."

"Yes, I do. Can she talk?"

"She's asleep right now. You may want to try her tomorrow."

"How are you holding up, Matt?"

"Okay, I guess. I knew this time was coming, but there's really nothing you can do to prepare. It kills me to watch her suffer knowing I can't do a thing about it."

"The FDA is going to approve experimental use soon. Just a few more months and she'll get some treatment that may turn everything around—a real cure."

"How many months?"

"I can't say for sure. Maybe six. It depends on the FDA. We've been on their ass every day to get the necessary approvals. The goddamn red tape is mind boggling."

"I hope and pray she makes it that long. She's been struggling."

"She'll make it, Matt. She just has to. We're so close."

"Thanks for all of your help and support, Michael. It means a lot to both of us."

"Don't worry about it. You know I'd do anything for my little girl," he said.

"Including trying to kill me with a golf club?" Matt said, trying to lighten the conversation.

"Are you referring to the time over summer break you brought Katie home two hours after curfew? From what I recall, both of you reeked of a brewery."

"Yeah, you took a 5-iron to the trunk of my car and told me not to come back unless I got a hair cut and a job."

"I think I improved the look of your car, didn't I? What was that piece of crap you were driving anyway?"

"Pontiac LeMans, and it wasn't all that bad."

"Would it help if I apologized after all these years?"

"I would appreciate that, Michael," Matt cracked.

"Well it's not going to happen," he laughed. "Your hair is still too long for my liking."

"Just keep it up, and I'll tell you what Katie and I were really doing the night she got home late."

"On that note, I'm terminating this conversation. I'll call back tomorrow."

"Goodnight, Michael."

37

Jessica struggled to open her eyes, still groggy from a long night's sleep. She was confused by her surroundings. After leaving the police station, Alex took her to Haney's house to spend the night. Still wearing an oversized T-shirt and some extra-large sweat pants Haney loaned her, she wandered down the small hallway toward voices in the kitchen.

"Good morning," Haney said. He and Alex were drinking coffee. "I guess we don't wear the same size," Haney commented. Both men had large circles under their eyes, as they took turns keeping watch during the night.

"I can't believe I slept this long," she said.

"You needed it. You were a wreck last night," Alex said.

"What a terrible place," she recounted. "I've never seen so many frightening people."

"The coffee's over there," Haney pointed to the counter. She grabbed a mug and filled it to the top. The warmth felt good. "I guess you didn't have any luck with the picture books at the station, huh?" Haney asked.

"No," she said. "We didn't have much luck with anything. The man who tried to kill us got away and the lead detective doesn't seem willing to do much about it."

"Yeah, Alex told me about your experience with Ferenz. He's not a bad guy. Pretty good cop, actually. He's just overworked, like all the rest. You have to understand, these guys have an unbelievable caseload. They just can't make everything a priority."

"So, what now?" she asked.

"We're going to get you out of town," Alex said.

"What do you mean?"

"He's right," Haney said. "You're not safe here. That maniac found you before, and if you're local, he's more likely to find you again."

"Just how did he find me?"

Alex and Haney looked at each other. "We don't know. Jim and I talked about it earlier. It's possible he followed me without me knowing," Alex answered. He felt bad about the possibility he led the killer to Jessica's location.

"Jessica," Haney said, "I think this guy is a professional. If that's the case, he could have found you in all kinds of different ways."

"Did you tell anyone where I was?" she asked Alex.

"Only Jim." He hesitated as he thought. "Wait, I also told Murphy."

"Anyone else?"

"No."

"Did you tell anyone?" she asked Haney.

"No ma'am. I did not."

"Alex, can you ask Michael whether he may have mentioned it to someone else?"

"I planned on doing just that."

Jessica sipped her coffee. "Where am I going?"

"Can't tell you right now," Alex answered.

"Why not? I . . ."

"Jessica, I asked Alex not to tell me or anyone else where you're going. Only you and Alex will know. It's one less leak for you to worry about. He'll give you all the details when you two are alone."

"How will I know what's going on? What if I need to talk to one of you?" she asked.

"I'll call you," Alex said. "You shouldn't try to contact either of us, or anyone else for that matter."

"Why can you call me, but I can't call you? How can you be sure he won't tap your phone?"

"I won't call you from home. I'll use payphones. No one can tap the phone in advance. They can't know what phone I plan to use."

"When are we leaving?"

"As soon as we pick up some things for you to take," Alex answered. "Jim's going to run out to get some things for you so you're not empty handed when you arrive. You can make a list if you like. There's a shopping center not too far from here." He handed Jessica a pad of paper and pen.

"Should I go with him?"

"No," Jim answered. "Too risky. Just make up the list and I'll do my best."

"How long am I going to be gone?"

"We don't know," Alex said. "According to the phantom caller, you have to disappear for at least a few weeks. If he's right about the timing, the heat might get turned up around here. Since they won't find you, they'll probably be breathing down my neck. Let's hope they make a mistake. Until then, we don't want to hear a peep from you."

"I can't believe this is happening," she sighed, shaking her head.

"You'll get through this, Jessica," Haney said. "Now, why don't you write me up that list?"

38

"So, where am I going?" Jessica asked. Alex checked his rear-view mirror for signs of trouble. His head had been on a pivot ever since leaving Haney's house.

"Ohio," he finally answered.

"Ohio? Where in Ohio? Who am I staying with?"

"My brother, John. He's in Columbus."

"Am I flying to Columbus or are you driving me there?"

"Neither. You're flying to Cincinnati."

"Okay, that almost makes sense." She rolled her eyes and turned her attention to her purse.

"If anyone tries to track your flight information, they won't have the right city."

"Am I taking a cab from Cincinnati to Columbus?"

"John's picking you up at the airport," he said. "Would you flip down your visor and use the mirror to watch behind us?" He was still bothered by the thought the killer may have followed him to the boat.

She did as he asked and watched the highway falling away from view. "Does anyone live with John?"

"Technically, no, but unofficially, yes. His girlfriend practically lives there. Lindsey." He pushed his visor against the driver's side window to deflect the harsh, afternoon sun.

"How much did you tell John about what's been going on?"

"Everything I could in a short call from the pay phone. Don't worry. He won't talk. He knows talking could get us both killed."

"What about Lindsey? What does she know?"

"Nothing."

"Oh that sounds really well thought out," she said. "How's John going to explain what I'm doing there when Lindsey comes over? That'll go over like a lead balloon."

"He'll just say you're a friend who's staying with him for a while." He tried not to laugh, but couldn't help himself. "Okay. Out loud, that doesn't sound good," he said, chuckling. The nervous tension flowing through his body needed an escape.

"Lindsey's out of town for six weeks," he said, trying to recover himself. "She's a senior at Ohio State and she's doing an exchange program this summer at the U of Hamburg in Germany. She has some relatives over there she's staying with."

"Okay. That'll work," she said.

"Did Jim find everything on your shopping list?" he asked. "John's apartment is close to some stores. You shouldn't have a problem finding clothes and other stuff you need. Female stuff."

He exited I-95 and hit the gas to Jacksonville International Airport. He stopped at the curb by the departing flights terminal and pressed his emergency flashers. He stepped out and scanned the area for anything unusual. Airport traffic was light. He grabbed Jessica's bags from the back seat and opened her door.

"Come on. Let's go," he said. After about three paces, a loud voice rang out behind them.

"Hey. You. BMW."

He turned to face the sound. A bulky airport security cop stood next to his car. "You can't leave this here," he shouted.

"I'll be right back."

"I'll call a tow truck," the officer shouted.

"I'll be back in a minute," he turned with Jessica and they moved quickly inside. The officer shook his head and lifted his ticket book from his pocket.

Alex thought, even if Lunden tailed him to the airport, he wouldn't risk being hassled by the police by parking illegally. He had time to hurry Jessica to the security line without being trailed.

"I can't go through there," he said at the first checkpoint. "You're on your own from here."

"What if something happens?" she asked.

"Airports are filled with cops and security. There's probably an Air Marshall on your plane. You know what the guy looks like. If you see him, scream like hell. Someone'll help you."

"How will I find John at the Cincinnati airport?"

"Here, take this." He handed her a picture of his brother. "He still has the shirt in the picture and I asked him to wear it."

"You will call me." She touched his chest.

"I promise. Now get going. Get out of here."

She gave him a hug and kiss on the cheek. "Thank you."

"You're welcome and go, Jess. Now."

She handed the security officer her boarding pass and I.D. and melded into the line. Soon, she was out of sight.

39

"Scotch?" Van Doren asked Murphy.

"Can't go wrong with a good bottle of scotch," he replied. As Van Doren poured two drinks, Murphy admired the handcrafted bookshelves that held up opposite ends of the stone fireplace mantle in Van Doren's study.

"Here you go." Van Doren handed Murphy a drink. "Ten-year-old Glenkinchie."

"Thank you."

"I appreciate your stopping by this evening, Michael. Please, sit down." Van Doren pointed to his saddle-leather barrister sofa. He sat opposite Murphy in a matching Kensington chair. The smell of burnt wood lingered in the air, signaling that the fireplace got some recent use.

"We're having some real problems with the girl," Van Doren said. "The job seems more difficult for our man than expected. My concern is we're running out of time. We have just a few more weeks."

Murphy fiddled with his tie. "I'm not sure I know what to say, Charles. Wet work is not my bag."

"No, I'm sure not. It seems, however, our Alex is making things difficult and, as far as I'm concerned, he qualifies as your bag."

"Frankly, I don't know what else I could have done. I got Jessica's location from Alex and managed to direct him away from the boat so your man could do the job."

"Indeed, Michael. Indeed." Van Doren motioned with a hand like a king. "You've been the one person I can count on and I appreciate that."

"What's the next step?" Murphy asked.

"We need to find the girl. See what you can find out from Alex. He trusts you. Get him to talk."

40

Dark clouds marched in formation over the city's morning glow. A southeasterly high collided with a westward low causing considerable violence. Lightning popped and cracked outside of Alex's office window, occasionally tapping on the river. He sat hunched over his desk with a pen in one hand and his head in the other. Three knocks hit his closed door. Foster walked in and stopped in his tracks when he saw Alex's face.

"What in the hell happened to you?" he asked.

"Other than someone trying to kill me, nothing much," he said. His stone face made it clear he wasn't kidding.

"What?" Foster slammed the door behind him and barreled toward the desk.

"It's Jessica," he said. "I told you something strange was going on . . . someone might be trying to kill her."

"What happened?" Foster sat, locking his eyes on his friend.

"Someone *did* try to kill her and I happened to get in the way long enough to fight him off. I stabbed the son of a bitch in the chest with a dull kitchen knife, but he managed to get away."

"Is this a joke?"

"No joke."

"You stabbed somebody?"

"Rob, the son of a bitch tried to kill me."

"Who was it? Who tried to kill you?"

"No idea. The police can't find him or even ID him for that matter."

"Why Jessica?"

"Don't know that either." He rubbed his hands across his face. "Rob, my life has become a fucking horror movie. I'm in the middle of something that belongs in Tinseltown, and I have no clue what it is." He hung his head and started massaging his own neck.

"Alex, this is a police matter. You have to get yourself out of this—now. You can't put your life on the line for someone you hardly know. Let Jessica and her family handle this. It's not worth dying for."

"It's not that easy."

"It is that easy. Just cut the ties," Foster said.

"She doesn't have a family. She has no one to turn to. The police are no help. They can't do a goddamn thing."

"That doesn't make you her savior," Foster snapped. "You've got to get out of this."

"I won't, Rob. I can't just walk away. She could die and I couldn't live with myself if that happened."

"You could die too. Don't . . ."

"I have a lot of work to do, Rob. Maybe you should go."

"Look, Alex . . ." Foster tried again.

"Just go," he snapped.

Foster stood and began to walk out before hesitating. "If you need anything, I'm here for you, man."

"I know," he nodded. "I know."

After Foster left, he tried refocusing on his work. Five minutes later, more knocks sounded against his door.

"What now?" he shouted, thinking Foster had returned. The door cracked open and Murphy's face pushed through.

"You have a minute?" Murphy asked.

"Sorry, I thought you were someone else. Sure, come in," he said, damping down his temper.

Murphy pulled up a chair in front of his desk. "You look like shit. Are you all right?"

"Someone tried to kill me and Jessica."

"Tried to what? What happened?"

"I guess I'd better get used to telling this story until the bruises go away," he said. "You're about the fifth person today and it's not even lunch."

He was more crass than usual, but the circumstances were anything but usual. Being fired was the least of his concerns. He recounted the story of what happened on the boat to Murphy, who listened intently.

"Surely the police can get a handle on this," Murphy said, "can't they?"

"I'm not hopeful. They don't seem to know anything."

"Does Jessica have any idea why someone would be after her?"

"No. That's the frustrating part. We have no clue why anyone would want to do this to her or her family."

"You mentioned the family again. Do you still think there's a connection between the death of her father and this latest incident?"

"I do."

"Why?"

"Because the person who tried to kill Jessica admitted to murdering her family when he was strangling the life out of her on the boat."

"Jesus Christ, Alex. I've known the McCall family for years, and I can't think of any reason someone would want to harm any of them. They're good people. I mean really good. You must have run into a deranged stalker type."

"Well, right now, we don't know what we've run into. That's part of the problem."

"Okay, I got you into this mess and I apologize for that," Murphy said. "The least I can do is get you out, and that's exactly what I'm going to do."

"What do you mean?" He sat forward.

"I mean I'm going to tell Jessica we can't continue to represent her.

I'm not going to put you in harm's way."

"With all due respect, Mr. Murphy, we're well beyond that now. She needs a friend who can help her. She's in real trouble and has no one else. I can't walk away now. I just can't."

Murphy sat back for a moment and stared out the window. His wheels were turning. "How is she?" he asked.

"As well as can be expected, I guess. She was banged up pretty bad during the struggle. Didn't suffer any serious injuries. More than anything, she's shaken up."

"The McCalls mean a great deal to me, and I appreciate everything you're doing. It's certainly well beyond the call of duty. If I can't get you to leave this situation, then tell me how I can help. What can I do to help ensure Jessica is safe?"

He thought for a moment. "Right now, I can't think of anything. She's tucked away out of sight until someone—the police or I—can figure out why this nut-job is trying to kill her."

"How long does she plan to hide?"

"As long as it takes, I guess. I don't know."

"Well, I've known Jessica for years. It might help if I talk with her. Where is she?"

He paused at Murphy's question. He didn't know how the killer found Jessica on the boat, and Murphy was one of the few people who knew her whereabouts. "I don't know."

"What do you mean, you don't know?"

"I told her to go somewhere remote where no one would suspect she'd go. And she was not to tell anyone, including me, where she went."

"How is she going to know what's going on? What if you find out something? How will you communicate with her?"

"We have a system in place," he said, thinking up answers on the fly.

"What kind of system? English, Alex."

"I'm not at liberty to say. She asked I not tell anyone."

"I'm not just anyone. She's practically family. And I'm very concerned about her health and safety."

"Let me do this," he raised a finger. "The next time I speak to her, I'll ask if she'd like to contact you and, if she does, I'll set up something."

Murphy face scrunched up. He didn't appear satisfied with the answer, but he didn't press it further.

"Fair enough" he said, not quite hiding his disappointment. He stood and began to leave before Alex stopped him.

"Mr. Murphy, we got sidetracked on Jessica. Was there another reason you stopped by?"

"Oh, yeah," Murphy searched his thoughts. "I wanted to talk about preparing for our trial next week. We still need to get the witness outlines put together and arrange to meet with Van Doren. I know you've been through a lot lately. Are you able to get the work done and refocus on this case?"

"Absolutely." He appeared more confident than he was.

"Good. I'll ask Francis to set up a time for us all to get together."

He leaned back and rocked in his chair, wondering about Murphy's visit. Something didn't fit.

41

A lex couldn't focus on his work. With his office door shut, he spent most of the day jotting down every fact related to Jessica or her case. He filled up page after page of blank paper with scribbles, diagrams, charts, and arrows, hoping words and thoughts appearing next to one another might point to some possible answers. Before long, his recycling bin was overflowing.

With his head in hands, Kathy popped in. "Sorry to bother you, but Jim Haney called. He needs to talk to you right away."

"Get him on the phone, please," he said while straightening himself.

"He's downstairs in the coffee shop. He wants you to meet him down there."

"Thanks, Kathy." He grabbed his note pad and pen and charged out. No wasted steps.

Haney chose a corner table in the small coffee shop on the concourse of Riverplace Towers. Only a few people were in the shop, which was typical late in the day. A maintenance man covered in sweat gulped a large ice tea. A man wearing a pin stripe suit was studying the Wall Street Journal. Neither person appeared to have any interest in Haney or Alex.

"Hey, Alex. Sit." Haney pointed to an empty chair. He folded up the newspaper he was reading and dropped it on the table.

"How are you, Jim?"

"Good." He slid a styrofoam cup across the table. "Coffee?"

"God, yes. This stuff is my life blood lately." He was chomping at the bit. "So, what did you find?"

"I hope you don't mind," Haney started, "but I called in a favor to a friend at the phone company. I had her run me off a call log for the two days you received calls from the man who warned you to hide Jessica."

"And?"

Haney slid some papers across the table. "Well," he began, "it wasn't too hard to find the number we were looking for. Either you spend a lot of time at work, or you don't have many friends. You don't get a whole lot of calls, do you?"

He grabbed the phone records. The same number on two different sheets was highlighted.

"This it?" He pointed to the highlighted marks.

"I believe so. The times match the calls you told me about and the number is the same. Like I said, you had only three other calls on the days in question and two of them were telemarketers. They're the 888 numbers . . . see?"

"So, whose number is this?"

"Don't know exactly, but I have an idea."

Alex sat back in his chair. "You going to enlighten me?"

"When my friend checked the number, it came up empty. The call originated from an unlisted cell phone."

"Great."

Haney continued, "Probably a disposable cell phone. You can pick one up in any drugstore. You pay for a set number of minutes and then toss it when you're done."

"You didn't come down here just to tell me you don't know who made the call."

"I came down here to tell you where the call originated." Haney's habit of stretching every detail before arriving at his main point was wearing Alex's patience thin.

"Jesus Christ, Jim. Can you please just tell me what you found?"

"All right, all right," he said. "Though we couldn't match the cell number to a name, we could match the calls to a fixed location. Cell phones give off a signal traceable by GPS. The phone company has new technology that shows where cell phone calls come from within a few feet of the caller's location. In this case, both calls came from the same place." Haney checked his notes. "1672 River Road."

"Is that a residence?"

"Yes and no," Haney responded. "It's a house owned by a company called CVD Holdings, Inc."

"CVD Holdings?"

"Every company that does business in Florida has to register with the Secretary of State. Those records are public. I looked up the company on the Internet. Get this, Alex," Haney leaned forward, "it's a subsidiary of Van Doren Pharmaceuticals."

"Of *what*?"

"The 'CVD' stands for Charles Van Doren," Haney said.

"I'll be damned," he said. "Van Doren doesn't live there, though. I've been to his house. He's not on River Road."

"No, it's a write-off for his company. He apparently lets his top executive live there. Nice perk for that guy."

"Who?"

Haney checked his note pad. "Wilson Gates," he said, glancing up at Alex. "Does that name ring a bell?"

"Yeah, but . . ." he responded, " . . . that's Van Doren's General Counsel. Why would he know anything about Jessica? Talk about bizarre."

"We don't know he made the call. We just know it originated from an area within his property line. It could have been his gardener for all we know."

"Well, whoever it was seemed to know me. He called me by name. I'm pretty sure I don't know Wilson Gates' gardener."

"How well do you know Gates?"

"Not real well. I've spoken to him a few times about the lawsuit we're working on and I met him socially on one occasion at Van Doren's house. That's it."

"You're right, Alex. This is bizarre," Haney said as he sipped his coffee. "So, what do you want to do now?"

"Talk to Gates," he said as if there was no other answer.

"You're just going to walk into Gates' office and ask him if he called you. Are you going to run it by Michael Murphy first? If you start annoying his biggest client, you might find yourself on the unemployment line."

"I'd rather wind up there than the morgue. Wouldn't you?"

Haney raised his brows. "Good point."

"Funny you should mention Gates. When I was at Van Doren's house for dinner, I overheard something between him and Van Doren. I couldn't make out the details, but the whole conversation just sounded strange, as if they were doing something illegal. When I asked Murphy about it, he just brushed it off. He did the same thing with the Trust Agreement when I asked him about that. I also noticed Murphy's been acting strange," he said. "Something's going on with him and I can't quite put my finger on it."

"That's a lot to swallow. What do you mean about Michael?"

"I mean I spent the better part of the last eight hours writing down every fact I could think of relating to Jessica. I was hoping to jar something loose from my brain. A theory—anything. One possibility came up every time—Mark McCall's Will."

"I'm not sure I follow. I thought you gave up on the Will theory?"

"That's the thing, Jim. I did feel like giving up on it after talking to Murphy. He had an explanation for everything. The problem is McCall's Will is the only theory that makes sense. If no one in Mark McCall's immediate family outlives him by 120 days, all of his property passes through a Trust to a charitable organization for which Murphy is a board member. The call I got warning me to move Jessica for thirty days came after Mark McCall had been dead ninety days, which, if you add the two, equals 120. I think the guy trying to kill Jessica is the same person who killed the other members of her family. Why else would someone try to kill Mark McCall and his immediate family?"

"Hold on here, Alex, saying McCall's Will had something to do with Jessica's troubles is one thing. It's a-whole-nother to accuse Michael Murphy of being involved in a murder triangle. I've known Michael for ten years, and the man I know has too much integrity to be involved in something like that."

"What about the fact you, me, and Murphy were the only ones who knew Jessica was on the boat. That leaves open the possibility Murphy disclosed her location."

"It also leaves open the possibility I told the killer where to find her. You're dealing with a professional, Alex. We've been through this before. You could have been followed without knowing it."

"True, but I'm trying to put together a theory that makes sense. Setting aside personalities for a second, the theory about McCall's Will makes sense, because it offers a motive. Murphy had more than motive—he had opportunity, which I gave him by mentioning Jess' location. Was it mere coincidence he called me away from Jess the night of the attack? He's never once called me at home before."

Haney sat back for a moment. "You'd make a hell of an FBI investigator. It's still a stretch."

"I didn't tell you what happened today," he pressed. "Murphy came by my office and grilled me about Jessica's location."

"He did what?"

"He wants to talk to her. He wants me to arrange it."

"Did you tell him where she is?"

"Hell no. I'm not telling anyone. I learned my lesson."

"I still think you're barking up the wrong tree."

"Answer me one question, Jim."

"What's that?"

"How successful of an FBI agent would you have been if you ignored criminal theories when the suspects seemed to be nice guys?" He watched Haney grasp for a reply. "For chrissake, Jim, I've seen enough news interviews with neighbors of homicidal maniacs. These people say the same thing every time—'He was a quiet guy who kept to himself. I can't believe he gunned down those twenty people at Wal-Mart.'"

The words hit home. Haney had arrested plenty of depraved criminals who appeared to be pillars of the community. "I never ignored a theory. I followed up on every one. This particular theory just makes me a bit ill."

"You want out?" He crossed his arms.

"Not a chance. I never quit on a case."

"Man, am I glad to hear you say that." He ran a hand across his forehead. "I couldn't do this without you."

"Okay," Haney said, "we need a plan."

"You're the expert. What do we do?"

"Well, we have one theory, so we need to start looking into it. You have a connection with Gates. Talk to him. Feel him out a bit. I'm going to do some digging into Horizon."

"Sounds good. I have to meet with Gates and the others to prepare for the trial with Judge Shelton. That might provide an opportunity. Is there anything else I can do?"

"If Murphy is the trustee for McCall, he's bound to have some documents at your office in addition to the Trust Agreement he showed you. Can you put your hands on his files?"

"I can try," he responded.

"Word of advice, Alex," Haney pointed. "We don't know what's going on here, so watch yourself. You can't afford to trust anyone."

He pushed aside his cup and stood. "I don't."

———

42

"Alex, I'm worried about you," Kathy said as she handed her boss a mug filled with Marine Roast. "You look tired and run down every day. You haven't been yourself." She moved to the window and adjusted one of the shades to block the bright morning sun that was minutes from passing directly across his face.

"Good morning to you too, Kathy," he said, the brew claiming his full attention. He knew she was right, which is why he ignored her prodding. He hadn't slept more than a few hours any night during the past two months.

"I'm serious, Alex. I really am concerned. You need to take some time away from work after what you've been through."

"I have a lot going on right now, that's all. I'll be fine. Nothing for you to worry about. Did you get the password?" he asked.

"Don't change the subject. Do you promise to take me with you to your next job when we both get fired?"

"Of course. Did you get it?"

"What in the world do you want with Mr. Murphy's computer password?" Kathy asked, dangling a slip of paper between her fingers.

"Please, Kath, don't ask. You don't want to know. How did you get it?"

"I'm not sure that's something you want to know. Let me put it this way—if you are caught with this, you didn't get it from me. Got it?" she demanded.

"Yes, ma'am." He held out his hand. She passed him the paper with seven letters and numbers mixed together: 952R3PQ.

"What about the docket sheet? Were you able to pull it up?"

"Yes, but I'm not sure why you want information about a case you're not working on." She handed him another document.

"You didn't tell anyone I asked for this stuff, did you?"

"No. What's going on here?"

"Sorry. I can't say right now. I'll fill you in later. For now, I need you to keep this between us. I know how the support staff network is around here. Tell one person and you may as well broadcast it on CNN."

"You know I can keep a secret," she bristled.

"I know," he said. "I didn't mean you couldn't. I'm just . . . I'm an ass, okay? I just have to ask to reassure myself I'm covering all bases."

"Okay," she said, "I'll leave you alone now. But I'll expect an explanation at some point."

"You got it," he promised. "Kathy? Did I ever tell you you're the best?"

"Not enough," she said with a smile and she closed the door.

He didn't waste any time. He picked up the docket sheet and studied its contents. The top of the sheet read: Friedman v. Wells Construction, Inc. He reviewed the entries and checked off dates on his calendar.

"Son of a bitch," he breathed after studying the document.

He made notes on the page and stuffed it into his briefcase. He grabbed Murphy's password and typed the search term MCCALL into the firm's database. A box appeared on his screen, which read, PASSWORD PROTECTED. He entered the letters and numbers Kathy gave him.

The hard drive groaned and grunted. A list appeared on the screen showing only two documents—Mark McCall's Will and the Trust Agreement of Mark McCall. He opened the documents. They were the same documents Murphy had given him.

He searched the name HORIZON. Once again, the screen prompted him for a password. He again entered Murphy's password and waited. Twenty-five entries popped up.

"You've got to be kidding me," he said. Each entry contained the same two words: FILE DELETED. He ran a finger across his office telephone sheet and dialed four numbers.

"Office Services, this is Don," a voice answered.

"Don, it's Alex Weaver. I'm looking for a file and I'm not sure where to find it."

"What's the file?"

"Horizon."

"Do you have a case or file number?"

"No."

"Just a minute and I'll check for you."

Muzak played in his ear while Don placed him on hold. Nearly five minutes passed before he returned. Alex's insides twisted and turned.

"Sorry about that," Don said, finally interrupting the Muzak. "That one was hard to track."

"What did you find?"

"The file was scheduled for shredding last Friday."

"Shredding?"

"Yeah. It's on the list. If the schedule is right, it should already be destroyed."

"What do you mean by 'if the schedule is right?'" he pressed.

"We've been running behind schedule on closed files lately with Gerald out sick. He was out after his surgery last week, so he may not have gotten around to it."

"Would you check? Now?"

"Hold on," Don's voice carried frustration at being pulled away from his work. The last sanitized verse of the Eagles' *Hotel California* played in Alex's ear as he was again placed on hold. After an even longer wait, the Muzak finally stopped.

"You still there?" Don asked. He was used to attorneys hanging up on him.

"Yeah, I'm here."

"I talked to Gerald about that file. It's still alive."

"For how long?"

"Hard to say, but I'm guessing it'll get shredded before the end of the week."

"Can I see the file before it gets shredded?"

"Just let me get the okay from Michael Murphy and I'll call you back."

"No, wait," he said before Don could hang up the phone. "Why do you need to check with Murphy?"

"That's the instruction he left on the file. We know better than to screw up one of his orders. It would be the last mistake we made."

"Where is the file?"

"Closed files warehouse," Don responded.

"I'm going to go talk to Murphy later, so don't worry about calling him."

"Okay. But you'll need to have him call me or send something in writing before I can give you the file."

"No problem," he said. "Where in there warehouse is the file now?"

"Probably sitting on a dolly waiting for pickup. But you don't need to worry about that. We'll find it for you."

"Okay," he said. "I'll talk to Murphy about it and get back to you."

Just as he set the phone down, it rang. "Jesus Christ," he jumped as Michael Murphy's name appeared on his Caller ID. His thoughts spun. Why was he calling? After the third ring, he picked up.

"This is Alex."

"Alex, it's Michael Murphy. I need to speak to you. Do you have some time?"

"Sure, what's up?"

"Come up to my office, please. I'll explain."

His mind tormented him on the way to Murphy's office. Did

Murphy find out someone pinched his password? Could Murphy possibly be involved in a murder plot? What connection could there be between Jessica and Murphy, Wilson Gates or Van Doren Pharmaceuticals? His heart knocked against his chest as he knocked on Murphy's closed door.

"Come in." Murphy had company. Charles Van Doren was on his couch. His face looked grim. Murphy circled his desk and pulled up a chair.

Van Doren's presence made Alex more uncomfortable. He wondered if they saw his fear.

"We learned some very disturbing news, Alex," Murphy said.

"What?" he asked, fearing the response. At least he could outrun the two older men if he had to.

"Wilson Gates died last night."

"I beg your pardon?" he asked, the words not quite reaching his brain.

"Charles received word late last night, Wilson was shot during a mugging. Convenience store parking lot. He was DOA at Baptist Hospital."

His stomach fell. "Omigod," he said. "Did they catch the killer?"

"No," Murphy answered. "From what we heard, there were no witnesses."

"If there were no witnesses, how did anyone conclude it was a mugging?" Alex asked. His question caught Murphy and Van Doren off-guard.

Murphy stumbled, "We're just going by what the authorities told us."

Van Doren appeared much calmer than Murphy. "How else can you explain someone getting shot in a convenience store parking lot?"

Alex kicked himself for asking the question. "You're right, Mr. Van Doren. Nothing else would make sense."

"Alex," Van Doren continued, "we are deeply saddened by Wilson's death, but we didn't call you in here simply to share our grief. Though we would love to stop the world from turning while we deal with this tragedy, we cannot afford to do so, especially now when the stakes are so high. I've asked Michael to fill the void left by Wilson's untimely demise. He's agreed to serve as my new General Counsel, at least for the time being."

"That's right," Murphy picked up. "As you know, we planned for Wilson to serve as the corporate representative for Van Doren at the trial coming up next week. Given the terrible misfortune, Charles asked me to serve as his interim General Counsel, and I accepted."

Alex was still shell-shocked by the news Gates was dead. "Shouldn't we ask the Court for a continuance?"

"Absolutely not," Van Doren burst out. "This is too important to delay," he caught himself and eased his tone. "Lives are at stake, Alex. People out there waiting for this drug can't afford any delays. Their lives depend on it. Our company's future depends on it. We need to get this drug to market as soon as possible. We need the Court's ruling the patent is ours, fair-and-square. We're going full speed ahead."

"So, what this means," Murphy continued, "is you are going to take over my role as lead counsel on this case." Murphy paused "I know it's a lot to ask, but you've shown you can handle pressure. While I don't mean to downplay the decision, you're the only person, other than myself, who has the detailed knowledge of this case to take the lead. We don't have a choice, but I know you can handle it." Murphy leaned over and patted him on the shoulder.

"Yes," Van Doren said, "I, too, have confidence in your ability, Alex." He turned his attention fully to the young lawyer. "Do you remember our trip to the wine cellar at my home? After everyone had gone home?" he asked.

"Yes."

"Do you remember what I asked you right before you left?" Van

Doren's eyes bored into his.

"You asked whether you could count on me."

"Very good, Alex. Very good," Van Doren said as a slow patronizing smile grew from his thin, pasty lips. "And what did you say?"

"I said yes. You can count on me."

"Can I still count on you?"

"Of course."

He wasn't about to say anything to the contrary.

"Can you think of any reason why I shouldn't trust you?"

Did he know something or was he bluffing?

"No."

He couldn't help himself. He had to ask the question. It was a logical question. One that might draw suspicion if not asked: "Have I done something to breach your confidence?"

"I certainly hope not. I want to make certain I can trust a man before I make him a millionaire."

"Excuse me?"

Murphy interjected, "if things go well, Charles may ask me to remove the interim title from the General Counsel label and make the position permanent. Charles has asked that a partner serve as lead attorney on all Van Doren matters. Given your performance with this case, and your expected performance going forward, Charles has urged Parker Jones to extend you an offer to become a full equity partner. In that capacity, you would receive all the origination credit for Van Doren's work. I think we both know what that would mean to you, financially."

"Well, yes. That's incredible . . . thank you, Mr. Murphy," he sputtered, trying to put on his best face. "I don't know what to say."

Van Doren stood, "I need to get going. I'll send over the details regarding funeral arrangements. You're going to call me about our meeting to prepare for trial. Is that right?"

"Yes," Murphy answered.

"Good. Walk with me a moment, Michael?"

"Sure."

Murphy and Van Doren walked out of the office and stopped after about five steps. Murphy seemed to listen intently as Van Doren relayed several messages. Alex couldn't make out what Van Doren said. Murphy nodded and shook Van Doren's hand. Then returned to his office.

"I know the circumstances are highly unusual, but the opportunity of a lifetime has just dropped in your lap. I hope you can appreciate what Charles has done for your career."

"Yes, of course," he said.

"Well, you sure as hell don't act like you appreciate it," Murphy said, catching him off-guard. "I fully expected you to show some more gratitude."

"Sorry, Mr. Murphy. I tried. It's hard to be excited after learning someone you know has been murdered," he shot back.

"Wilson's death is an absolute tragedy, no question about it. We all feel terrible, but as Charles said, life goes on. This is a critical time for VDP. Transviazine will not only put the company back on top, it'll save thousands, if not millions, of lives. That's why we are so passionate about pressing on with the case. Some very sick people are hanging on for their lives right now, and we can't afford any delays."

"I understand. It's just a lot to swallow right now. I need some time for all this to sink in."

"I don't mean to crash down on you. Just make sure you get your head cleared for trial. We need everyone to be focused."

"Of course."

"Oh, and Alex?"

"Yes," he turned at the door.

"Have you had a chance to arrange for me to talk to Jessica?"

"Oh, uh, no, sir," he responded. "Not yet."

"I thought I made myself clear on that issue," Murphy said. "I want something set up by the end of the week. I have a responsibility to Jessica's father to look after her. Do I make myself clear?"

"Yes."

"Good. Make it happen." Murphy walked behind his desk. "That's all for now."

He hurried back to his office, grabbed the telephone, and dialed as fast as he could. "Jim? It's Alex. We need to talk."

43

water taxi pulled up to the south bank of the St. Johns River. From a shaded bench, Alex watched several passengers climb off and negotiate the wooden planks that made up the River Walk. The downtown lunch crowd was out in full force on this hot and sunny afternoon.

"Turkey club all right with you?" he asked, lifting two sandwiches out of a bag.

"Yeah, thanks," Haney answered, taking the sandwich. "After talking to you this morning about Gates," Haney said, "I made some calls. The police have no ID on the shooter. No witnesses. Nothing."

"What in the hell is going on? Gates was our biggest lead and now he's dead. I can't believe this shit."

"It's not good. Something tells me we weren't the only ones who figured out Gates called you. Did you tell anyone other than Jessica and me about it?"

"Yeah. Murphy. Goddamn, Jim. Is it me, or does everything point back to Murphy? I haven't even told you what I found at the office. It gets worse."

"What do you mean?"

"On the night Jessica and I were attacked, Murphy had me run down to the office and overnight a pleading he told me was due the next day."

"What about it?"

"The case was Friedman vs. Wells Construction, Inc."

"Okay." Haney bit into his sandwich.

"I pulled the docket sheet. The answer wasn't due for another week. There was no need to file it the night Murphy called me. I think he made up a phony deadline to get me off the boat."

"I'll be damned." Haney brushed crumbs off his pants.

"That's not all. I looked to see whether the firm had any files on Horizon. Since Murphy was on Horizon's board of directors, I figured he'd have files at work that might answer some questions, one way or the other. Curiously, all the Horizon files were password protected. Firm files are hardly ever password protected between attorneys. Only personal stuff gets password protected. Anyway, I managed to get Murphy's password to look at the Horizon files we had on the system."

"Hold on," Haney interrupted. "How did you get his password?"

"My assistant got it for me. She didn't exactly tell me how." He wiped away a bead of sweat from his forehead.

"I don't like this. If Murphy is involved in something as bad as murder, you sure as hell don't want him finding out you snagged his password and started prying into Horizon."

"I have faith in Kathy, but even if I didn't, it's too late now."

"From now on, run this stuff past me before you decide to act. Jesus Christ, you're going to get yourself killed if you're not careful."

"Do you want to hear what I found or not?"

"Of course. What?"

"We had twenty-five documents on the system. That means Murphy was probably very involved in drafting legal documents for Horizon. Each and every one of the documents on our system has been deleted."

"Completely?"

"Yep. Finito. I called our office services people to ask about the Horizon file and, get this, the entire file was supposed to be destroyed—shredded."

"When?"

"It should have already happened, but the file clerk who handles that was out sick, so they haven't gotten around to it yet."

"Did you get a look at the files?"

"Nope. Murphy gave the order not to release the file to anyone without his express permission."

"We need to get a look at that file."

"Yeah, I'm going to take care of it this afternoon."

"And just how do you plan to get the file without Murphy knowing?"

"Oh, I have something in mind," he said.

"I bet you do," Haney shook his head and attended to his lunch.

"I need you to do some more digging on Horizon. We need to find out what that organization is all about."

"I'll look into it." Haney inhaled nearly half of his sandwich in one bite.

"Jesus, Jim, when's the last time you ate?"

Haney chewed only five times before swallowing. "Sorry, but I'm used to eating fast. In my business, I never know if I'll get lunch or supper during surveillance. It seems like every time I start to eat, the person I'm watching moves and I have to follow. You know, Murphy's law."

He watched Haney swallow half a Coke to chase down his sandwich and shook his head. "Yeah, I'm learning all about Murphy's law."

The two men finished their lunches without talking more about the case. Alex gazed across the river at a large yacht heading east toward the ocean and thought about taking a long cruise away from the city and all his problems.

"I'll get back to the office to see what I can find out on Horizon," Haney said, standing to leave. "Let me know what you find in the files."

"Will do."

"And Alex," Haney said, "be careful."

44

lex rang his assistant. "Kathy, it's almost three. What's going on?"

"Be right there," she responded. She entered his office and closed the door. "Same rules apply as earlier: if you get caught, I was not a part of this."

"You know I wouldn't do that to you," he said. "I owe you big time."

"Okay." She looked uneasy. "Murphy's board meeting starts at three. They'll be up on twenty-six. Maryann Fiedler, Ben Johnson's secretary, told me their past meetings have lasted at least an hour or more, so I'm guessing you have until around four."

"Good, what about Murphy's assistant?"

"I asked her to stop by my desk to review files in the Van Doren case. I'll have you know, Mr. Weaver, I groveled to get her to come down here to my desk. That woman has quite an attitude, even worse than Murphy. Nobody can stand her. Anyway, I'll ring your office as soon as she gets here and you'll know to leave."

"Great," he ignored his assistant's commentary. "If she breaks away and starts back to her office, call me up there. I'll see your name on the Caller ID and get out."

"You're nothing but trouble, have I told you that?"

"Many times."

"It's a good thing I like you," she said on her way out.

A minute later, his phone rang. "She's coming down the hall," Kathy announced.

He hung up and made his way up to the twenty-sixth floor. Rushing out through the stairwell door, he practically ran right into Murphy passing in the hallway.

"Hey, Alex," Murphy said. "Were you coming up to see me?"

"Ummm," he sputtered, thinking of a response, "Not really, I was just looking for a file from your secretary."

"I'd help you find it, but I'm running late for a board meeting," Murphy answered. "She just walked down to see Kathy about something. You won't find her at the desk."

"Great. If you don't mind, I'll just see if the file is on her desk."

"Suit yourself." Murphy checked his watch. "I have to go. If you don't find it, check back later."

He watched Murphy disappear.

Coast clear.

He slid into Murphy's office and closed the door. He confiscated Murphy's chair and clicked the computer on the credenza behind the desk.

He opened the e-mail program, punched NEW MAIL and entered "Don Jansen" in the addressee box, and copied himself. He typed:

Don,

I sent down the Horizon file last week, and it's my understanding from Alex Weaver the file has not yet been destroyed.

Do not shred the Horizon file yet.

Alex needs to review it. Please have the file delivered to Alex's office, ASAP. He'll get the file back to you later.

If you have any questions, please contact Alex. No need to respond to me.

He reviewed the message and pressed "send." He waited anxiously and watched the screen in case Don ignored his instruction and replied.

After five minutes, a knock sounded on the door.

"Shit." His pulse doubled.

"Mr. Murphy?" a voice from the hall asked.

He crouched behind Murphy's desk and slid his body under the cutout as far as he could. He stayed perfectly still and waited.

No more knocks.

After a long minute, he crept out of hiding and clicked the e-mail properties, which told him the e-mail he sent had been opened. If Don hadn't replied by now, he probably wasn't going to.

He opened Murphy's SENT e-mail folder and located the e-mail to Don, which he promptly deleted. Next, he opened the DELETED mail folder and deleted the same e-mail a second time, permanently erasing it from Murphy's computer.

He checked his watch and bit his fingernails. He'd give it another few minutes before leaving. "So far, so good," he whispered.

Murphy's phone rang. It was Kathy.

He snatched up the receiver. "Kath?"

"Get out of there. Murphy's on his way back. The meeting was postponed. I couldn't call you right away, because the wicked witch was here. She just left. Go. Now."

"Shit." He jumped up out of Murphy's chair, ran to the office door and opened it. He scanned the room, which was perfectly clean—no loose papers, nothing. He pulled open Murphy's desk drawer and grabbed a pen and yellow sticky pad. He ran around the desk and began scribbling on his pad. Just then, Murphy entered.

He looked startled. "What are you doing here?"

"Just leaving you a note."

He stripped a sheet off the sticky pad and flashed it to Murphy, which read: "Give me a call. Alex."

Murphy took ownership of his office, moving behind his desk. Alex's shirt dampened from the sweat rolling down his body.

"What did you want to talk to me about?"

"The trial," he answered, frantically searching for something intelligent to say.

"What about it?" Murphy asked, looking across his desk. He couldn't see the computer screen on the credenza behind him.

Before he could answer, an e-mail alert popped up on Murphy's screen with the name in bold letters DON JANSEN. "Fuck," he thought.

The firm's e-mail system produced a pop up message with the sender's name every time a new e-mail arrived. The pop-up lasted only a few seconds before disappearing.

"I wanted to know whether you had any additional files," he said, clearing his throat. "It was my impression we were waiting on some additional discovery from Hudson." He struggled to stay calm. The e-mail alert finally disappeared from the screen. But Don's e-mail was there. Waiting. Murphy would see it as soon as he checked his mail.

"More with the goddamn files. Didn't we already go through this about fifteen minutes ago?" Murphy wheeled his chair around to face his computer. "I need to get some work done and return some e-mails, so if you don't mind." He began playing with his computer.

"Wait, Mr. Murphy," he said, stalling.

"What is it now? I have work to do." Murphy's face frowned.

Before Alex could answer, a lanky teenage boy wearing khaki pants and a golf shirt stuck his head in the office.

"I'm sorry to interrupt, Mr. Murphy," the boy said, "but you wanted me to get something filed over at court and they're about to leave for the afternoon run. You need to sign the original for filing."

"Oh, yes, Kevin. Thanks for reminding me. I forgot I hadn't signed it," Murphy said.

"I knocked on your door a few minutes ago, but no one answered," the boy said. He handed Murphy a few documents, which he promptly signed.

"Hmm?" Murphy glanced at Alex. "I was upstairs at a meeting. I just got back to my office. If you came by, you must have seen I wasn't behind my desk. That should have told you something," he said with more venom than necessary.

"Umm, no, sir, Mr. Murphy, your door was closed," the boy responded clumsily. "It sounded like someone was in your office. I heard some typing on the computer from out in the hall."

Murphy shook his head and threw his reading glasses on his desk. He stared down Alex, whose stomach was knotted. "Do you have any idea what in the hell he's talking about? Was my door closed when you came by?"

"No, it was open."

Before the conversation could go any further, Murphy's phone rang. "Oh, shit," he said, studying the Caller ID. "I need to take this."

He picked up the phone. Alex and the young man started to leave the office. "Bill, how are you?" Murphy spoke into the receiver. "Hold on a second," Murphy put his hand over the phone. "Alex," he said.

"Yes?" He stopped his forward progress.

"That was Tom Penders' kid," Murphy said quietly as he pointed toward the hall. "If you didn't already know it, that last conversation clinched it. He's a fucking moron." Murphy put the phone back to his ear and waived him out.

He high-tailed it down the hall to the stairwell, opened the door, and raced down the steps. Seconds later, he appeared at Kathy's desk, trying to catch his breath.

"Come with me. Now," he said, pulling her along by the arm to the elevator banks.

"What's going on?" she demanded as they stepped into the elevator.

"We're going down to the concourse. Jesus Christ, I hope we're not too late."

"Late for what?"

"Just listen," he said, "we're going down to Office Services. I need you to distract Don. Get him away from his work area."

"How am I supposed to do that?"

"I don't know, but you'll think of something, and quick."

The elevator doors opened on the concourse level. He hurried Kathy through two swinging doors into a freight hallway and approached a set of double doors. "Go on," he said, pointing her through the doors leading to office services.

"I don't like this one bit," she hesitated.

"Go," he nudged her through the door.

Don sat behind a service counter reviewing some paperwork. He was in his late twenties and had a pudgy frame with longish red hair and a thick mustache. He always wore blue jeans and a button-down shirt with a firm logo stitched on the pocket.

"Hey, Don, how are you?" She showed a broad smile.

"Good, Kathy. You?" He spoke with a thick Louisiana drawl.

"Just fine. I hate to trouble you, but I need to look for the Cordova file we sent down a few weeks back. I need some documents."

"Cordova, hmm, let's see here." Don fingered through a stack of papers. "I don't see anything about a Cordova file. Could it be under another name?"

"Actually, I might be able to save you some time. I had one of the mailroom guys help me carry it down here when you weren't around. I think I can find it with your help. It's just back there," she pointed to the storage room in the back.

"Sure."

Don got up from his seat and Kathy followed him to the back room. Alex rushed in and infiltrated his computer. He worked the keyboard hard. He pulled up the "Sent" file and saw the e-mail to Murphy, clicked on the e-mail, which showed Don's reply: "No problem."

"Dumb shit."

He opened the Properties page, which caused the computer to grumble. "Come on, come on," he mouthed to the monitor.

The account finally popped up. There it was. The e-mail had been delivered to Murphy, but not yet opened. Murphy hadn't gotten around to reviewing his e-mails.

"Fuckin-A." Murphy was probably still on the phone.

He banged on the keys until he completed all the steps to retrieve the unread e-mail and delete it from both Don's and Murphy's system. He re-clicked the Properties key to confirm the e-mail was gone.

"Thank you so much, Don. I don't know what happened to that file," Kathy said loudly.

Alex jumped back across the service counter just as they reappeared.

"Well, hey, boss," she said. Her performance could have won an Oscar. "What are you doing down here?"

"So this is where you're hiding," he responded playfully. "I couldn't find you, so I came down to ask Don for the Horizon file."

He turned to Jansen. "Michael Murphy said he was going to e-mail you to get that file for me. Did he do that?"

"Oh, yeah. He did. I sent the courier over to the closed files storage to pick it up. You're lucky. I just got off the phone with Gerald and he said Mr. Murphy's e-mail came just in the nick of time. That file was about to disappear forever."

"When do you expect the file to get here?"

"Before the end of the day."

"Can you give me a call when it does? Murphy's in a really bad mood and doesn't want to be bothered."

"Sure."

"Good." He walked Kathy out of the room. In the hallway, he stopped and leaned up against the wall. He put his head in his hands and took a deep breath.

"Do you want to tell me what the hell is going on?" she asked.

"Not now. But I will when it's over. Just trust me."

46

Alex's phone rang. "Don's bringing up the file now," Kathy said. "He just called."

He jerked his head up from his catnap and wiped his eyes. "Thanks, Kath." He leaned back in his chair and released a sigh.

"I'm going home now," she said, "do you need anything else?"

"No, I'm fine. Have a good evening."

"You, too. Try to get some sleep—in a bed," she said.

A minute later, another knock sounded on the door. "That was quick," he thought.

"Come in."

The door opened up, but it wasn't Don Jansen.

"Mr. Murphy," he said, "what can I do for you?" He sat up straight and ran his hand through his disheveled hair.

"I hope I'm not interrupting," he took a seat in one of the chairs in front of the desk.

"Oh, well," he fought for a clear thought. He needed to shuffle Murphy out of his office before Don arrived. "I'm actually scheduled for a conference call at 5:30," he said, looking at his watch, "which is in a few minutes. I have to pull some notes together before the call, so this really isn't a good time."

"I'll be quick," Murphy said, showing little concern for the fabricated conflict. "First, I wanted to make sure you had all the files you need for the trial. You seemed concerned about it earlier. Do you?"

"Yes, actually, I do. I got with Kathy earlier and straightened everything out." He kept one eye on Murphy and the other on the door. Sweat flowed down both sides of his ribcage.

"Good. The other thing I wanted to talk to you about is Jessica. I've been thinking a lot about her situation and feel I really need to be more involved. Her father placed his confidence and trust in me for many years, and I know he would expect me to watch after her under the circumstances." Murphy observed Alex and waited for a response.

"I'm sorry, I'm not sure I follow. What are you saying?"

"I'm saying I need to know where she is. How to contact her and what her plans are. In good conscience, I can't sit back and do nothing if she's in danger."

"Mr. Murphy, I don't know where she is. She didn't tell me. I expect she'll contact me at some point, but I can't be more specific right now."

"Alex," Murphy tried a different tack, "I don't mean to be difficult here. I'm concerned. I hope you understand."

"I do. As soon as I hear from her, I'll let you know."

"Please do. This is very important to me."

"Sure," he said, checking his watch. "If you'll excuse me, Mr. Murphy, I really do need to gather some materials before the conference call."

"Oh, yes, I'm sorry. I'll let you get back to work." He stood.

Alex approached the door to hasten Murphy's exit. Before Murphy made the doorway, Don appeared holding a banker box.

A swarm of butterflies filled Alex's stomach.

"Hello, Don," Murphy backed up to let him through.

"Just set that box against the wall there for me, thanks," Alex pointed to the side of his office.

"Boy, you guys got lucky we didn't already get to this box," Don said, looking at both men.

Murphy appeared confused. "What did you say?"

"This is that file . . ." Don started to respond.

"Sorry to cut you off, Don," Alex interrupted, "but I have a conference call I need to make in just a minute."

The last thing he needed now was for Jansen to run off at the mouth about his trouble retrieving this particular file.

"Okay," Don said. "Well, let me get going."

"Hold on for a sec, Don," Alex motioned him back inside, anything to separate him from Murphy. "I just remembered I do have a couple quick questions about some additional files I need. Would you stay a second?"

He turned to Murphy. "I'm sorry, Mr. Murphy. Were we finished? I don't mean to hold you up."

Murphy looked at Jansen and the box. "Yeah, I guess we're finished. I'll talk to you tomorrow." He turned and left.

"What is it you needed to talk to me about?" Don asked.

"Hold on. Let me take a look real quick at a file on the computer system to see if I have it before I ask you to go get it."

He surfed his computer to kill time. "You know what, Don, never mind. I found what I was looking for."

"You okay?"

"Sure, yeah. Fine. Why?"

"You seem a bit worked up, that's all. I haven't seen you like this before."

"Really, I'm fine. But thanks for asking."

Don left.

He fell back in his chair and covered his face with his hands. "What a seriously fucked-up day," he moaned.

He closed the door, moved the file to his desk, opened the cover, and rummaged through the stack of documents inside. The papers were as thick as a clenched fist. He snapped off the clips and rubber bands and began to study the contents.

His eyes widened. "Oh, Jesus Christ."

47

Murphy stared blankly at the tall pines swaying in his back yard. It didn't take him long to fill his fourth glass with bourbon.

A warm east wind rushed in and blew off the bottle cap from the end table. It fell to the ground and bounced unevenly against the brick deck like a fumbled football.

"Are you coming in soon?" His wife poked her head out of the sliding glad door. "It's getting late."

"I'll be there in a bit," he said. His voice carried no life.

"You're doing everything you can for her, Michael," she said. "You have to stop torturing yourself."

Murphy didn't respond or, for that matter, even look in her direction. He just gazed into space and raised his tired glass again, emptying its contents.

"Well, drinking yourself to death isn't going to save your daughter, either." She turned back inside and slammed the door.

Unfazed, he tilted the bottle and filled his glass. "God help me."

48

"Where's the 501(c)3 filing you mentioned?" Haney asked Alex as the two men hunched over Haney's small kitchen table.

"Right here."

He slid several papers across the distressed pine. A flash of lightning lit up the sky, followed seconds later by a thunderclap. The downpour banged off Haney's roof like a cattle stampede.

"I'll be goddamned," Haney said. "Rabinowitz was on Horizon's board of directors?"

"Yeah," he said. "It was the three of them, McCall, Murphy, and Rabinowitz. The IRS requires three board members to qualify for the charitable exemption. Murphy told me about McCall, but he conveniently forgot to mention Rabinowitz was on the board. We've been working on the Van Doren case day and night for months and that son of a bitch somehow forgot to tell me he served on a board with the man at the center of the Van Doren litigation."

"I'd call that a pretty big omission," Haney said. "No way he would have left out that little nugget if he was legit. Any idea how the three men hooked up together on this charity?"

"Not yet. But we're going to find out," he said. "Wait until you see what else I found."

He retrieved additional documents from the files and thumbed through them. "Look at this," he said, handing Haney another paper cluster.

"Board meeting minutes," Haney scanned the headings.

"They had quarterly meetings," Alex said. "The company was formed two years ago, so there aren't that many of them. Take a quick look at the highlighted portions. I think you'll get the picture pretty fast."

Haney picked up his coffee mug and sipped as he studied the pages. Alex doodled on a note pad.

"Transviazine?" Haney's asked.

"That's Horizon's drug," Alex said. "Rabinowitz and McCall formed Horizon with Murphy's help to treat HIV and AIDS patients with Transviazine. They were going to use the proceeds from the drug to start a free clinic. Look at this," he said, pointing to highlighted terms in the meeting minutes.

Mar. 03

. . . . David reported the Patent Office processed the applications for Transviazine. Horizon filed an Investigational New Drug ("IND") application with the FDA, which should reduce the typical 8-9 year drug evaluation process to 3 to 4 years. . . .

"Jesus Christ. I can't believe Murphy played possum on this."

"There's more," Alex slid forward on his seat. "Look at this entry from June of last year."

June 2004

. . . . Michael continues to field inquiries from drug companies interested in purchasing rights to Transviazine. Some want to contribute R&D dollars through joint ventures and others want to purchase the patent outright. Van Doren Pharmaceuticals is coming on the strongest. David and Mark remain firm in their positions that Horizon will not sell the rights to the drug. They want the revenues generated from the drug to stay with Horizon and used for free health care for those who cannot afford it. Their goal is to open related clinics across the country. Michael stressed entering a joint venture or selling the patent would expedite the experimental phase associated with the FDA's pre-market approval process and, in turn, make the drug available for widespread treatment sooner. . . .

"Murphy was pushing like hell to sell to Van Doren. Look at the next group of highlighted minutes," Alex said.

Sept. 2004

Michael reported on his meeting with Charles Van Doren and Wilson Gates in Jacksonville last week. VDP continues aggressively to pursue Transviazine. As an alternative to sale, Van Doren suggested Horizon sell the majority of its shares of stock to the company. David and Mark refused to sell their interest in Transviazine under any circumstances. They believe selling majority control of the organization to a for-profit company would conflict with Horizon's charitable goals and lead to Horizon's eventual shut-down. Michael again stressed selling to VDP would get the drug to market faster through the addition of corporate resources available for the clinical trials. Michael pointed out VDP has connections through its relationships with the FDA, which may eliminate some of the red tape. Michael vigorously argued for the board to consider selling. Mark and David refused to continue negotiations with any of the interested drug companies.

* * *

Dec. 2004

Michael called a second special meeting, held by telephone conference, to request Horizon allow VDP to make a proposal regarding Transviazine. David rejected Michael's proposal and the discussion became heated. David called for a final vote to terminate all discussions with drug companies. David and Mark voted against the sale and resolved to terminate all further discussions with VDP and other pursuers. The board directed Michael to advise VDP that Horizon would not sell its ownership interest in the drug. The meeting was terminated abruptly.

"Mary, Mother of God," Haney shook his head. "McCall and Rabinowitz turned down Van Doren and the next thing you know, they're dead and the deal somehow gets done." Haney stood and started pacing back and forth across the kitchen. The small room afforded him only three paces before he had to turn around.

"And now Van Doren has the patent," Alex added.

"Wait a minute," Haney said. "I just thought of something." He hurried out of the kitchen.

"What?" He heard Haney rustling through papers in a back room.

Haney returned to the kitchen with a stack of note pads. He dropped them on the table and flipped quickly through his notes.

"Here it is."

"What?" he asked a second time.

"H" Haney answered, "Fucking H."

"Come again?"

"Remember when I told you I went to Chicago to investigate Rabinowitz? I was in his house?"

The light bulb went on in Alex's head. "Oh, yeah . . . Yeah, I do remember that discussion. The missing files in Rabinowitz's house."

"Exactly," Haney said. "Someone got to Rabinowitz's house and purged all of his files on Horizon. That's why the 'H' filing space was empty and the computer files were deleted. I suspect that's also why his killer burned down the office. The killers didn't want anything about Horizon known."

"Shit. This keeps getting worse. Check this out: I reviewed Horizon's by-laws, which showed Murphy had limited voting authority in the business affairs. He served on the board primarily in an advisory capacity and had no ownership interest. The company was Rabinowitz's baby. He served as chairman and had veto authority even over McCall, who served as vice chairman." He paused for a moment. "There is one circumstance, however, that would grant Murphy authority to act."

"What's that?"

"Look at Article 13(b)," he pointed to the text:

In the event the Chairman becomes incapacitated as a result of death or disability and/or becomes incapable of fulfilling his duties hereunder, the Vice-Chairman shall assume the position of Chairman and have the authority to perform all duties and responsibilities as of the date of death or disability, until such time, if any, the Chairman is no longer incapacitated and is able to return to his position. The third board member shall assume the position of Vice-Chairman should the existing Vice-Chairman be required to assume the position of Chairman under this paragraph.

Haney looked as if he was just diagnosed with cancer. "I've known Michael Murphy for ten years, Alex. We've worked on a lot of cases together. He's pushed the envelope a few times—we all have. But I never imagined him being involved in something like this. There's no reason. The man has everything. Makes no sense."

The room went silent as each man soaked up the grim facts.

"I'm afraid to ask, but is there anything else?" Haney asked, glancing at the files.

"A couple things," he responded.

"Oh, great," Haney said. "I've had about enough of this fucking coffee."

He slammed the mug down in the sink basin. Surprisingly, the ceramic cup didn't break.

"Can I interest you in something a bit more appropriate for the circumstances?"

Haney pulled a bottle of Jack Daniels from the cabinet above his refrigerator. "It's cheap, but effective."

"Yeah. Load me up."

Haney tossed a handful of ice cubes in two water glasses and filled each glass half way with straight bourbon. The ice struggled to keep its form, crackling and popping as it shrank. He chugged half the contents of his glass and handed the other glass to Alex.

"Okay, what else you got?" Haney asked, grimacing from the fire in his throat.

"The first thing Murphy did as acting chairman was to sell Horizon."

"To Van Doren?"

"No. A company called Hinsdorf Holdings, Inc. It was a simple asset purchase deal for one million. The purchase agreement is only three pages long. I haven't ever seen one so short. I checked the Secretary of State's web site. The company is registered to do business in Florida, but it's incorporated in Switzerland."

"I'm guessing this holding company doesn't have any offices in Florida?" Haney asked.

"No, just a registered agent—CT Systems."

"Not surprising. Swiss companies are a royal pain in the ass to investigate. Terrorist operatives in the States use Swiss shells all the time to fund their networks, you know. I bet there are a few other countries in the mix, too. I have some friends at the Bureau who might be able to get some additional info on this. Dollars to doughnuts the trail comes right back to you know who." Haney scribbled notes.

"What else?"

"One other thing," he responded. "Horizon's by-laws reference an agreement between Mark McCall and David Rabinowitz that's not contained in the file. Look at this:"

Nothing in these By-Laws shall be construed to alter or amend the Agreement entered between Mark McCall and David Rabinowitz, M.D., on May 24, 2001 (the "Agreement"). To the extent any terms in these By-Laws are deemed inconsistent with the terms of the Agreement, the terms of the Agreement shall prevail. Furthermore, at all times the authority of Horizon's officers and board of directors shall be carried out in a manner consistent with the Agreement.

"We need to find that Agreement, Alex."

"Any ideas? Murphy deleted all the McCall files at work. Jessica gave me all of her dad's papers and I didn't see this Agreement in there."

Haney continued to study the documents while he pondered Alex's question. Alex leaned back and sipped his bourbon. He didn't like the taste, but the alcohol felt good flowing through his system.

"Look at this," Haney said, holding up the last page of one of the meeting minutes.

"What about it?"

"Did you see this?" He pointed to the bottom of the last page. Alex sat up and focused his eyes at the end of Haney's pinky. After the text of the minutes ended, the letters "KJ" appeared.

"I'm a little tired, Jim, so you may want to spell it out for me."

"You have a secretary?"

He traded the blank look on his face for one of shock. "Shit. How did I not see that?"

"Somebody other than Murphy, McCall, and Rabinowitz typed up these minutes and initialed the bottom of the last page. We need to find this person."

"Can you do it?"

"I can sure as hell try. I'll start digging first thing in the morning."

Haney noticed Alex rubbing his red eyes. "It's late. We both need to get some sleep," he said. "Why don't you crash here tonight?"

He gladly accepted Haney's invitation. He wasn't sure he could have stayed awake for the drive home.

49

Murphy rolled into his office Friday morning at 11:20 a.m. wearing khaki pants and a golf shirt. The red tint on his face eliminated any doubt as to his whereabouts.

"Would you please get me a sandwich from downstairs," he asked, lifting a stack of messages from his assistant's desk. "I need to get caught up on these and go through my e-mails."

"Yes, Mr. Murphy." Despite having worked for Murphy for the past twelve years, she still referred to him by his sir name.

He closed the door to his office and perched himself in front of his computer. "Be a slow day," he said.

No such luck. Forty unread messages popped up on the Outlook screen. He steered his mouse arrow to the delete bar and got to work.

"Fucking junk mail. They need to do away with this shit." He immediately deleted a dozen e-mails without reading them. Bake sales, general requests for information, reminders of upcoming firm events and similar messages didn't survive long.

One e-mail, however, caught his attention. Three quarters of the way down the list, the subject line "Horizon File." Don Jansen was the sender. He clicked on the message.

We received the Horizon file back this morning. Just wanted to make sure you and Alex didn't need it for anything else before we shred it.

He didn't waste any time picking up the phone and dialing four numbers.

"Office Services, Don speaking."

"It's Michael Murphy."

"What can I do for you?"

"I just got your e-mail about the Horizon file. I'm a bit confused. What did you mean by saying you just got the file back?"

"I don't understand, sir?" Don became defensive. "You told me not to shred the file yet and to give it to Alex Weaver."

"When did I tell you this?"

"You're e-mail," he replied.

"What e-mail?"

"The one you sent Wednesday. Hold on a second and I'll find it."

A pause. "That's weird," he said.

"What?"

"It's not here."

"You don't have it?" Murphy pressed.

"No. Don't you have it on your system?" His question was met with dead air.

"Uh, yeah. I should have it on mine," he said, not wishing to draw any more attention to the topic. "I'm sorry Don. I have a lot going on. It must have slipped my mind."

"You still want the file shredded?"

"Yeah. Go ahead. Make sure it's done today. Let me know as soon as it's finished. And nobody else needs to see the file, not even Alex. Are we clear on that?"

"Yes, sir."

Murphy leaned back in his chair and shook his head. "Goddamn it, Alex. You have no idea what you've done."

He picked up the phone and dialed.

"It's Michael. We have a problem."

50

lex steered into a convenience store on the south side of town. Though rush hour ended two hours earlier, traffic was still heavy in this popular quarter. He opened his door and a strong breeze carrying the smell of gasoline brushed his face.

Nothing suspicious.

"How in the hell am I supposed to know that a professional is following me?" he kept asking himself.

He moved cautiously into the store. The pavement under his feet still smoldered from the sun's earlier pounding.

He grabbed a bottled water from the cooler. He eyed the activity in the parking lot as well as the people coming and going. The face of the man who attacked him was permanently imprinted into his mind. His gut told him he would see this man again. He wanted to be prepared when he did.

"That'll be a dollar-five," the young blonde working the register said. "Working late tonight?" she purred.

"What?"

Her attempt to flirt was lost. "I asked if you were working late," the girl repeated. "It's after eight, and you're still in a suit."

"Oh," he looked down at his tie as if he had forgotten what he was wearing. "Yeah, it's been a long day." He forced a return smile and handed her two dollars.

He returned to the parking lot, continuing to pan his surroundings. He found a payphone outside the store and loaded a handful of quarters in the coin receptacle.

"Hello?" a male voice answered.

"John, it's me."

"How are you?" His brother's voice carried concern.

"I've been better. I'll fill you in on everything later. I don't want to talk too long. How's Jessica?"

"She's okay."

"Good. You know I appreciate everything you're doing, man."

"Don't worry about it. Just stay safe."

"I'll try. Can I talk to her?"

"Yeah, hold on."

A familiar voice appeared. "Hi, I've been dying to hear from you."

"Are you okay?"

"I just want this to be over so I can get my life back."

"I need you to hang in there a little longer. We're getting close to figuring out what happened."

"What did you find out? What's going on?"

"It's a long story, but our suspicions were correct. Murphy's involved, along with others."

"You must be joking. Why?"

"It involves the charity your father was serving on and probably your Trust, but we still have some more investigating to do. I don't want to talk long right now, so I'll have to give you the details later." He continued scanning the lot. "I don't know if I'm being followed. I don't know if someone is listening to what I'm saying right now. I don't know how far these people will go, and it scares the shit out of me."

"Can't you go to the police?"

"Not yet. Need more evidence. You saw what happened the last time we went."

"How much longer?"

"I don't know. Not long. Jim is on his way out of town right now to follow up on a lead that could break things open."

"What about you?" Her voice softened. "I'm worried about you. You have to work with Michael. How can you do that knowing he's involved?"

"It's not easy, but he doesn't suspect I know anything. Our relationship has been business-as-usual."

He wasn't about to tell her he had to meet with Murphy and Van Doren the next day. His stomach was in knots over it.

"Is there anything I can do?"

"Yeah, stay safe and pray for all of us."

51

The bright morning sun pierced the rental car's window in a spot that rendered the visor worthless. Haney had one eye on the road and another on the crinkled map of Huntington, West Virginia, spread across his passenger seat as he drove along I-64.

Up, down and all around, Haney winded his way along rolling hills freshly painted green by a late spring. Stilted, wooden houses speckled the countryside to his north. The highway hugged the Ohio River to his south. The morning mist on the river was heavy enough to make the coal barges disappear.

He veered off the Interstate when he reached Huntington's meager city limits and drove due north. He found himself in the parking lot of a rustic brick hospital in the heart of the small river town.

"Excuse me, sir, good morning. Where's your lab?" Haney asked the old man sitting behind the main information desk.

"Good morning," the man spoke with a heavy Southern accent. "Just go down the hall, take the first elevator to your left to the lower level, take a right out of the elevator and you can't miss it."

"Thanks."

Haney made his way down the checkerboard hallway passing staff and patients along the way. He navigated the dungeon-like corridor in the lower level. He pushed through a set of double doors and entered some kind of waiting room with an unmanned counter. He searched for help, but didn't see anyone. He noticed a small bell at the end of the counter.

"Cutting edge healthcare technology," he said softly. The bell brought a heavy-set woman wearing a white hospital coat out from the back room.

"Can I help you, sir?" Like the older man in the reception area, she also carried an accent too rough to be charming.

"I'm looking for Karen James. Is she working today?"

"Sure is, honey. Hold on just a sec and I'll get her for you."

The woman picked up the phone and dialed four numbers. "Ray, hey, how're you? Will you tell Karen she has a visitor up front?"

The woman eyed Haney and smiled. She continued listening with the phone to her ear. "Okay, thanks," she said and hung it up. "She'll be right out. You can have a seat over there if you like," the woman pointed to a warped vinyl couch that sat against the concrete wall.

"I'm fine standing," he replied.

A slender, young woman with dark hair emerged from the back. Her brown eyes met Haney's. She glanced at the woman behind the counter and then back again at Haney.

"Ms. James?" he asked.

"Yes." She didn't speak with an accent. She wore a professional pantsuit that distinguished her from the other hospital employees.

"Can I help you?" she asked.

"I'm Jim Haney, ma'am. Private investigator from Florida," he said, holding out his hand. "I'm working on a civil case in Florida and need to ask you a few questions."

"About what?"

"Is there someplace we could speak privately?" he asked. The woman behind the counter didn't hide the fact she was eavesdropping.

"Maryann, would you please go in the back for a minute?" Karen asked her co-worker.

"No problem, honey. I'll be in the back if you need anything." The rotund woman eyeballed Haney and shuffled out of the room.

"I don't understand what I have to do with a case going on in

Florida, Mr. Haney. You must have me mistaken for someone else. I've never lived in Florida and don't have any family there."

"No mistake, Ms. James. The case involves a patent for a drug called Transviazine sold by your former employer, David Rabinowitz, to Van Doren Pharmaceuticals. You used to work for Dr. Rabinowitz, and I think you might have some relevant information."

Karen's face reddened. "How did you find me?"

"My job is to find people. I just have a few questions is all. It shouldn't take long." He was surprised at her apparent distress.

"I told the police everything I know, Mr. Haney. I don't want to get involved. I told them that."

"Ma'am, I'm not here . . ."

"How many people know I'm here?" she asked.

"Right now, just me."

"I don't want to talk to you or anyone else, Mr. Haney. Please just leave me alone," she demanded.

As she turned to leave, Haney grabbed her arm and stopped her forward progress. "What is it you're afraid of, Ms. James. I might be able to help."

"Let go of me." She jerked her arm away.

"Ms. James, before you leave I need to tell you something," he said. "I know what happened to Dr. Rabinowitz. If you don't talk to me voluntarily, I'll be back with a subpoena and your name and address is going to be part of the public court file for everyone involved with Dr. Rabinowitz to see."

She stood silent, staring at the ground. "Take this," he said, handing her his business card. "I'm staying at the Holiday Inn downtown and I'll be here until tomorrow morning. If you change your mind, give me a call."

She reluctantly took the card and paced quickly to the back door. She swiped her access card and shot him a cold glare before slipping through.

52

A lex paced back and forth in the roundabout in front of his
office building. Murphy asked him to be out there at 9:30 a.m.
to ride over to Van Doren's office. The meeting was originally
scheduled to take place in Murphy's office, but the location was
changed. He had been dreading this day, wondering how he could act
normal in the presence of two cold-blooded killers.

The morning sun was already melting him in his suit. To make matters worse, his only clean dress shirt had a neck size a half-inch too
small. He tugged at his collar to stretch it. No relief.

Murphy's Mercedes stopped abruptly where he was standing. He
threw his briefcase in the back seat and hopped in. "Hello, Alex,"
Murphy said.

"Good morning," he smiled, trying to appear normal.

"We have a lot of work to do to get ready for trial."

"We do."

Murphy's blast of air conditioning wasn't the only thing keeping the
inside of the car cold. He hadn't looked at Alex.

Murphy adjusted his radio to a talk news program as he drove. "I
didn't get a chance to read the paper this morning," he said. "Hope
you don't mind if I get caught up on some news while we drive."

"Not at all." He was relieved to have the pressure of making conversation lifted from his shoulders. The two men drove without speaking.

"Shouldn't we have gotten off at the last exit?" Alex asked, breaking
the silence. .

"Oh, didn't I tell you about the change of plans?" Murphy asked.

"You told me the meeting was changed from our office to Van Doren's," he said.

"Charles preferred to hold the meeting at his weekend house," Murphy answered.

"Weekend house?"

"Yeah, it's an incredible place. Ten acres just south of town on the river."

"How far out is this place?"

"Fifteen miles off of I-95."

Murphy exited the busy interstate onto a rural highway and pressed the gas. "We're running behind."

He accelerated to seventy-five miles an hour. The strip malls, grocery stores, and residential neighborhoods quickly disappeared from sight, replaced by undeveloped woodlands.

Enough time passed for the news to get repeated twice.

"I think this is it, up here to the left," Murphy announced, slowing the car to check his bearings. "Yeah, this is it."

He wheeled left onto a dirt road and passed through an open metal gate with two signs marked NO TRESPASSING on either side. A trail of dust followed the car down the path. The Mercedes' suspension struggled to keep the ride smooth over the rough terrain.

The thick forest opened to a sprawling lot with a shingled house tucked neatly between tall yellow pines. The house sat just fifty paces off the river and had a wrap-around porch with rustic chairs, potted plants and a porch swing. A separate garage was set off to the south.

"Good morning. Did you get lost?" Van Doren approached from the garage wearing a pair of jeans and a blue dress shirt.

"Hello, Charles," Murphy said. "This place is out here a bit."

The men exchanged greetings and Van Doren invited them inside. Both Alex and Murphy lugged their oversized briefcases behind Van Doren through the front door into the foyer. The house had a simple, country style with wooden floors, open rooms, and high ceilings.

"Let's go to my office to talk," Van Doren said. The men followed him down the hallway, past the staircase.

Van Doren's study was larger than most family rooms. Mahogany bookshelves covered two walls. Another wall had a brick fireplace flanked by large windows that showcased the river. The beams crossing the ceiling gave the new house a bucolic feel.

"Please, have a seat. Make yourselves comfortable." Van Doren closed the door to the office. Alex sat on the couch and opened his briefcase. Murphy found a chair next to the couch.

"Relax just a minute, Alex." Van Doren moved behind his desk and melted into his oversized leather chair. "Before we get into the legal jargon, I want to chat."

Alex glanced at Murphy, who was busy studying the patterns of the rug covering the floor.

"Okay," he responded. His collar tightened.

Van Doren leaned back, crossed his legs, and focused his intense eyes on Alex. "I've come a long way since I was a young man like you. I learned many hard lessons. First from my father, who started this company from scratch, then in the business world. You know the saying, only the strong survive. Sometimes you have to do whatever it takes to not only be successful, but to help society."

He had no idea where Van Doren was going. He eyeballed Murphy again, who seemed dazed.

Van Doren continued his lecture. "Don't worry, Alex, I'll spare you a detailed discussion of my life. Instead, I want to talk about the present, which is the drug Transviazine and what we're trying to accomplish. Do you actually know how widespread AIDS is?"

"Not specifically."

"Last year, five million people across the world became infected with the disease. Five million. Just last year, over three million people died of AIDS. I don't know about you, but to me those numbers are staggering."

"I didn't know."

"We can save these people. But we need to get Transviazine approved. I've been in this business long enough to know the word *efficiency* has been removed from all governmental timelines." Van Doren looked to Murphy, who nodded half-heartedly.

"VDP can throw the weight of a billion dollar company at the FDA to speed up their pathetic approval process. We can get to production faster than Rabinowitz ever could have. You know what that means, Alex, don't you?"

"The faster the approval, the faster people can get treatment, and the more lives can be saved," he answered.

"Exactly," Van Doren patronized his guest. "With the number of lives at issue, it's critical we do whatever it takes to get the drug to market fast. And if it happens to make us rich in the process, so be it."

"With all due respect," he asked, "wouldn't the FDA be just as anxious to get the drug approved for Rabinowitz as your company? Why are you so sure you can get the drug approved quicker?"

Van Doren laughed. "If we played by the rules, we'd fall well behind the competition. It's really quite amazing what a government employee making forty-two thousand a year will do for a little tuition help for the kids, a great lease deal on a car, a few airline tickets, or some adult companionship at a seminar."

"I see," he responded.

"For the system to work, you need people you can count on. Like Michael. Like the people who run my company. Like my friends at the FDA—I can trust them." Van Doren's tone deepened. "I find it troubling when someone I thought I could trust starts working against me."

Alex's insides twitched. He eyed Murphy again, who refused to meet his gaze. Then he heard the front door to the house open and close.

They had company.

"Attorneys are bound by ethics, aren't they Alex?" Van Doren asked.

"Yes, of course."

"If an attorney believes his client is doing something illegal or contrary to the attorney's ethical standards, the attorney has a duty to bring it to the client's attention, doesn't he?"

"Yes."

Van Doren stood and moved around his desk. He leaned back against it and folded his arms. "Is there anything you'd like to bring to my attention?"

"No," he answered, betting Van Doren was bluffing.

"I was afraid this is where we'd end up," Van Doren said. "It's a shame. You could have been a rich and successful young man. Maybe you still can if you cooperate."

"What's going on here?" he asked. "Mr. Murphy?"

Murphy stayed quiet.

"We're going to need you to decide, Alex," Van Doren continued. "Whether you're on board."

"Can someone please tell me what this is all about?" He shot Murphy another look, which was finally returned.

"We know you took the Horizon file," Murphy said.

"That's right, Alex," Van Doren added, re-taking control, "why don't you tell us your interest in that file and what you found."

"I needed that file for another case," he answered. His heart pounded his chest.

"Well, then, tell me about this other case," Van Doren pressed.

"It's confidential. Privileged. I can't discuss it. I'm sure Mr. Murphy understands I can't discuss the case."

Murphy may as well have been dead. He said nothing.

"Jessica McCall. Is that the case you're talking about?" Van Doren asked.

He turned to Murphy again. "You have to tell him we can't discuss other client matters. It's confidential. You need to tell him that," he pleaded. His senses were functioning at an all-time high. The human fight or flight mechanism was working well.

"Alex," Murphy asked, "why the fuck did you have to get so involved? Why didn't you just do what I asked instead of going behind my back? It didn't have to be this way."

"What way is that?" he asked, half-scared to death and half-enraged.

"Where's the girl?" Van Doren cut Murphy off before he could say anything.

"Please, Alex," Murphy begged, "answer his question. We can work this out. You have to understand, everything we're doing is for the best. We're going to save thousands of lives."

"Yes, Alex," Van Doren said. "If you can just answer a simple question, I'm prepared to make you a very wealthy man. Your career will takeoff. I can promise you that. Then we can forget all the unpleasantness and get down to preparing for the trial. You won't need to worry about anything anymore."

Floorboards creaked in the hallway.

"And if I don't answer your questions?" he asked. "What are you going to do?"

Van Doren moved within inches of Alex's face. He could practically taste the bitter coffee on Van Doren's breath. "You really don't want to find out."

Alex backed up a step. "How rich of a man would I become if I cooperated?"

Van Doren smiled. His shoulders dropped and he left Alex some space. He laughed, shaking his head, "you had me fooled for a moment. I though you were as stubborn as Rabinowitz. You've restored my faith in the American system, that everyone has a price."

Van Doren snatched a paper off his desk. "I have five million dollars I'm prepared to wire into a Swiss bank account under your name. As soon as you tell me what I want to know, I'll make the call and it's yours. You can keep practicing law if you like or you can go sit on a beach somewhere and sip umbrella drinks."

"Five million dollars," Alex repeated, shifting his eyes all around the large room.

"Yes, and all you have to do is just answer one simple question. Where's the girl?"

He walked closer to Van Doren. "You don't know where she is, do you?"

"No, Alex. I don't. If I did, we wouldn't be having this discussion."

In one motion, he released all the tension in his body with an uppercut into Van Doren's right cheekbone.

The elder man fell backwards over the side of his desk to the floor, taking a few books and papers from the desk on the ride down.

Murphy jumped up out of his chair with a dropped jaw. Alex turned quickly and charged him like a linebacker doing tackle drills. The force of the two men hitting the wall knocked out Murphy's wind. He fell, gasping for air.

The doorknob to the room twisted. As the door fanned open, Alex kicked it as hard as he could, slamming it into the person entering. The man on the other side toppled with a grunt.

He scooped a lamp from the end table and launched it through one of the picture windows, shattering glass. He kicked loose pieces still hanging from the frame and jumped through the opening. A shard ripped open his left arm on his way through. He escaped in a sprint.

"What now?" Murphy shouted at Van Doren.

Lunden entered the room, clutching his bloody face. Spotted red stains covered his plain, white shirt.

Van Doren grabbed the end of the desk and pulled himself up. "He dies," he shouted, rubbing his bruised cheek. "That's what."

"Get him," Van Doren yelled at Lunden.

Lunden didn't say a word. He disappeared through the broken window.

53

"Table for one?" the young hostess asked Haney as he entered Heritage Station Restaurant with his briefcase.

"I'm meeting someone. A woman. Thin with dark hair, shoulder length," he answered.

"Are you Mr. Haney?"

"Yes."

"She's back in the Pullman room," the hostess said with a smile.

The restaurant was a historical landmark in Huntington, West Virginia. The city thrived on the shipping and rail industries and the place had a rail theme with an old locomotive and caboose affixed to the front of the property. The interior resembled an old saloon with detailed woodwork and railroad memorabilia scattered about.

The hostess led Haney to a dimly lit back room with only enough space for a few tables, all of which were occupied. "Is that her, sir?" she asked.

"Yes, thank you."

Karen James sat alone with a cup of tea.

"May I?" he asked, placing his hand on the chair across from her.

"Please," she answered, "sit down, Mr. Haney."

"Call me Jim."

He flagged the waiter and ordered coffee and a refill for Karen. "I appreciate you agreeing to meet with me. I was surprised you called," he said.

"I didn't have a choice, did I?"

"I'm sorry, but I have to know whether you have information relevant to this case. I tried to do this in the least intrusive way possible. Please understand I'm just doing my job." He stopped talking as the waiter returned with his java and set it on the red and white checked tablecloth.

"How did you wind up in Huntington?" He went for small talk to break the ice. "It's quite a change from Chicago."

"Is this relevant to your case?"

"No, I . . . I was just making conversation."

He added four packs of sugar to his coffee, stirred his cup and set the spoon on the saucer. "Karen, what are you afraid of?"

"What do you mean, *afraid of*?"

"You looked like you saw a ghost when I came to the hospital to see you this morning. And, no offense, but you seem uncomfortable right now. What is it? Why are you afraid?"

She sat still, only her fingers moved along the rim of her mug. She turned her head briefly, then leaned back in her seat. "Just ask me your questions?"

"Are you all right?"

"Please, Jim, I'd like to finish as soon as possible."

He pulled a pen and notebook from his briefcase. "My memory is fading a bit with old age. I have to make some notes or I'll forget everything." He gave a reassuring smile, but the blank look on her face told him it didn't work.

"How long did you work for Dr. Rabinowitz?"

"Five years."

"What did you do?"

"Office Manager."

"For Horizon?"

"Yes."

"Are you familiar with the drug Transviazine?"

"Yes. That was the only drug we were developing."

"Transviazine was a cure for HIV or AIDS, is that right?"

"Yes, a real miracle."

"Did the drug actually come from a person's DNA?"

"From what I know, it was modeled after a real person's DNA, but David had to make it work by applying science. The man was brilliant."

"Whose DNA? Do you know?"

"No, none of us knew. David wouldn't say."

"Tell me about Horizon's board of directors. You were the recording secretary, right?"

"Yes, David asked me to take notes at the annual meetings and type up the minutes for the company records. We typically had an annual meeting and sometimes met more often if there was a need," she offered. "The board members were David, Mark McCall, and Michael Murphy. I think Mark asked Mr. Murphy to join the board since they were friends."

"How did Mr. McCall become affiliated with Dr. Rabinowitz?" he asked.

"Mark played football for the Bears and he was active in a lot of different charities. He was sympathetic to people who had terminal illnesses like AIDS and I think he met David during some fundraisers, at least that's what David told me."

"Fair enough," he jotted more notes. "Do you recall a time where drug companies approached Horizon to purchase Transviazine?"

"Yes, I do," she said. "Those were not pleasant times in the office."

"What do you mean?"

"David hated big drug companies. He told me he started his career working as a research physician for one of them. I can't recall which one, but he used to tell me how much they cut corners to rush drugs to market. He got fed up and quit after a few years. He said he'd never give up control of Transviazine. When they started making offers, he wasn't happy about it."

"Did that set off some fireworks between the board members?"

"The fireworks were between David and Michael Murphy," she said. "Mark agreed with David about not selling the drug, but as a favor to Mr. Murphy, Mark convinced David to listen to a few offers and be done with it."

"From what I know, it seems VDP pushed the hardest," he said.

"Oh, yeah, by a long shot. They were relentless. They kept calling, writing, and even tried unannounced visits. It drove David crazy and, of course, his mood rubbed off on the rest of us. We couldn't wait for VDP to go away."

"When did they finally go away?"

"I couldn't say for sure, but I think it was just a few weeks before David was killed," she recalled.

"Did something happen? Anything that stands out?"

"Happen . . . with the drug companies? Or are you talking about David's death?"

"Well, let's start with the drug companies, Van Doren in particular. Was there a final event that terminated the discussions between VDP and Dr. Rabinowitz?

"The thing I remember was a phone call David had with the president of the company. I think his name was Van Doren. Things must have gotten ugly during the call, because I heard David yelling and cussing in his office like I never heard him before. He came out red-faced and said something about being harassed and intimidated and that he was going out to meet with a lawyer about it. It was a bad day."

"Did he tell you any specifics about what he meant?"

"No, and I didn't ask. He wasn't the type of person you'd push when he was in a bad mood."

"Do you know whether he talked to a lawyer?"

"Yes, I believe he did. He left the office a few times during the next week and told me he was going to meet with his lawyer. I may have spoken to someone at the lawyer's office to arrange a meeting, but I can't be certain of it."

"Do you remember the lawyer's name?"

"No, I don't. I might recognize it if I heard it, but I don't remember right now. I'll probably think of it ten minutes after you leave knowing me." She picked up her mug and raised it cautiously to her lips. "What does Mark say about all this? Wouldn't he be a better source of information than me?"

"You didn't hear? I thought it was in the national papers."

"Hear what?"

"Mark McCall died."

"Died? What happened?" Her eyes widened.

"The coroner said it was a heart attack." He wasn't about to disclose his murder conspiracy theory to a witness who was already shaken.

"Oh, that's terrible. I didn't know him well, but the few times I spoke to him at the board meetings, he seemed like a very nice man."

"I hate to ask this, Karen," he said, "but what about David's death? I didn't want to mention this before, because you seemed upset, but I know you saw something the night David was murdered. You gave a statement to the police, didn't you?"

She had warmed up a bit during their conversation, but his question cooled her right back down. "I'm afraid if I talk to you tonight, something bad will happen to me and my . . ." she stopped herself, " . . . something bad might happen to me."

"Were you going to say daughter? You have a three year old daughter, right? Ashley?"

"How did you know that?"

Haney raised a hand and waved her to stay calm. "My job is to investigate witness backgrounds. It's simple to do a court docket search. You got divorced two years ago. The file is public—anyone can look it up." He ratcheted down his typically loud voice. "Please, believe me when

I say I'm on your side. I'm not here to hurt you. I promise."

"I beg your pardon, but I don't know who you are. Why should I trust you?"

"Because sometimes you don't have a choice but to trust someone you don't know. This is one of those times," he said matter-of-fact. "Now, please talk to me. Tell me what you're afraid of and let me help you."

She focused on the checkered lines of the tablecloth and then Haney. Her eyes welled. "You have to promise me nothing will happen to my little girl. Please, promise me that," she demanded.

"Karen, if you and your daughter need to be protected, I'll make sure it happens. But you have to talk to me."

She snatched up a sugar packet and twirled it in her hand. "It was a Wednesday night," she said, "and David asked me to work late, because he knew I'd do it without complaining like the others. We were buried in paperwork from the FDA trying to set up clinical trials. I needed the extra money and I got overtime for doing it."

"I left work at my normal time, five-thirty, to pick up Ashley from day care. I drove her home and my neighbor came over to watch her. While driving back to work, David called me on my cell. It was strange. He said his car was hit in the parking lot at work and the man who hit him was waiting outside to exchange insurance information. He wanted me to know he wasn't in the office in case I showed up to work and couldn't find him."

Her hands trembled.

"Just take your time."

"When I got to the office," she continued, "I pulled around back to the parking lot. There was a small side street along one side of our building. When I turned into the lot, my lights flashed on a man standing over David," she started crying, "I'm sorry," she said.

He handed her a spare napkin.

"I saw a gun in his hand. A pool of blood was spread out under David's head. He wasn't moving. I knew he was dead."

"What did you do?"

"The man standing over him gazed at me and I think we both froze. Then he moved toward the car. I slammed it in reverse and hit the gas as hard as I could. I don't know whether he ran after me or not. I was looking out the rear window trying to drive the car."

"What happened next?"

"I shot out of the lot right into the intersection. Luckily, I missed the oncoming cars. I flew home as fast as I could. I ran inside, grabbed Ashley, and called the police. I couldn't stop shaking."

"I have a copy of the police report," he pulled additional documents from his briefcase. "You described the killer as tall with a large build. He was wearing a baseball cap with long, dark hair showing out the back of the cap. He had glasses and a dark beard. He wore an old, bulky jacket and dark pants. Is that right?"

"Sounds right, from what I recall. It all happened so fast."

"Anything else you can tell me that's not in the report?"

"She wrapped her hands together tightly. "A few days after David was killed, I was cooking breakfast for Ashley and heard a knock at my door," she continued. "I must have jumped three feet when I heard it. Every little noise scared me. I looked out the window and saw a man in a suit standing on my front porch. He had a badge."

"Who was he?"

"Said he was with the FBI. Said his name was agent Richards."

"What happened?"

"He told me he was following up on the police report to see if there was anything I may have left out of my description. He asked a bunch of questions. He seemed professional, but I remember something being . . . off. Something he said wasn't right."

"What do you mean?"

"He asked me why I flashed my brights as I turned into the parking lot."

"What about it?"

"I flashed my brights because we had a couple broken lights outside in the back lot. I was so used to doing it in the winter months when it got dark early; I didn't think to mention it to the police."

He picked up the police report and studied it in detail. "You're right. There's nothing in here about brights."

"The man standing in my living room wouldn't have any reason to know I flashed my brights when I rounded the corner. I hadn't told anyone. The only way he would have known is if he was there . . . that night."

"Did you realize this as you were speaking to him?"

"Oh-yeah. I thought I was going to die right then and there. I thought he was going to kill me."

"What did you do?"

"I told him I needed to get Ashley to school and asked if we could finish up another time. He said he was done with his questions and then he said something I'll never forget."

Her shakes returned. "He said 'the people suspected of this crime are very dangerous. You need to be aware, if any arrests are made and you're called to testify, you and your daughter may not be safe.' He told me 'your little girl is very pretty. I know you don't want to have anything happen to her.'" Her eyes watered.

"Did you ever see this person, Agent Richards, again?"

"No."

"Did he leave anything with you? A business card?"

"No, nothing."

"What did you do after that?"

"I called the FBI and asked if they had an Agent Richards in Chicago. They said they did and gave me the number for his office. I called the number they gave me and his secretary told me he was on assignment out of state. She kept his calendar and didn't know anything about him coming to meet with me. She didn't even know about Dr. Rabinowitz's death. I asked her to describe agent Richards and she told me he was in his mid-fifties with a receding hairline."

"What did the man who came to your house look like?"

"He was about six feet or six-two and had short, red hair, a buzz cut. He had a mustache and wore small, rounded glasses with a slight tint, just dark enough to cover his eyes. I couldn't really see his eyes. He looked to be in his mid-thirties."

Haney wrote as fast as he could. "Did he look like the man you saw standing over Dr. Rabinowitz's body?"

"Hard to say," she said. "He looked different, but he was dressed differently, too. I don't know if it was the same man, but even if it wasn't, the man who came to my house wasn't who he said he was, and he had information only someone at the crime scene would have known. I just know I don't want to see either of them ever again."

"What did you do next?"

"Left town. I moved down here to this small town where I didn't think anyone could find me. My mom grew up here years ago and spoke of it fondly. I still can't believe you found me."

"Do you know why anyone would want to kill Dr. Rabinowitz?"

"The only thing I know is the police asked me a lot of questions about some hate mail we'd been getting at the office from some anti-gay crazies. There were a few newspaper articles that talked about David and his miracle drug. And we used to get some hate mail from people after the articles ran. There are a lot of weirdoes out there. That's the only reason I knew people didn't like him."

He closed his notes. "Is there anything else?"

Her eyes peered up and focused on a wooden beam stretched across the ceiling. "No, I think that's it."

"Now listen to me, Karen, you can't tell anyone about our conversation. You will be safe as long as certain people don't believe you can hurt them, and right now they don't think you can."

"What people? Do you know what's going on?"

"The less you know the better right now," he answered. "The day will come in the near future where you won't have to be scared anymore."

He stood from the table. "I know you have a little girl waiting on you at home. Why don't you get out of here and go see her."

He threw a ten-dollar bill on the table to cover the coffee and tip and escorted her to her car.

"If you think of anything else, please call me," he said. Don't call me from home. Use a pay phone or work, just to be safe. Otherwise, I'll be in touch."

54

Alex's legs had never carried him this fast. Then again, it wasn't every day that he was running for his life.

He needed fifty yards to get past the cleared portion of the lot into the thick brush. He shot a glance back at the house and saw a man leap through the window. It wasn't Murphy or Van Doren.

He was fast. Faster than Alex. Gaining ground with every step.

Alex charged straight into thick woods. Branches, palmettos, and thorny vines carved into his face and body like little razors.

As he tore through the heavy brush, he heard someone else enter the woods.

His pursuer continued gaining ground.

Alex skipped through a thicket and rambled downhill into a gully. His loafers were no match for the steep, sandy terrain. He lost his footing and tumbled ass over heels, then ricocheted off some scrub pine.

"Idiot," he moaned.

He clutched his side to check for broken parts. Sharp pain radiated through his body. He found himself in a dried creek bed at the bottom of the hill.

Silence.

He sat up and scanned every direction. Nothing. He listened for footsteps. Nothing. The forest was still. He spotted a jagged stone nearly the size of his fist nestled down in the creek bed. He dug it out of the soft muck.

An adrenaline burst magnified his senses. As he stood, he heard something move directly behind him. He jumped up to his feet and spun around with his arms raised, which effectively scared off the squirrel roaming through the brush. The tiny creature headed for cover up the nearest pine.

"Goddamn," he said, releasing a deep breath. He rubbed the mix of sweat and dirt from his forehead.

Through condensed brush to his east, he spotted the dirt trail leading off Van Doren's property. The creek ran in the direction his eyes focused, which would provide a direct path. Nerves on edge, he charged forward along the creek bed.

As he rounded a corner, the end of a thick branch swung out from behind a clump of bushes and smashed into his forehead, dropping him in his tracks.

He hit hard. Unable to see. Dizzy from the blow. Suddenly, an image came into focus. A man stood over him, holding a branch.

"Remember me, asshole?" Lunden jabbed his leg with the makeshift weapon. "I was hoping we'd meet again."

His ears rang and his vision was blurred. Blood rushed down the side of his face from a cut that opened up over his eye.

"Get up," Lunden said. "I'd just as soon cut your throat right here," he detached a hunting knife from his belt. "But we don't want your body buried here, and I sure as shit ain't gonna tote your ass for a mile."

"We're going to walk." Lunden grabbed his arm and yanked him up with one hand, holding the knife steady in the other.

"Come on, boy, walk. That way," he pointed the opposite direction Alex had been running. "This old creek'll take us to a lake with a few big gators. They're waiting for you."

He put a boot to Alex's rear. "Move it!"

Cobwebs filled his head. He struggled to regain his senses. He stumbled forward, Lunden following right behind.

"Since we have some time for a chat, why don't you tell me where Jessica is?" Lunden asked. "Where did you hide her?"

Alex's jacket sleeve hung loose at the rip in the shoulder. The extra material provided just enough cover for his right hand to shield the rock from Lunden's view.

"Did you hear what I asked you?" Lunden pressed. "Where's the girl?"

"Why would I tell you if you're going to just kill me anyway?" He wobbled forward.

"'Cause if you tell me, I'll hurt you a lot less," he answered. "Don't worry, you're going to talk. Trust me on that. We'll have us a little fun when we get to the lake."

"You mind if I take off my tie? It's hot as hell out here."

Lunden laughed, "You're a different kind of animal, that's certain. Going to your own funeral and you're worried about the heat."

Lunden grabbed him from behind. "Stop right where you are and stand still," he walked around front to face Alex, lifted the knife to his throat, pushed the sharp blade underneath the knot, and slid it through the material like butter. The tie fell to the ground.

"Pick it up and put it in your pocket," Lunden demanded. "I don't want to leave a trail."

He bent down to pick up the shredded tie, grabbed his forehead with his left hand, moaned, and then fell to his knees.

"Come on, goddamnit," Lunden growled. "Get your ass up."

"I'm not sure I can," he said.

"Jesus-fucking-Christ," Lunden reached down and put a vice grip on Alex's arm and jerked him off the ground.

His feet grabbed hold of the ground in a wide stance. He firmed his grip, swung his right arm as hard and fast as he could and caught Lunden with edge of the rock deep into his temple.

"Fuuuck!" Lunden wailed and put his hands on his bloody head. The blow sent him down.

Alex jumped over his body, barely avoided a wild swing of Lunden's blade and took off.

***

Lunden struggled to his feet. "You're dead, motherfucker. Dead," he shrieked; and then he chased.

Alex's tired legs churned as hard as they could. He made the dirt road that led off Van Doren's property and sprinted toward the gate.

He could see the highway. He glanced back and saw Lunden coming out of the woods.

Gaining fast.

Alex shot past the entrance gate to Van Doren's property, turned right, and bolted down the shoulder of the two-lane highway.

A tan SUV approached from the opposite direction. He straddled the yellow line and waved his arms. The middle-aged woman behind the wheel squealed to a stop, which gave him a chance to run to the passenger side and yank open the door.

"What's going on? What are you doing?" the woman shouted. He jumped in, slammed the door shut, and hit the locks.

Lunden jumped on the hood and pounded the windshield with the metal handle of his knife. His powerful blows cracked the glass, and it was about to give way.

The woman shrieked.

"Go." He reached his foot across the floor panel and jammed the gas. The force caused Lunden to fall forward. His bloody face smeared the windshield.

"Get off. What are you doing? Who are you people?" the woman shouted.

Alex hit the brakes hard and turned the wheel. The inertia spun the vehicle 180 degrees and threw Lunden off the hood onto the road. He switched back to the accelerator and left Lunden behind in his tracks.

"Drive," he commanded and removed his foot from the accelerator. The woman, no doubt afraid for her life, complied.

"What do you want with me?" she asked. "Where am I supposed to go?"

"The police."

55

"Do you need some help?" A young woman asked Alex at the reception desk on the third floor of the Jacksonville Sheriff's Office. The tattered clothing and blood and dirt smeared across his face made him stand out from the others milling around the receiving area.

"Detective Ferenz," he said. "It's an emergency."

"What's your name?"

"Alex Weaver."

"Do you have an appointment?"

"Do I look like I have an appointment? Somebody just tried to carve me up into little pieces. I didn't have a chance to make an appointment, no."

His back felt the stares from virtually everyone in the room.

"Just a minute please," she picked up the phone and dialed a number. "I'm sorry, his line is busy. Have a seat and I'll try him again in a few minutes."

"Oh, like hell. Forget it. I know where he is." He brushed past her desk toward the back of the room. As the sergeant in charge of the homicide unit, Ferenz was the only detective to have his own office.

"Hey," the receptionist shouted, "you can't just go back there."

A burly deputy fell into pursuit and snagged him just as he burst through Ferenz's office door. Ferenz jumped when the door flew open.

"What in the hell is going on here?" he put the phone to his thigh to block the racket.

"I need to talk to you—right now," Alex ripped his arm away from the deputy's grip.

"You know this guy?" the deputy asked.

"Yeah, I know him," Ferenz said. "Let him in."

"I'll be right outside," the deputy squinted his disapproval all over Alex.

"You look like shit," Ferenz pointed him to a chair. He terminated his call and asked his assistant to bring some damp towels and bandages from the first aid kit. Back in his chair, he lifted an unlit cigar from the glass ashtray on his desk, and chewed on the butt.

"What in the hell happened to you?"

"The same son of a bitch who tried to kill Jessica McCall and me on the boat last week just came after me again. He tried to cut me to little pieces and feed me to the alligators."

"Where?"

"South of town. St. Johns County."

"Okay," Ferenz said, "take a breath and calm yourself. I can't hear as fast as you're talking. No one's going to get at you here. Just take a load off and tell me what happened."

He followed the advice and took a deep breath. "I had a meeting this morning with Charles Van Doren at his second house. It's a huge place south of town. I'm working on a case for Van Doren Pharmaceuticals with one of my firm's partners, Michael Murphy."

"Alex, I'm telling you, you're going to have to slow down. I've got arthritis in this hand," Ferenz wrote as fast as he could on pad in front of him.

"What time was your meeting?"

"Ten."

"Now we're getting somewhere. What were you meeting about?"

"Parker Jones represents VDP. I'm lead counsel on a patent case."

"All right, now, how did you get from a meeting at Van Doren's to getting yourself nearly killed?"

Before Alex could answer, a middle-aged woman with a puffy hairdo entered the room loaded down with a damp towel, a plastic bag filled with ice, and bandages. She placed the items on the edge of Ferenz's desk.

"Thank you, Mary," Ferenz nodded.

"Yes, thank you," he said.

"You're welcome," she answered. "Do you need anything else?"

"Actually some water would be great, thanks," Alex answered.

"Hold my calls if you would, Mary," Ferenz asked his assistant.

Alex wiped his face as he spoke. "This is going to sound crazy, detective, but it's true."

"I'm ready," he said, "go on."

"Charles Van Doren is trying to kill Jessica McCall, and I believe he is the person responsible for the death of Jessica's father and grandparents. He hired the killer. The same guy who tried to kill me today."

"Charles Van Doren. A killer. Mm-hmm. I thought we covered this already. Those murders are solved and you're trying to tell me the culprit is Charles Van Doren. *The* Charles Van Doren."

"I have proof."

"You damn-sure better."

"First off, there's a woman downstairs, her name is Judy Waters, filling out an incident report right now. She saw the maniac who tried to kill me this morning. His blood is smeared all over her windshield."

Ferenz's bit through his cigar.

"Check her report. He was at Van Doren's house and not by chance. Second," he continued, "Jessica is linked to a patent Van Doren stole from a doctor in Chicago. I know, because I'm Van Doren's attorney and I have documents to prove it."

"Wait, wait a minute," Ferenz struggled to write down everything he said. "I got it. Okay. Go ahead," he said.

"After Jessica and I were attacked on the boat, I moved her to a hiding place to keep her safe. When I was at Van Doren's house this morning, he demanded I tell him Jessica's whereabouts and he offered me five million bucks to tell. Now, he sure as hell wasn't asking so he could send a Christmas card."

"Did you tell him where she is?"

"She'd be dead if I did."

"Was your partner, Murphy, present for the conversation?"

"Yeah."

"Will he confirm what happened?"

"He's in on it."

Ferenz threw down his pen and leaned back in his chair. You mean to tell me," he scratched at his head and shot a glance at the ceiling, "the wealthiest and probably most powerful exec in this city, not to mention his fancy attorney from the fancy law firm, are co-conspirators to murder? You have got to be kidding me."

"I know how it sounds," he said, "but yes, that's what I'm saying."

"All right," Ferenz massaged the back of his neck, "let's take this whole story one step at a time. Go back to the beginning. Like I never heard it before."

Alex told him everything he knew about the drug patent, Rabinowitz, Horizon and Mark McCall. After an hour of question and answer, Ferenz's phone interrupted.

"I thought I said no calls," he barked into the receiver. "What? Okay . . . uh-huh. I see. I'll be right there."

Ferenz threw his cigar down. "Something just came up," he said. "I need to step out. Don't go anywhere. This'll only take a minute."

"Is it about me?"

"Just hold your shirt. I'll be back."

Alex padded the towel with ice and dabbed his face and neck. He leaned his head against the chair and set the makeshift ice bag on his forehead.

"I can't fucking believe this is happening," he muttered.

Drops of condensation trickled down his face. The cold felt good. With eyes closed, he felt every scrape, itch, cut, bump, and bruise on his body.

Ferenz finally returned.

"This is one fucked-up situation we got here," he said. He plopped down hard in his chair fished out his cigar.

"What do you mean?"

"Van Doren's been burning up the phone lines to the Mayor, Sheriff, and Chief Judge Baxley over at the courthouse. He claims you went crazy and attacked him. He's putting pressure on the DA to press charges."

"That's bullshit." He propped himself forward and dropped the ice-bag to his lap.

"Look, Alex, I'm not taking sides here. I checked downstairs. Ms. Waters, the woman who drove you here, confirmed there was someone else out there who scared her worse than you did. He fits the description you gave, so at least that part of your story checks out. All that aside, we may both have a bigger problem right now."

"What?"

"Judge Baxley's office just faxed us an order the judge entered against you. A temporary restraining order."

"From who?"

"According to Baxley's judicial assistant, at some point between the time you left Van Doren's and the time you arrived here, Van Doren got the judge on the phone and convinced him to write this . . ." He handed over a piece of paper still warm from the fax machine.

O-R-D-E-R

Pursuant to Florida Rule of Civil Procedure 1.610, and upon hearing the evidence and arguments presented by counsel for the moving party, the Court hereby issues a temporary restraining order against Alex J. Weaver, restraining him from breaching the attorney-client privilege by discussing any information pertaining to Charles Van Doren individually or Van Doren Pharmaceuticals, Inc., if such information was discovered during the course of Mr. Weaver's professional relationship with the aforementioned parties. Any persons with knowledge of this Order who elicit, use, or disclose any information subject to protection under this Order shall be held in contempt and subject to fines and/or imprisonment. This Order shall become effective immediately and remain in force for ten (10) days or until the restrained party has an opportunity to be heard.

/s/ Chief Judge Baxley

"Un-fucking-believable," he tossed the Order across Ferenz's desk.

"You're the lawyer. You want to tell me what that means?" Ferenz asked. "I've seen lots of restraining orders in my day, but not like this."

"It means Van Doren paid a shit-load of money to the judge's re-election campaign and got him to sign off on this as a return favor," he said. "Van Doren probably told the judge a bogus story about how I threatened to disclose attorney-client privileged information. So, the judge entered a gag order against me. According to this," he pointed to the paper, "I'm not allowed to discuss anything about Van Doren to anyone for the next ten days. The judge probably thought 'no big deal, it's just ten days. I'll do my buddy a favor.'"

"How can the judge do that without giving you advance notice? Isn't that a due process violation?" Ferenz asked. "It is in criminal law."

"The judge has discretion to enter restraining orders without notice if it's some kind of emergency situation. This piece of crap goes one further, though. It threatens to throw people in jail who listen to what I say about Van Doren if they know the order exists. That's why Van Doren had it sent over here."

"And after ten days?" Ferenz asked.

"By law, the judge has to hold an evidentiary hearing attended by all affected parties before extending the order beyond that time-frame," he answered.

"I would think the last thing Van Doren would want is an evidentiary hearing on what you've been telling me. He'd have to be an idiot to go to court with something like this."

Alex studied the floor and shook his head. He refocused on Ferenz. "He doesn't expect me to live more than ten days," he said. "In his mind, there won't ever be a hearing."

"Mmm," Ferenz said.

He looked at the Order and ran his fingers across his chin. He picked up the telephone. "Mary, if anyone calls looking for Mr. Weaver, and I mean *anyone*, tell them he's gone and we don't know where he went. I'm not here, either, if anyone asks. And would you brew up a fresh pot of coffee and fill up two mugs for me? Oh, we still need that glass of water. Thanks, Mary."

He hung up the phone. "Now, where were we?"

"What about the restraining order?"

"Fuck Van Doren and Baxley. Finish your story."

56

aney turned sharply at an intersection. "I'm not losing those guys us, am I?" he asked, checking his rear view mirror.

"No, they're still back there," Alex answered. He and Haney accepted a police escort to Alex's condo.

"We have to get in and out. No screwing around. This freak isn't going to hesitate killing a couple of cops to get to you. Don't waste time packing."

"Didn't plan on it."

Two deputies escorted them into the building. They took the elevator to the twelfth floor and exited right toward Alex's unit.

"Which one is it?" one of the deputies asked.

"1215," Alex answered. "Down the hall on the left."

As they closed in, the lead deputy held up his fist to stop the group.

"Door's open," he mouthed to his partner.

Both officers drew their firearms and hugged the wall. They crouch-walked toward the open door.

Haney wasn't about to be a sitting duck in the hallway. He reached into his jacket and removed a .38 caliber Smith and Wesson.

"Stay behind me," he told Alex.

The two cops straddled the doorway. "What's the layout of the unit?" the cop closest to Alex asked.

"Living room first. Kitchen to the left. Hallway straight back to two bedrooms on the right and a bathroom on the left."

The lead cop pushed open the door. The living area was trashed.

Shelves emptied. Furniture tossed. Papers and files scattered about.

The officer crept through the doorway, followed by his partner. The lead officer put a fist in the air. He put a finger to his ear and pointed down the hall. He knelt at the head of the hallway and aimed his pistol.

"Police. Whoever's in the back room, come out slowly with your hands in the air."

A male voice responded: "I'm coming out. Don't shoot."

Haney heard the exchange and entered the room for backup. Alex stayed close and followed him in.

"Slow, goddamnit. Slow," the cop shouted. "One wrong move and we'll drop you where you stand."

"I'm coming out," the voice answered. A short, rumpled man in his late twenties appeared in the hallway with his hands raised.

"Down on the ground. Now. Arms in front where we can see them." Both deputies shouted orders over each other. The man obliged and hit the ground.

"I didn't do this," he said. "I live next door."

The deputies pounced on him, bent his arms behind his back, and clicked on the cuffs.

"Is anyone else in here?" one of the officers asked.

"No," the man answered.

"You sure?"

"Yes, I'm sure. Damn, these are tight."

One officer guarded the suspect. The other scanned the back rooms. "Clear." He walked back to the subject. Each officer took an arm to hoist the man off the ground. The back-up officer patted him down and escorted him out to the living room.

"Mike," Alex shouted to the man in custody. "What in the hell is going on?"

"Alex, tell them who I am," he pleaded. "I got home from work and saw your door cracked," he said between breaths, "I figured you were home and I stopped by. I've been holding a UPS package for you for the past week. I just got back from my conference today."

"Slow down, sir," the cop said. "You vouch for this guy?" he asked Alex.

"He's my neighbor, Officer," he said. "I've known him for two years."

"It might help if you took the cuffs off," Haney said. "This isn't the guy you're looking for."

The deputy removed the cuffs. "Let's all calm down and let the man tell us what happened."

Mike rubbed his wrists, looked at both of the officers, and started talking to Alex.

"I came by to drop off the mail and, like I said, the door was cracked. I knocked and you didn't answer, so I pushed it open. When I saw your place, I figured you might be hurt. So, I walked in and called your name a couple times. The next thing I know, some linebacker charged me from your bedroom. He went through me like I was nothing."

"What were you doing in the back when we got here?" the lead deputy asked.

Mike turned to the officers. "I went to see if Alex was back there. He could have been bleeding or something. Next thing I know, you guys show up."

"This just happened?" Alex asked.

"Yeah. Five minutes ago."

"Can you describe him?" the deputy asked.

"He was tall, solid as a rock, had a crew cut. It all happened so fast, I didn't get a better look than that."

"Race?"

"White."

"Clothing?"

"Black shirt and pants from what I could tell."

The deputy called for backup and put out a description.

"Paul," Haney said to one of the deputies, "The man you're after is a professional. As long as Alex is here, we're all sitting ducks. We need to get him out of here ASAP and make sure he isn't followed."

"What do you have in mind?"

Haney looked at the other deputy. "You're about Alex's size, aren't you?" He sized up the deputy's uniform.

"You can't have the uniform I'm wearing," the deputy said, "but I have some spares I picked up from the dry-cleaner in the cruiser. I can lend you one."

"Good," Haney said. "You guys have some extra evidence bags?"

"Yeah, out in the car."

"Alex," Haney continued, "use the bags to pack your things. If our man is out there waiting, he'll think it's business as usual."

"Paul," he continued, "do you mind running the lights and siren when you get out of here with Alex? So no one can follow."

"Sure, Jim. No problem."

"Alex, I'll reserve you a room at the Holiday Inn on Baymeadows Road under the name Jeff Albers. I'll put the room on my business credit card, so they shouldn't hassle you for a credit card or ID."

"Thanks, Jim," Alex said. "Are you staying or going?"

"I'm going to stick around here with these guys and see if we can dig anything up. I'll touch base with you later."

Alex bagged some clothes and personal items. He changed into a police uniform, grabbed the bags and walked out the door.

"Alex," Mike shouted after him, "let me at least give you the box." He emerged from his condo carrying a package he handed over. The cover was handwritten in black marker with no return address.

Alex stuffed it in a bag and headed out of the building with his escort.

57

"How is she?" Murphy asked, out of breath from the run from the parking lot to the emergency room.

"We don't know, Michael," his son-in-law, Matt, answered. "We're still waiting to hear something."

"What happened?"

"Something in her chest. It's been getting worse. She woke up this morning with a fever we can't get under control. She was 101°. She had trouble breathing and started coughing just a little while ago. I called Dr. Carter and he said to get her to the ER as soon as possible. He's with her now."

"Christ, Matt, she has to get through this. We're so close to the experimental phase."

"Calm yourself, Michael. You're doing everything you can."

"I told her not to get mixed up with AIDS patients. I told her that. You know I did." Murphy ran his hands across his face, stretching his pale skin.

"You know Katie better than anyone. No way she was going to shy away from patients who needed help. She didn't go to med school for the money. You know that too." Just as Matt finished his sentence, a man in his thirties wearing a white coat and green scrubs approached.

"Matt," Dr. Carter grabbed his shoulder. His body language was stiff.

"How is she?" Matt asked with Murphy listening intently.

"It's touch-and-go right now," the doctor answered. "She has Pneumocystis carinii Pneumonia, or PCP. A fungus causes it. Most people's immune systems can fight it off, but Katie's T-cell count dropped below 100, which is bad."

"What are you saying? I'm not sure I understand."

"We're going to admit her overnight and put her on antibiotics. I've prescribed trimethoprim and sulfamethoxazole. We hope that will control the PCP and get her T-cell count back up."

"She's going to be all right, isn't she?" Murphy interrupted. "I'm Katie's father," he shook the doctor's hand.

The doctor eyed both men. "I can't make any promises right now. I'm sorry."

* * *

Alex sat up in the hotel bed. After clearing a few cobwebs from his mind, he called his friend.

"Rob? It's Alex."

"Where are you? What the hell's going on?"

"You tell me. What's going on there?"

"All hell broke loose, that's what. We got a firm-wide e-mail from the new managing partner saying you were no longer employed here and a restraining order has been entered against you. The e-mail said anyone who heard from you should contact him immediately."

"Unbelievable," he said.

"It gets worse."

"How?"

"I passed by your office earlier and they had security up there tearing it apart. They were going through everything: desk drawers, files, computer hard drive, you name it. No one's working this morning. You're the talk of the office."

"Fuck."

"Rumor has it you assaulted Charles Van Doren and Michael

Murphy. Is it true? What the hell happened?"

"Long story, Rob," he answered, "but the short version is Van Doren and Murphy tried to kill me. I had to defend myself."

Silence.

"You heard me. If they knew where I was, they'd try again."

"Holy shit, why would they do that?"

"Van Doren ripped off a patent worth billions and had some people murdered in the process. I uncovered evidence he did it. He doesn't want me around to talk. Murphy's in on it, too."

"Murphy."

"Yes, Murphy."

"That's nuts, Alex. Murder?"

"I know. It's a fucking nightmare."

"Have you gone to the police?"

"Of course."

"What did they say?"

"They need more proof. Van Doren covers his tracks pretty well."

"Where are you now?" Foster asked.

"Not at home, that's for sure. My place was trashed. They'll be looking for me there. It's better you don't know."

"What the hell are you going to do?"

"Don't exactly know. I need to get my head together and figure out something."

"Shit, Alex. What can I do?"

"You did it already. I wanted to know what was going on at the office. I know to steer clear."

"Well, call me on my cell if you need anything, you hear?"

"Thanks, Rob."

"Take care of yourself."

"I will."

Alex stood and kicked one of the bags he filled the night before.

"Goddamn," he shouted. Half of the bag's contents spilled out over the floor, including the UPS package.

The package lay face-up on the floor. He snatched it up and peeled it open. Inside was a small stack of papers clipped together with a handwritten note on top.

Dear Alex,

If you received this letter, it means I am dead. My fate is not undeserved. An apology to those whose lives I destroyed would serve no purpose. It would not bring back the people who were killed, nor cure the pain of family and friends. The only act that might make a difference now is revealing the truth.

I hope the enclosed documents will serve as a means to that end. I am sending them to you because the authorities would not know what to make of them. You are the only person who will likely understand their meaning and who is not an active participant in the scheme. As I cannot trust anyone else involved with this case, I am placing my trust in you. I hope you will do the right thing.

Sincerely, Wilson Gates

Alex's knees gave way. He fell into the chair at the desk and studied the papers Gates sent him. After finishing, he pushed the pages away and ran a hand across his face.

"I'll be damned," he said.

He dialed Haney's number. "Jim? It's Alex. I need you to meet me at the airport. We're going to Chicago."

58

"Corner of Wacker and LaSalle," the cab driver cut across several lanes of traffic to get to the curb. The maneuver triggered a symphony of horns to which he mumbled profanity under his breath. Alex paid the cabby as he and Haney exited.

"It's a block on the left here," he told Haney. The sidewalk was filled with early rush hour bodies.

"You sure you want to do this?" Haney dodged people coming from the opposite direction. "You could get disbarred. We should take the materials to Ferenz and let him investigate."

"By the time Ferenz did anything," Alex answered, "Judge Shelton will have already entered an order declaring VDP the lawful owner of the Transviazine patent. I'm not going to let that happen. As for getting disbarred, that's the least of my worries."

"Here it is, 200 N. LaSalle," Haney said.

A blue-glass and steel starburst reaching straight into the clouds covered their view. They took the elevator to the thirty-second floor and entered the *Sebold & Hudson, Attorneys at Law* suite.

A receptionist led them down a plush hall to Hudson's office. Glass block walls filtered natural sunlight into the corridors. City views belonged to the money-makers. Partners hoarded the best views with floor-to-ceiling insulated glass walls.

Hudson's office faced south, into the financial district. Like most litigators, he had papers and files scattered across every available surface.

Alex felt right at home.

Hudson skirted his desk to greet his guests. "This is an unexpected surprise," he said.

"I apologize for popping in like this Gary, but it's important we talk. This is Jim Haney. He's a private investigator helping me on the Van Doren case."

"I see. You're a long way from Florida. What gives?"

"Let me cut to the chase, Gary," Alex said. "We're here to talk about the Van Doren case and you'll be very interested in what we have to say."

Hudson's poker face gave away nothing as he migrated around his desk and sat. "Please," he said, pointing to the chairs.

"You have a trial in three days on whether VDP is rightful owner of the Transviazine patent," Alex said.

"You didn't come all the way here to tell me that."

"I'm here to give you evidence that hasn't yet been produced," he said.

He held a manila package in the air. "I know who produced the DNA that led to the discovery of Transviazine, and I know Dr. Rabinowitz never intended to sell the drug to Van Doren or anyone else. The evidence I brought establishes VDP obtained the patent illegally. Only one person owns the patent rights and that person is not one of your clients."

Hudson swiveled back and forth. His body language announced his skepticism. "Before you go any further," he said, "I need to tell you I know about your situation."

"What situation?"

Hudson turned and shuffled through papers on the credenza behind his desk. "I received a letter from Michael Murphy yesterday informing me you're no longer employed by Parker Jones. You're off the case, Alex. I also received notice a Florida court entered an injunction against you, which prohibits me, or anyone else for that matter,

---

from discussing the case with you." Hudson leaned back. "Based on the order I reviewed, I'm not sure this conversation can go any further."

"The injunction is bullshit, Gary," Alex said. "It hasn't been domesticated in Illinois and can't bind anyone outside the State of Florida. That's why I came here personally."

Alex looked to Haney. "Jim, give him the subpoena."

Haney slid a document across his desk. Hudson reviewed it. "This is an unsigned subpoena issued out of the Northern District of Illinois."

"Exactly," Haney answered. "A person with relevant evidence in one of your cases is currently present in this district and planted here in your office. You can issue him a lawful subpoena and take his evidence. Just sign the document."

"I don't know about this," Hudson said. "This smacks of malpractice or an ethical violation. You're Van Doren's former attorney and you're giving me evidence that hurts your client. Don't you think this is problematic? Or perhaps illegal?"

"When this evidence comes out, the people who need to worry about illegal conduct are sitting in the Van Doren camp. I'm producing evidence Van Doren tried to conceal as part of a criminal conspiracy. I'd be in more trouble if I didn't turn it over."

Alex stood. "I'm not going to argue with you about this, Gary. I'm offering to give you the name of a prospective client who will assure you a multi-million dollar payday. If you don't want what I'm offering, I'll find someone who does." He nodded to Haney. "Let's get out of here."

"Hold on a minute," Hudson motioned them with his hands. "I need some time to think about this. Have you told anyone else about this?"

"You saw the injunction. I can't do anything with this evidence for another week. But you can use it right now, because you acquired it through a lawful subpoena and the injunction isn't enforceable against you up here."

Hudson picked up the subpoena again and flipped through it. "Okay, gentlemen," he signed the document and handed it back to Haney. "I'll take a look at the documents."

Alex dropped the package on Hudson's desk. "I'll contact you after I review the records," Hudson said. "How do I get in touch?"

"You don't," Alex answered. "I'll call you."

"When?"

"Tomorrow afternoon." He checked his watch. "Same time."

"Until tomorrow," Hudson said.

59

"It was a beautiful service, Michael," Matt patted Murphy on the shoulder. "Thanks for all your help with the arrangements."

Murphy clutched a glass of scotch in his son-in-law's kitchen. He hadn't spoken more than a handful of words since the funeral.

"Why don't you try to eat something?" Matt tempted Murphy with a deviled egg.

"Not hungry," he said.

"There's nothing more you could have done."

Murphy didn't answer. He raised his glass and stared into space.

"Katie knew how hard you tried to help her, but the drug was a long shot from the start. She didn't have much time. Why don't you come out to the family room and join everyone else?"

"No, you go ahead."

"Suit yourself."

He started out, but stopped short of the doorway. "I'm not sure anyone could have been more proud of a father than Katie was of you. She's watching over us right now. She knows what kind of man you are, Michael. We'll see you in a bit." He left the room.

Alone, Murphy put his head in his hands and started sobbing. It was the first time he broke down and bawled in thirty years; the day his daughter was born.

60

Alex knocked three times on the apartment door and waited. The hallway was quiet. He heard footsteps. A familiar face stood behind the door.

"Alex," his brother bear-hugged him. "How the hell are you?"

"Still alive," he said. "It's good to see you, man. It's been a while."

"You, too."

Alex patted his brother's belly. "I can see you've been eating well."

"Yeah, med school hasn't been kind," he said, rubbing his stomach. "I haven't had much time to work out. How was the drive down?"

"Not bad. Passed through a couple storms, but they died down after sunset."

"Is Jim with you?"

"No, he flew back to Jax. He's going to meet with the detectives tomorrow morning."

"Well, shit, let's not stand around here in the hall. Come inside."

John grabbed Alex's bag and led him through his small college apartment into the kitchen. "Let me get you a beer." He grabbed two bottles of Sam Adams from the fridge. "You made pretty good time. We didn't expect you for another hour."

"You can spot trailers easier when you drive with a lead foot. I can't believe the way my mind works now. I feel like I'm in the witness protection program."

"God, this is all so crazy. I'm still having trouble getting my mind around what's going on," John said. "It doesn't seem real." He took a swig from the bottle.

"Where's Jess?"

"Shower."

"She okay?"

"For the most part. She's stir-crazy from spending most of her time in this shoebox, but she's tough."

Alex smiled. "Yeah, I figured that out a while back."

"You're flying out of Cincinnati tomorrow morning?"

"Nine-fifteen. We need to get out of here no later than six."

"Let me throw your bag in the back. Make yourself at home."

John walked off and Jessica appeared from the hall. "Alex," she wrapped her arms around him. She smelled like strawberries and her touch was warm. "I'm so glad you're here," she said. Her damp hair left drops of water on his cheek. "How are you?"

"Good," he said. "You?"

"Ready to get my life back. I can't stand this anymore." She turned to John who had reappeared. "I didn't mean it like it sounded."

"Don't worry about it."

She turned to Alex. "I want to hear everything that's going on."

"Let's sit down and I'll fill you in," he pointed to the old beige, cloth couch in the living area. She sat close to him. John slid into his rustic recliner and eased it back.

"Jess, we know what's going on. I didn't want to tell you over the phone."

"Tell me now."

"Do you remember us talking about your father's Will and how it was related to the attempts on your life?"

"Yeah."

"We were right. You know your father was on the board of directors of Horizon. Right?

Jess nodded.

"Horizon was set up to do AIDS research as well as provide health care for the indigent. He formed the company with Dr. David Rabinowitz. I'll spare you the legal formalities, but they needed a third member on the board to keep their charitable status, so they asked your father's friend, Michael Murphy, to sit. It made sense, because he was an attorney who could also provide legal advice."

"I remember my dad telling me about Horizon," she said.

"Did you know Dr. Rabinowitz?"

"No, but I heard his name mentioned a few times. He sounded impressive."

"Yeah," Alex said. "Do you know how your father and Dr. Rabinowitz met?"

Her eyes leaked sideways. "Now that you ask, no, I really don't."

"Rabinowitz was your father's treating physician for a period of time. He never told you about that?"

"Dad played pro-ball. Do you know how many doctors that entails? I couldn't possibly know them all."

"Dr. Rabinowitz treats AIDS patients."

Jessica's eyebrows shot up. "I beg your pardon?"

He swallowed hard. "Your dad had AIDS."

"That's impossible," she said. "If dad had AIDS, I'd have known about it. That's not something that's easy to hide."

"Back in 1987, he was hospitalized for internal bleeding after a game. He had surgery and received blood, bad blood. Blood with HIV. A few weeks later, the hospital figured it out and had him tested. Sure enough, he tested positive for HIV."

"You know this, how?"

"We finally got our hands on Rabinowitz's confidential files. It's all in there—treatment history; everything."

"I . . . I . . . ," she covered her mouth with her hand. " . . . I had no idea. He never said he was ill and he seemed perfectly healthy. He kept playing. That makes no sense."

"He *was* perfectly healthy," Alex answered. "That's what this mess is all about. When your father went for treatment, he was referred to Rabinowitz who was one of the few AIDS specialists in town at the time. Your father kept going in for treatment. A year later, there was no more trace of the virus in his body."

"The treatment cured him?"

"No."

"I'm not a doctor yet," John chimed in, "but I know enough to tell you there isn't a cure for AIDS."

"Not until now," Alex said. "Jess, your father had a unique DNA structure that rendered him immune from the virus. I don't understand all the science behind it, but the Cliff's Notes version is HIV attacks the immune system by invading white blood cells, destroying them, and replicating itself. Sound right, John?"

"So far, so good."

"Your dad's DNA was different than most, and for whatever reason, the virus couldn't get through the outer core of his white blood cells to replicate itself. I heard it described before as having the wrong key to your house. You can't get in. If the virus can't replicate itself, it becomes weak and defensible."

Jessica snagged the beer out of Alex's hand and took a swig. "Okay. I'm confused now. You want to translate that?"

"Once Rabinowitz figured out your dad's cells blocked the virus, he started doing research. Your father agreed to be a guinea pig, and the two formed a partnership, which became Horizon. They were never in it for the money. They both wanted to do something good for society. Rabinowitz used your dad's DNA to find a cure for AIDS. And that's when all of this started."

"Why didn't he tell me?"

"That, I can't answer. Maybe he didn't want to worry you that he tested positive for HIV. Maybe he didn't want to make it public, because of his career. From what I know about pro ball, players and coaches aren't exactly understanding of the AIDS virus."

She stayed quiet, soaking up the information.

John's curiosity broke the silence. "How do you get from a cure for HIV to murder? What does this all have to do with you and Jess?"

"You've heard of Van Doren Pharmaceuticals, right?"

"Sure."

"They were one of the drug manufacturers hot and heavy after Transviazine. Everyone wanted a piece. The problem was neither Rabinowitz nor Mark McCall was interested in selling. We think that's when Van Doren tried working behind the scenes to use Murphy to push a resolution through Horizon's board to sell."

"What was in it for Murphy?"

"Money and power. Murphy used to be a partner with Parker Jones. Van Doren just hired him as General Counsel. His compensation package includes stock options that push his income above most Fortune 50 CEOs. Ten million a year."

"Did Horizon sell to VDP?"

"No. Once Van Doren realized Horizon wouldn't sell, he had Rabinowitz and Jess' dad murdered and forged the documents to transfer the drug rights to VDP."

"You're telling me Charles Van Doren had my father murdered."

Her tone was just below a shout. "I can't believe this."

"Incredible," John commented. "Do you think Van Doren is also responsible for killing Jess' grandparents? And what about Jess? Is he trying to kill her too? This is all convoluted."

"That's where the Will comes into play. The Will transfers the bulk of his assets to Jess and his parents. It also contains a survivorship clause that says the family members must outlive him by at least one hundred-twenty days to collect. With them dead, no one in his family has a claim to enforce Mark's legal rights, and Van Doren gets away with stealing the drug."

"When does the one-twenty run out?" John asked.

"Five days," Alex answered.

"What do we do now?" she asked. "On the phone, you mentioned the lawyer in Chicago we need to meet with."

"Right. Gary Hudson. He filed a class action against Van Doren challenging the company's rights to Transviazine. Van Doren hired Parker Jones to defend the case and I was working on it with Murphy when all this shit happened."

"What's the basis of the claim?" John asked.

"Hudson represents a group of AIDS patients Rabinowitz treated. The gist of the lawsuit is Rabinowitz used these people's blood and DNA for research that helped invent Transviazine without getting permission to use their DNA in his research. The legal term is lack of informed consent. Hudson argued Rabinowitz had no right to sell the drug, because his former patients have an ownership interest based on the research. The judge dismissed most of the claims on grounds that patients don't have a property interested to their DNA. The judge didn't want to set a precedent that would limit a doctor's ability to conduct research."

"Makes sense," John agreed.

"The judge gave Hudson a chance to see if he could find the person whose DNA led to the cure to determine whether that person had an agreement with Rabinowitz that would trump Van Doren's agreement to purchase the patent rights. Van Doren went to great lengths to hide or destroy all of the proof your father was the DNA donor. We didn't know who the donor was until just this week."

"You're telling me my father had an agreement with Dr. Rabinowitz," Jessica said.

"Right. That's why we need to get you for the trial. If Hudson can't present you as a witness on your father's behalf, the judge is going to enter a judgment for Van Doren granting it all of the rights to Transviazine. Once the judgment is entered, you could be permanently barred from enforcing your father's legal rights."

"Why should I let the attorney from Chicago represent me? Why can't you represent me? You're my attorney."

"I'm conflicted out. I represented Van Doren in the past."

Jessica's mind churned. "I have a hard time trusting anyone after what Murphy did. But if you think Hudson is our best option, I'll meet with him."

"It's the right decision. Look, it's getting late and we have an early morning ahead of us. Why don't you two get some sleep? We can talk more tomorrow."

"This is only a two bedroom, Alex," John said. "You take my bed and I'll crash out here on the couch."

"I appreciate the offer, little brother, but I'll be fine out here. I'm still wired. Haven't slept much lately and I don't plan on starting tonight."

"Suit yourself," John responded. "Don't say I didn't try to do something nice. I'm going to bed. I have an early day myself." John loped back to his bedroom.

"You mind if I stay up with you for a while?" she asked. "I haven't slept well either."

"I'd like it if you did."

She pulled a blanket from the edge of the couch and draped it over her legs. She leaned her head against his shoulder and clicked on the television. "I missed you," she said quietly.

"I missed you too."

61

"Please hold," Hudson's assistant told Alex. As promised, his call came twenty-four hours after his visit. He heard a click.

"Gary Hudson."

"Have you reviewed the files?"

"Yes."

"And?"

"I agree with your assessment. Van Doren doesn't own Transviazine and it looks like he and his henchman are liable for a host of legal and ethical violations, including spoliation of evidence, fraud, tampering, and perjury to name a few. This case could bring the entire company down, not to mention a handful of criminal indictments."

"The documents we provided don't tell the whole story."

"Meaning?"

"Van Doren is a murderer."

"Excuse me?"

"He killed Rabinowitz and Mark McCall. He's also behind several other murders associated with this case."

"What makes you say that?"

"For starters, some crazy son of a bitch tried to kill me twice, once at Van Doren's house. I can't explain everything right now. As far as I know, people are listening to our call. I'll explain everything when we all meet in person with the true owner of the Transviazine patent."

"Jessica McCall?" Hudson asked.

"Yes."

"You realize the trial in Van Doren's case is this Friday. If this is going to happen, I'll need to meet with her beforehand. We have an awful lot of work to do between now and then."

"Will you represent her?"

"I don't want to wind up on a slab in the morgue. Is this going to make me a marked man?"

"They won't know what hit them until the trial. At that point, it'll be too late. Just make damn sure you keep everything quiet until then."

Hudson didn't speak for a moment.

"Gary, you there?"

"Yeah, I'm here. I'm thinking. You dropped a bomb on me."

"If you don't want to get involved, I understand, but the evidence is going to come out at the hearing one way or another. I don't mean to pressure you, but under the circumstances, I need an answer. Now. If you can't do it, I'll find someone else."

Dead air.

Hudson sighed. "I'll do it."

"I appreciate this, Gary. Just to let you know, there've already been several attempts on Jessica's life. She's in a safe place right now, but we can't take any chances. I'll touch base with you to set up the meeting when you arrive in Jacksonville. Can you get on a plane tomorrow?"

"I'll have to clear some things off the calendar, but yeah, I should be able to do that. I don't suppose you can give me a contact number for you."

"No. I'll find you. And remember what I said, Gary. Not a word to anyone.

"I'll wait to hear from you."

* * *

Karen James held the receiver to her ear and listened past the five rings. She got the machine. "Mr. Haney? This is Karen James. You asked me to call if anything else came to mind. I remembered a name you asked me about."

62

"Welcome to Jacksonville, Mr. Hudson. Let me check your reservation." The perfectly pressed hotel clerk punched the computer keyboard. "Yes, we have you right here. I see there's a package for you. If you'll just give me a moment."

She opened a safe under the desk and came up with an envelope. "This came for you an hour ago."

"Thank you," he slid the envelope into his suit jacket.

The clerk scanned a plastic key card and handed it to him. "The elevator is through the lobby and to your left."

"Thanks."

"Would you like a bellman to help you with your luggage?"

"I got it." He picked up his bags and lugged them to his room. As soon as the door closed behind him, he reached for the envelope and peeled it open.

A handwritten note read: "Jessica and Alex are staying at the Sea Turtle Inn, Atlantic Beach, Room 528. We'll see you there at eight o'clock sharp tomorrow morning. Keep this confidential." Haney's signature was on the bottom.

Hudson studied the note and opened his cell phone. He pressed a program button and a number automatically dialed.

"Charles, it's Gary," he said.

"I've been waiting for you to call," Van Doren's voice crackled from the static. "Have you heard from them?"

"Yes. She's at the Sea Turtle Inn, room 528. She's staying with Alex. I'm scheduled to meet with them tomorrow morning."

"Excellent. We'll take care of everything from here."

"Do you want me to go over there in the morning?" Hudson tossed his suitcase on the king-sized bed and unzipped the outer shell.

"There won't be anyone left to meet with."

"Do you need anything else?" Hudson strolled to the window to collect the city view.

"Just lose the goddamn trial like we planned."

"You make sure Jessica and Alex don't show up to the trial, and I'll make sure I lose it."

"The only place they'll be showing up is the morgue. You can count on that."

"Well then, we have nothing to worry about."

"See you in court."

63

L unden approached the front desk wearing khaki shorts and a light blue dress shirt. "Checking in," he said. "Name's Gil Winstrom. I requested room 428."

"Yes, Mr. Winstrom, welcome to the Sea Turtle," a chipper young man responded. "One night?"

"Yes, just the one."

The clerk studied his screen, "room 428. That's a two-bedroom suite. Do you want to put this on your charge card?"

"Cash." Lunden threw five one-hundred dollar bills on the counter.

The clerk's eyebrows raised. "Uh, okay. May I see a picture ID, please?"

He politely removed a driver license.

"From Indiana, huh?"

"Yeah, down on business for the day."

"Welcome to Florida. Enjoy your stay."

Lunden slung his overnight bag over his back and climbed the stairs to his suite. He waited for a young couple to clear the hall before he opened his door. As soon as they left his sight, he slid into the room. He locked the deadbolt, dropped his bag on the kitchen counter, and did a walk-through. He checked all closets, bedrooms, and bathrooms.

Inspection passed.

He paced off the dimensions of each room in all directions, noting the precise placement of every piece of furniture and object: desks, couch, beds, tables, stools, light fixtures, armoires, lamps, and even kitchen appliances. He then wrapped a blindfold around his head and walked through the suite five more times. By his third trip without the benefit of sight, he made it through every nook and cranny without bumping into anything.

Satisfied, he snatched a bottle of Johnny Walker Red out of his bag and filled a highball glass. He emptied his bag onto the coffee table. A black semi-automatic .25 Browning ACP hid inside a folded shirt. He unraveled it and reached back for another piece of cold steel, a suppressor he screwed on the barrel.

He dug deeper in the bag and found a long piece of rope with a rubber hook on the end. He inspected it for frayed edges.

It was clean. Perfect.

He grabbed the bottle and meandered to the balcony. The ocean breeze made the humidity bearable. He peered over the side, up and down, and snapped a mental picture

Now came the wait.

He returned inside and set the alarm for 4:00 A.M. He finished off a stiff drink, turned off the lights, and rested his head on the pillow.

The alcohol warmed his body. Eased his tension. The killing didn't bother him. The prospects of a mistake did. He didn't make mistakes.

His eyes opened at 3:55 A.M. He didn't need an alarm. Deep sleepers didn't live long in his business.

He splashed cold water on his face and picked up the goodies on the table. Dressed in black, he returned the balcony. The rhythmic ocean was the only sound. The cloudy night sky would blend him into the darkness.

He swung the rope back and forth. Controlled momentum. He cast it up to the balcony directly above. The rubber hook caught the railing without a sound. He tugged three times. Ready.

He free-scaled fifteen feet, grabbed the rail, and pulled himself up just enough to poke his head over the balcony.

No light. No movement. All clear.

He climbed over the rail, peered through the window, and then pressed his head against the glass to listen.

Quiet.

He removed a glasscutter from his belt and carved a semi-circle next to the handle of the sliding door. His hand slipped through and turned the lock.

He glided through the living area to a bedroom.

The door was cracked. Lights off. No sound.

He pushed it back and entered, pistol drawn. Long dark hair spread across white pillows at the head of the bed.

"You're mine, you troublesome bitch." He aimed the pistol.

Three muffled shots ripped into the target: two to the body and one to the head.

He approached the victim and yanked back the sheets.

"What the fuck?"

A plastic dummy.

The lights flicked on. "Drop the fucking gun, now," Detective Ferenz shouted from the doorway, pistol drawn. A uniformed cop stepped out from the bathroom.

"You so much as breathe and I'll blow off your fucking head."

He stood absolutely still. A statue.

"Nice and slow," Ferenz said, "and I mean really slow, I want you to put the gun on the bed and lay face-down on the floor."

No movement.

"Are you deaf? Put the fucking gun on the bed and get your god-damn face on the floor."

"I give all my clients the same guarantee," Lunden said with a smirk, "they won't have to worry about me testifying in court." He faced Ferenz.

"Put the gun down," Ferenz demanded.

"No can do," he said, raising his arm.

Gunshots rang out like firecrackers.

Pop, pop, pop.

Then quiet.

Lunden's body lay motionless, face-down on the floor.

"Don't touch anything," Ferenz told the cop in blue "and notify the ME. We'll need a bag for the stiff."

He left the bedroom and called Haney on his cell phone. "Jim, you were right," he said. "We got him."

64

erenz, Haney, Alex, and Jessica traversed the medical examiner's office downtown. "I can't believe he was killed in the hotel where we were supposed to stay," Jessica said.

"You can thank Karen James for that," Haney said. "If she hadn't called when she did, I'd have never got Ferenz over there in time."

"There must be a God up there," Alex chimed. "What are the chances of her remembering Gary Hudson was Rabinowitz's attorney the day we were to check in? Unbelievable."

"You can thank her personally," Ferenz said. "She's flying in to see if she can identify the body. We also contacted the FBI to alert them of a possible connection between Rabinowitz's death and Van Doren."

"I still don't understand why you connected Hudson to a conspiracy just because he was Dr. Rabinowitz's attorney?" Jessica asked Haney.

"I didn't know for sure, but I had a strong hunch. If Rabinowitz hired Hudson to help him fend off Van Doren in the past, then Hudson probably knew that the miracle DNA belonged to your dad. Why would he then bring a lawsuit on behalf of people he knows don't have legal rights to what they are claiming? Also, Hudson's lawsuit accuses Rabinowitz of being dishonest with his former patients. Because Hudson represented Rabinowitz before, he was prohibited from taking a case adverse to his former client. The law would have required him to disclose the conflict. It didn't add up. So I changed our hotel reservations and had Ferenz stake out the room just to be safe. If Hudson was in on it, I figured he'd make sure you were paid a visit by the guy we're about to see."

The elevator doors opened to the lower level in the medical examiner's office. "It's an ice box down here," Alex said as they entered the autopsy room.

"Ugh," Jessica cupped her nose. "God, this smells," she said.

"This ain't nothing," Ferenz said. "The old office had a lousy ventilation system that carried the stench all over the building. At least in the new building, it's just the rooms down here."

The room was large and sterile with plain, concrete floors and several surgical tables. An older woman with a shock of gray hair and purple scrubs bent over a body on the table. She turned at the sounds of footsteps and raised a sheet over the corpse.

"Jack, how are you?" The woman asked Ferenz.

"Good, Janey," he said. "You?"

"Better than this guy," she pointed to the covered body. "Are these folks here for the identification?"

"This is Alex and Jessica. Guys, this is Janey Higson. Medical examiner."

"Nice to meet you. I'd shake your hands, but you might not like that much." She waved her bloodstained surgical gloves. "Would you two be more comfortable behind the glass?" She pointed to the viewing room behind the operating table. Alex looked at Jessica, who shook her head.

"Suit yourselves."

Higson folded back the sheet and stepped away.

"You recognize this guy?" Ferenz asked.

"That's him," Alex said.

Jessica nodded and turned away. She covered her mouth.

Alex escorted her out of the room. Haney and Ferenz would probe the examiner.

"What did you find, Janey?" Ferenz asked.

"A whole lot of lead for starters," she joked. "But you already know that, since you put it there."

"Drugs?"

"Nope. Clean. I found a small trace of alcohol, but he wasn't impaired. Who is he?"

"Prints came back to Robert Lunden. Special Forces. A real bad ass. They kicked him out four years ago after he assaulted his commanding officer. Nearly killed the guy. He accepted a dishonorable discharge in lieu of a court-martial. After he got out, his personal history vanished. No trace of him anywhere. No credit history. No driver license. Nothing. He had a couple good fake IDs on him. We think he's been working as a mercenary."

"I'll be damned," Higson said. "How does he know your two friends?"

"Oh, he just tried to kill them a few times, that's all," Ferenz sipped his coffee.

"Do you know who's behind it?" Higson asked.

"Brace yourself," Haney said. "Charles Van Doren."

Her jaw dropped. "The pharmaceutical guy?"

"Yep. And he's had a couple other people killed already."

"I'll be damned. Why would he want to kill someone?"

"Oh, take a guess—money. He wanted to buy a patent on a drug worth billions and the guy who made the drug wasn't selling. Van Doren elected self-help. He hired this lunatic and dead bodies started turning up."

"Holy-moly, can you prove it?"

"We're close. It would have been nice to take this piece of shit alive and get him to talk," Ferenz pointed to Lunden's body, "but that turned out not to be an option."

"Is there anything else you need from me?"

"Yeah," Haney said. "We need you to hold the body on ice for a bit. I have another witness flying in today to try to ID this guy. He may have killed a doctor in Chicago and she witnessed it."

———

"Gets around, doesn't he?" Higson said. "Okay, I'll put the body in the cold room when I'm done here. Just give me a ring when she gets here."

Ferenz and Haney left the room and caught up with Alex and Jessica in the lobby.

"What now?" Jessica asked Haney.

"We get ready for trial."

65

Murphy, Van Doren, and a team of Parker Jones attorneys huddled around counsels' table. With Murphy as Van Doren's General Counsel and Alex no longer working on the case, he assigned the trial counsel role to Lou Dells, one of the firm's seasoned litigation partners. A large, distinguished-looking African-American man with a gravelly voice, he had the reputation as a calm player, but not one who'd back down from a sparring match.

Dells brought two associates to assist. A handful of other Parker Jones attorneys came by to observe, including Rob Foster, who had an idea the day's activities might provide some fireworks. Hudson was hunkered down across the aisle from Van Doren's team, talking to a few witnesses he brought for show.

"All rise," the bailiff announced. Judge Shelton emerged from chambers. "The United States District Court for the Middle District of Florida is now in session. The Honorable Franklin Shelton presiding."

"You may be seated," Shelton tapped his gavel and unloaded the thick files under his arm.

"Good morning. This is a bench trial, so we don't need to deal with jury selection. Is everyone ready?"

"Yes, Your Honor," Dells stood. Hudson also stood and agreed.

"I've read the pretrial statements. Are there any issues we need to take up before opening statements?"

"No, Your Honor," both attorneys chimed.

"Very well. I'll hear the openings, starting with counsel for Van Doren Pharmaceuticals."

Dells stood and buttoned his suit-jacket. He moved gracefully to the podium. He spread a stack of papers and notes across the raised surface.

"Good morning, Your Honor. I'm Lou Dells and I represent Van Doren Pharmaceuticals." Dells was smooth and polished. He had obviously done this many times before.

He spent twenty minutes on his opening statement, which was enough time to make his key points, but not too much time for him to lose his audience's attention.

He droned on about the wonderful drug VDP purchased and how it would change the world. He talked about patent rights, clearly and precisely explaining the law. He even threw in a story about how a sick AIDS patient is waiting for the red tape, including this lawsuit, to clear so VDP can move forward with the clinical trials and begin treatment. His presentation was immaculate and left the listeners to wonder how anyone could possibly disagree with VDP's position.

"Thank you, Your Honor," he said as he gathered up his papers from the podium.

"Thank you, Mr. Dells," Shelton said. "Mr. Hudson, would you care to make your opening now?"

"I'll reserve the opening for the beginning of our case in chief."

"Very well. Mr. Dells, call your first witness."

Dells stood. "We call Michael Murphy to the stand." Murphy settled himself in the witness box. The bailiff approached and gave him the oath. "Do you swear the testimony you are about to give is the truth, the whole truth and nothing but the truth, so help you God?"

He paused for a moment and stared at both Hudson and Van Doren before answering. His eyes were worn and tired. "I do."

"Will you state your name and occupation?"

"Michael Murphy. I currently serve as the general counsel for Van Doren Pharmaceuticals."

"In what capacity are you here to testify today?"

"I am testifying as VDP's corporate representative."

"Will you tell the Court how you prepared to give testimony today?"

"I reviewed all relevant corporate documents and gathered evidence in the ordinary course of business for the purpose of testifying on behalf of the company."

"Very well." Dells shuffled his papers when the courtroom doors opened.

Ferenz, Haney, Alex and Jessica pushed their way through, followed by four uniformed officers. Alex carried a banker's box filled with documents. He stopped short of the wooden gate that separated the attorneys from spectators and leaned the box against the rail. He shot a glance at Van Doren who paled.

"I'm sure you read the signs out front on the door that say 'Court in Session.'" Shelton glowered. "I don't appreciate distractions."

Van Doren grabbed a notepad and scribbled furiously. He handed the pad to his attorneys.

"Your Honor, I apologize for the interruption," Alex said, "My name is Alex Weaver and this is Jessica McCall. Ms. McCall is here to intervene in this trial. She just filed a brief downstairs with the clerk's office and she is prepared to deliver a courtesy copy to the Court." He held the brief in the air.

Dells erupted. "Your Honor, we object to this intrusion."

The judge waved Dells off.

"Mr. Weaver," Shelton barked, "you previously represented Van Doren in this case. I received Parker Jones' notice you were removed as counsel of record. Now you show up to disrupt my trial and tell me you've filed a motion to intervene on behalf of a client different from Van Doren. If you'd like to avoid a contempt order, you'd better have very good explanation."

Sweat beaded on his forehead. "Yes, Your Honor. May I approach the podium? What I have to say is of immense importance."

Dells and Hudson both exploded. This time Hudson's voice overrode Dell's. "Your Honor, Mr. Weaver's conduct violates the rules of procedure as well as every ethical rule in the book. It is completely inappropriate."

Alex interrupted. "Please, Your Honor, a few minutes is all I ask."

"Your objection is noted, Mr. Hudson," Shelton responded, "but I'll give him five minutes to explain himself. And it better be good."

"Thank you, Your Honor." He passed through the waist-high swinging gate and confiscated the podium. Dells returned to his seat.

"I'd like to address the points you raised. First, I represent Ms. McCall in another matter, but not in this case. Ms. McCall is here pro se, because she has not yet had time to locate other counsel and time was of the essence to intervene. With respect to my participation today, and my former representation of Van Doren, the rules of ethics require me to come forward with evidence to prevent Charles Van Doren, as well as the attorneys representing both sides of this case, from perpetrating a criminal fraud on this Court."

"This is outrageous," Van Doren cried. "This man tried to assault me and should be thrown in jail."

Dells and Hudson shot out of their chairs. "Your Honor," Hudson spoke first, "these allegations are scandalous. Mr. Weaver formerly represented Van Doren in this litigation. He was fired not only from the case, but also from his firm. He obviously has an axe to grind and has come in here today with reckless claims worthy of disbarment. We ask he be immediately removed from the courtroom and held in contempt."

"I agree, Your Honor," Dells said. "We add that the Duval County Circuit Court entered a temporary restraining order against Mr. Weaver as a result of his prior misconduct in the case. The order specifically prohibits Mr. Weaver from discussing Van Doren's case to avoid precisely what's happening here, which is violating the attorney-client privilege and attempting to destroy Mr. Van Doren's reputation." Dells scrambled through his papers to locate a copy of the restraining order.

"That restraining order is a crock and they know it," Alex shot back. "The evidence I have in this box proves this entire trial is a sham, Your Honor. The attorneys on both sides are placing false evidence before the Court to rig the case for a Van Doren victory, and worse, they conspired to murder Dr. Rabinowitz and members of Ms. McCall's family so they could steal Transviazine from the rightful owner. The reason I'm not on the case anymore is I figured out Van Doren's plot and wouldn't go along with it. Ms. McCall is the owner of Transviazine because of her father's partnership with Dr. Rabinowitz. We have a written contract to prove it. Van Doren had Jessica's father murdered and made several attempts on her life, and because I was trying to help her, he tried to kill me, too. He's a cold-blooded killer," he pointed at Van Doren.

"Mr. Weaver," Shelton barked. The veins across his forehead bulged. "You have the nerve to come in here during of a trial and accuse respected members of the professional community of a murder conspiracy and cover-up—your former colleagues, no less. I'm inclined to have you thrown in jail right now."

"Look at the police sitting in the back of the room," he told the judge. "They didn't come here to watch a civil trial, Your Honor. They're here to make arrests based upon the probable cause sitting right in this box and through the testimony of the people standing before you. It's all spelled out in the brief and the back-up is in here," he tapped the box. "The Court has nothing to lose by considering it and that's all we ask."

Dells jumped back in the fray. "Your Honor, this has to stop right now. The Court cannot allow these baseless allegations to continue. We ask Your Honor to immediately remove these people from the courtroom and hold Mr. Weaver in contempt. We're confident what-ever he told the police is a lie."

"I would add, Your Honor . . ." Hudson started to interrupt.

"Enough," the judge slammed his gavel. "Everyone shut up."

The courtroom rang silent.

"Bring me his motion and the box," Shelton directed the bailiff. "Mr. Weaver, did you bring copies for the attorneys?"

"Yes, Your Honor." He pulled two more copies out of the box and put them on top. Alex handed his files to the towering bailiff, who dropped a copy with each of the attorneys and carried the rest of the materials to the judge.

Shelton studied the motion and shuffled through papers.

Dells and Hudson also pored through the motion papers as quickly as possible. Van Doren couldn't sit still. "Your Honor," he said, "I'd like to be heard on this."

"When I said shut up, I meant you too, Mr. Van Doren," the judge spat. "Mr. Dells, control your client or I'll have him removed and locked up."

"Yes, Your Honor." Dells patted Van Doren on the back and whispered in his ear.

Shelton continued to study the documents. "I'm going to need a recess. Let's take thirty minutes so I can get a handle on this. I'd like everyone to stay put while I'm gone."

"Excuse me, Your Honor," Dells said. "My associate found the gag order entered by the Duval County Circuit Court against Mr. Weaver."

"Give it to the bailiff." The judge grabbed a stack of papers and dis-appeared to his chambers.

Van Doren looked at his attorneys and scribbled frantically on the legal pad in front of him. He whispered raging orders until his face purpled.

Hudson said something to the people sitting with him and then stood to exit the courtroom. Ferenz and two officers blocked his path. "You can just sit your ass right back down in that chair, Mr. Hudson," Ferenz flashed his badge. "You're not going anywhere."

After a long break, Shelton reappeared and pointed to Alex and Jessica. "I want to see the two of you in chambers. Where are Mr. Ferenz and Mr. Haney? Are they here?"

"Yes, Judge," Ferenz answered. He and Haney stood.

"You come, too. As for the rest of you, no one leaves the courtroom. John?" he looked at the Bailiff, "make sure everyone stays put."

"Yes, sir."

"Your Honor," Dells said, "with all due respect, counsel of record has a right to be involved with any communications involving the parties in this case. I ask permission to attend the conference in chambers."

"Denied."

Foster watched the group of four follow Shelton into chambers. "What I wouldn't give to be roach in that room," he whispered to an associate next to him.

Dells continued to study the motion he just received, his body language broadcast his ill ease. He made eye contact with Murphy as if to ask, "Is it true?" Murphy's head shifted down.

After a longer break, Shelton returned to the courtroom and directed Alex and Jessica to sit next to the bailiff at a side table. Ferenz and Haney joined the other officers.

The judge carried Alex's box and set it on the bench. He reclaimed his seat and rubbed his hands across his face and through his white hair.

"Mr. Murphy," Shelton said, "Take your place in the witness box. I have some questions."

"Your Honor," Dells said, "we object to this line of questioning. We're concerned the Court might direct questions to our witness based upon documents Mr. Weaver just produced that Van Doren has not yet had an opportunity to review and respond. This is trial by ambush and we ask for a recess to allow our witnesses to review the documents just produced. Furthermore, the Duval County Circuit Court entered an order barring Mr. Weaver from discussing Van Doren's case with anyone and, based upon the discussions we imagine just happened in chambers, we believe Mr. Weaver violated the order."

"Let's just clear the record right now about this restraining order, Mr. Dells. As best I can tell, the order was entered based upon the false and fraudulent testimony of Mr. Van Doren, not to mention misrepresentations by your firm. I'm not going to follow it and, as you know since we're in federal court, I don't have to follow it. Motion denied. As for your request for continuance to review these documents, that's also denied. They came from your client and I'm very interested in hearing what he has to say about them."

"In that case, Your Honor," Dells stood up once again, "given the accusations made by Mr. Weaver, I would like to remind the Court and Mr. Murphy that he has rights under the Fifth Amendment to elect not to testify. Furthermore, because he is testifying as VDP's corporate representative, and because the company is accused of criminal conduct, the privilege against testifying belongs to Mr. Van Doren as well as Mr. Murphy."

Shelton leaned back in his chair and turned his head to the witness box. "Do you want to assert the privilege, Michael?"

Murphy eyed Van Doren, whose return gaze could have burned a hole in the wall. "Mr. Weaver is telling you the truth, Your Honor." Murphy finally said. "And I can't do this anymore."

"Liar," Van Doren leapt from his chair. "You're going to pay for this."

Dell grabbed his client's arm and shoved him back into his chair. "We object to Mr. Murphy's testimony and move to strike," Dells shouted. "He can't waive the company's privilege. He can't do it."

"Is that your position, Mr. Dells? Are you telling me Van Doren Pharmaceuticals has elected to assert a Fifth Amendment privilege against self incrimination and, as a result, refuses to testify concerning the ownership rights to Transviazine?"

Dells huddled again with Van Doren. He turned back to the judge. "We would like to request a continuance of this matter, Your Honor."

"Denied." Shelton's face smoldered. "Answer the question. Are you going to present a corporate representative or aren't you? It's a simple yes or no."

Dells panned to Van Doren, who shook his head. "At this time, we will not present testimony from our corporate representative."

"Okay, then. Here's where we are," Shelton said. "We have a motion to intervene, properly supported by affidavits and legal documents. We have Mr. Van Doren, who filed this case, but refuses to present evidence, because he was caught in a web of lies and criminal conduct that may include murder. And we have Mr. Hudson, a co-conspirator who dragged people down here from Chicago to make it look like he's defending when, in truth, he intends to lose this case. Does that about sum it up?" Shelton's glare dared anyone to argue with him.

Silence.

"Very well," he continued. "First, as to Van Doren, I'm entering an order to strike your pleadings. Your case is over and your contract with Dr. Rabinowitz is declared null and void. I direct you to withdraw all of your patent applications with the patent office and restore the patents to their rightful owner, who I believe is sitting in the courtroom today." He pointed to Jessica.

"You folks with Mr. Hudson," the judge said, "you need to go straight to the Illinois and Florida Bar Associations and register a complaint against Mr. Hudson, Mr. Dells and their law firms and then file a legal malpractice claim. I'll be your star witness. Do it fast, though, because they will be going away for a long time. As for this case, your claims are dismissed."

"Finally, Ms. McCall, your motion to intervene is granted. I'm giving you sixty days to find legal representation and present your case. If you need more time, let me know, but considering no one's left to oppose you, I like your chances."

The judge shook his head and rubbed his face. "Ms. McCall," he said, "I offer you my sincerest apologies for the tragedies dealt you by people we thought were trusted members of this community. This is the worst day in my thirty years practicing law, and it could be the worst day for jurisprudence in the State of Florida. I'm embarrassed to be a part of it."

He focused on the attorneys. "You people make me sick. And for you younger attorneys out there with Parker Jones," he eyed Foster and the others sitting around him, "get your resumes together. Your firm won't be around this time next year."

He hit his gavel so hard the top flew off and bounced halfway across the courtroom. He ripped himself from his chair and stormed off the bench.

"All rise," the bailiff announced.

Judge Shelton carried the files Alex brought quickly into chambers. By the time the chamber door shut, the officers were handcuffing Doren, Murphy, Dells and Hudson.

Alex watched them get marched out of the courtroom. Heads down. No eye contact. They moved in a straight line out the door.

"I can't believe what I just saw," Foster told Alex. "Are you all right?" He put his hand on Alex's shoulder.

"I am now, my friend," he said.

He turned to Jessica and wrapped both arms around her tight. "It's over, Jess. It's finally over."

11/07

OLD CHARLES TOWN LIBRARY
CHARLES TOWN, WV 25414
(304) 725-2208